CAMPION'S GHOST

By the same author

LE THÉÂTRE EN GRANDE-BRETAGNE
FRENCH THEATRE TODAY
DIFFERENT CIRCUMSTANCES
DIALOGUE BETWEEN FRIENDS
THE PURSUIT OF PERFECTION: A LIFE OF MAGGIE TEYTE
RALPH RICHARDSON: AN ACTOR'S LIFE
DARLINGS OF THE GODS: ONE YEAR IN THE LIFE OF LAURENCE
    OLIVIER AND VIVIEN LEIGH
OLIVIER IN CELEBRATION (editor)
SEAN O'CASEY: A LIFE
THE MAHABHARATA
DARLINGS OF THE GODS [novel, Coronet, 1990]
WILLIAM SHAKESPEARE: A LIFE

CAMPION'S GHOST

The Sacred and Profane Memories of John Donne, Poet

GARRY O'CONNOR

Hodder & Stoughton
LONDON SYDNEY AUCKLAND

British Library Cataloguing in Publication Data
O'Connor, Garry
  Campion's Ghost.
  I. Title
  823.914 [F]

ISBN 0-340-55374-X

Copyright © Garry O'Connor 1993

First published in Great Britain 1993

All rights reserved. No part of this publication may be
reproduced or transmitted in any form or by any means,
electronic or mechanical, including photocopying,
recording, or any information storage and retrieval
system, without either prior permission in writing from
the publisher or a licence permitting restricted copying.
In the United Kingdom such licences are issued by the
Copyright Licensing Agency, 90 Tottenham Court Road,
London W1P 9HE. The right of Garry O'Connor
to be identified as the author of this work has been
asserted by him in accordance with the Copyright,
Designs and Patents Act 1988.

Published by Hodder and Stoughton,
a division of Hodder and Stoughton Ltd,
Mill Road, Dunton Green, Sevenoaks, Kent TN13 2YA
Editorial Office: 47 Bedford Square, London WC1B 3DP

Typeset by Hewer Text Composition Services, Edinburgh
Printed in Great Britain by St. Edmundsbury Press, Bury St. Edmunds

In memory of
my sister-in-law

HEATHER

who died 14 December 1991

Contents

At the Height of my Celebrity ... 1

Part One: To Anger Destiny

1. It Begins in York ... 7
2. The Lord Keeper ... 16
3. Jezebel ... 26
4. The Citadel ... 32
5. Margaret in Arcadia ... 35
6. Underhill Shows Some Force ... 40
7. To Lie in Oblivion ... 48

Part Two: The Marriage Temple

8. Sex and Sovereignty ... 53
9. My Brother Henry ... 62
10. Kate Ferrars ... 66
11. The Golden Needle ... 73
12. Division ... 75
13. The Fox in his Lair ... 81
14. Mother and Son ... 91
15. Venus and Mars ... 98
16. The Turning ... 104
17. Hatfield Follies ... 109
18. Women are Angels Wooing ... 121

Part Three: A Falling Star

19. Riders ... 133
20. The Infiltration ... 138
21. A Convert ... 144
22. Quelque Chose from Court ... 149
23. Prisms of the Flesh ... 153

24	Captain of the Guard	158
25	Likeness Glues Love	168
26	In my Albany Lodging	172
27	The Boar Hunt	177
28	Infinity's Sunrise	178

Part Four: The Torch of Flesh

29	Underhill's Secret	187
30	Royal Divorce	194
31	The Incubus of Terror and Examination	207
32	The Race Is On	213
33	Caesar Shall Go Forth	218
34	The Iron Man	224
35	Death's Second Self	229
36	The Great Collector	234

My Play's Last Scene – February 1631   237

Historical Note   243

'Tis much that glass should be
As all confessing, and through-shine as I . . .
But all such rules, love's magic can undo
Here you see me, and I am you.

At the Height of my Celebrity

In the bleary darkened mirrors of Whitehall as I pass along the covered ways, I catch sight of myself. My eyes are wide and hollowed out, my hair, once full and dark with black and manly beard, now icicled and grey. Still tall and straight, I am gaunt in look and build. I am nearly sixty in this plaguey time when most men cannot hope to see thirty.

The date is February 1631. My memory stretches back to two or three people gathered together under the same plodding, one-syllable name. Donne. Forename John. John Donne. That's me.

The "Doctor" – cough, cough, or cynical, throat-clearing sound – of Divinity preaches his first sermon of Lent direct to Charles I of England, as if he is alone with him. I have done so for six years. I preached my first sermon to him only seven days after he became King. His Queen, Henrietta, sits beside him. And some of her delectable handmaidens. Yet I speak as if only to him. I did so with Scottish James, the present King's father.

The King reposes in a plain black cloth cloak to the ankle. He is as pale and impassive in the face as white tulip petals past their best.

I begin my blather.

"First as the God of power the Almighty rescues his servants from the jaws of death . . ."

Is this my canticle of glory? I call my homily "Death's Duel", and this is not far off the truth! All my life he's been my sparring partner. Ever since I can remember I have fought this bloody duel. Recently it's no longer been a game.

The printer has his copy ready for the press. Samuel Cooper has engraved a frontispiece. I have been so scurvily ill that not even the daily and copious swallowing of milk – how I loathe the filthy stuff – will stop fever from coming back or the vapours of my spleen from rising and choking me.

At last I am losing the fight. Or am I? I mean to cheat to the very end. Why not, when I have such a gift for theatricality? Court and stage are one, and everyone is a player. I have already rehearsed my own appearance in my death shroud. For my biggest moment of all I mean to be ready, engraved and drawn. I have ordered the wooden urn – the one on which in death I am due to stand – and procured a plank the size of my body. The charcoal fires in my study will be glowing.

Then I will strip bare these thin and emaciated shreds of flesh with which, alas, I can no longer pursue the sins of my hungry and thirsty youth. With knots tied at head and foot, I will put on my shroud.

And so I will stand, eyes closed, on the urn while the artist sketches my life-size figure on the plank. O yes, make no mistake, I mean to defeat death. And I will keep the drawing by my bedside, to remind me of what I am soon to be.

Only a little while ago I lost my mother; and then my Lucilla, perfect replica of my dead wife Anne, who died many, many years ago. Lucilla died at eighteen, just a shade older than Anne when I married her.

Here we go. Today I will give it to Our divine Majesty straight.

"All our periods and transitions in this life are so many passages from death to death. We have a winding sheet in our mother's womb which grows with us from our conception. We come into the world wound up in that sheet, for we come here to seek a grave . . ."

The King does not turn a hair. Is he as polite and attentive as he looks? I do not think so. He is a pious man and, secretly, I suspect, a Catholic, like my own mother. What a charade religion is.

Yet I play at just as artificial a deceit, trying to concoct, with elaborate flourishes, a magnificent coda to my own life. This is indeed Death's Duel! An intimate tête-à-tête on death with a great king.

I try to keep to my prepared text, but I am frightened. Malice breaks free in my heart. Ferocious thoughts swell and flood below the public repentance. I hook my sight in vain on Henrietta's flanking ladies, young luscious fruits juicily attired in simple, long, white gowns open at the front where they show well-cupped and turreted loveliness which my bony old fingers ache to close around.

Long ago, so long ago now, this is what would have happened. Words of that earlier self, long squashed in clerical dignity, leap to flash like salmon out of the dark waters where my shaky faith is anchored. "License my roving hands and let them go. Before, behind, between, above, below . . . Full nakedness, all joys are due to thee. As souls unbodied, bodies unclothed . . ."

Hush! I must put an end to this inner raving. Desperately I intone

At the Height of my Celebrity

the words, "Sin of fear". I hold on to my only hope of salvation. I cling to my prepared words as a gesture to my divine master and that divine master's representative on earth.

Can I not still lie on my back to feel their tongue and lips, or suffer their velvet leaves to drain my old sacs of long-idle joy?

"How much worse a death than death is this life . . ."

PART ONE
To Anger Destiny

1

It Begins in York

The strong sun's rays streamed down in triumphant gold splendour on the city of York. Stained glass in the Minster diluted its sovereign eye with mysterious alchemy, darting gentle fingering intimations into the dark recesses of stone. It was a day when everything on earth promised fair, when meadows which lay outside the city walls hummed with the enticement of honey, when summer flowers began their brief but glorious blazoning forth, when everything was governed by rising sap.

But Elizabethan England was ideological. Fear and distrust ate out its heart. About forty-five years in the past, in my poor reckoning, is that fatal day – fatal in more ways than one – on which there began the fight which rages in my divided soul.

In Master O'Hearne's schoolroom, above the civic chamber in the Guildhall, O'Hearne was instructing his small class of mixed ages and abilities made up entirely of the male sex. The oldest were eleven or twelve, but they, in spite of pale womanish faces and effeminate sighs, were already mature young men. Some of the youngest, at seven or eight, were fully fledged in theology and Latin.

"Mmm . . . Hugh, just run through the passage you learned last night."

Hugh Morton, a fat red-headed boy, stood in a gilded shaft of motes and began:

"Even they who are superiors of some are inferiors to others. The wife, though a mother of children, is under her husband. The husband, though head of the family, is under public magistrates. Public magistrates are under another, and all under the Queen. The Queen herself is under God."

Morton, who was fluent in this hogwash – or so O'Hearne believed it – swayed and almost yawned. O'Hearne pulled himself together. The boy was negligent, his manner not obedient: there was to be no slipping or he would lose his twenty pound a year and end by being fined as a recusant or for going to Mass in secret.

He knew one of the boys, Napesley, was a spy. No matter what you did in Yorkshire they fined you for recusancy. It had been rumoured, not long before, when the imprisoned Mary Stuart plotted with foreign agents to overthrow her cousin, that the whole of Yorkshire was taking up arms against the sovereign Queen.

No such thing will happen, thought O'Hearne. He rose laboriously to fetch his birch: cruel infliction on such a perfect morning, but small boys had little cave-keeping evils that needed rooting out.

There was bustle from the far side of the market square: signal for a public punishment. More political coercion; a nasty male growl of anticipation, disputes on the nature of the crime – such as there always were – some bawled words of command from bailiff, beadle or constable. Something very small, like fixing a pinching coe or stray beggar woman in the stocks for begging; everything had its ceremonial enforcement.

The sounds of the crowd swelled and swelled so that soon all O'Hearne's boys were at the lattice-windows of the Guildhall schoolroom, gaping at the sights below.

O'Hearne would have done anything not to let them go; but it was for them as much as their parents that such shows were put on. So he smiled, fawning upon those whose summer of life would soon be over. "Off you go." He exchanged with Napesley a look which said, "I know you approve."

What more could O'Hearne's Protestant masters of York want? He would stay in, read, mind his business and hope for better times. Until then he could dream of the good old days of the friars, the benign and erudite men in black and grey.

He did not hear the two Sheriff's men who stole into his empty schoolroom when his back was turned.

"Master O'Hearne," one addressed him. O'Hearne spun round; it was the moment he had long feared. Yet, now it had arrived, he felt joyous and light-hearted.

"By the order of the Council of the North we've been sent to arrest you on the charge of high treason."

One of the boys had denounced him to a friend of the evil and celebrated Richard Topcliffe, who had arrived in York. Napesley, of course. He sighed.

This was the Saturday when I rode to York to stay with O'Hearne, who a few years before had been my tutor in London. My mother often encouraged me to visit him. But my presence in York had another purpose. This was the day ordained for the execution

It Begins in York

of a Catholic traitor. Such dark events, well known in advance, held a peculiar fascination for me, and I would do my best to attend.

It was not entirely out of sick, unholy curiosity. I needed to know the answer to certain questions. Was the blood of the martyr just blood, or did it have magic powers, such as the cure of epilepsy, or impotence? Could it really make the lame walk? Even when I was at Oxford – I had matriculated there when I was twelve – I had identified with those who did not conform.

My mother had sent me to Hart Hall where, as the college had no chapel, I managed to avoid Anglican services. Some Catholics I knew were forced to attend such services to escape the fines, with dire results. One had his stomach turned to fire and drank eight gallons of beer to put it out, but the heat could only be quenched by a shriving priest. Another had cast off his clothes and run naked through the city, dying a few days later in agony of mind in the confinement of his room.

Despite this persecution my days in Oxford had been exciting. The glories of Edmund Campion were still on everyone's lips. Protégé of Lord Burghley, dazzling satellite of the Earl of Leicester, Campion had been the exemplary English scholar and gentleman. The impact of his startling conversion to Catholicism had, with the passing of a few years, hardly lessened. Vivid accounts of his life, of his ordination as a priest and his entry into the Jesuits, still provoked violent dispute, even fist fights and duels.

For ten years Campion had travelled abroad. His return to England as a Jesuit missionary priest and his "Brag" to the lords of Her Majesty's privy council in which he confessed to his faith and modestly set out his purpose, had brought the kingdom to a state of panic and alarm. At the time I had been eight. At Hart Hall years later I had secretly been shown a copy of his *Decem Rationes* or "Ten Reasons", which had so terrified the authorities on its unlawful publication that they had ordered the Bishop of London *and* the Regius Professors at both Oxford and Cambridge to refute its arguments. By the time I was at Oxford more than a score of works attacking Campion had been printed.

These only served to give the Jesuit even greater lustre. Those known to have slipped away quietly to meet Campion at secret hiding places a few miles outside Oxford were eagerly sought out and questioned. Much circulated were those resounding words with which he had rebuked his Queen: "There will come, Elizabeth, the day that will show thee clearly which have loved thee, the Society of Jesus or the offspring of Luther."

II

In front of the iron-clamped oak door which served as jail next to the courthouse there now swirled a large collection of the people of the town.

More than usual in that crowd were numbered the goodwives of middle age, from twenty to thirty-five, well nourished on beef and ale, with round and ruddy cheeks, broad shoulders and well-developed busts: bold and rotund matrons with a grievance to vent.

"If she is to be pressed for feeding a papist priest, then I might as well be disembowelled for keeping my chalice indoors!" said one fiery dame of forty with deep trenches in her beauty's field. Her neighbour growled assent.

"Anyone's entitled to worship what they feel. There's old Wendy Lean – she worships her dog, but they don't chop off her head for it!"

"This woman has brought shame upon us all!" barked a severe and dismal voice.

There was a knot of hardfaced men close by. Grave, bearded, sable-cloaked, they spurned the frivolous ruff of middle-class fashion and hid black brows from the sun under steeple crowns. They bore grim and rigid expressions.

A woman turned and spat, which provoked pleasure enough to crease one beetlebrow.

By now the grass plot before the doors was trampled into mud by thrashing feet. The crowd had long passed a hundred as, still growing, it argued the merits of the case.

"I think pressing's too good for her – she should be burnt."

"Surely a turn in the pillory's enough?"

"Tie her to the whipping post and flog her within an inch of her life!"

While the victim or guilty party was eagerly expected by this growing herd; and while it was joined now by the boys, apprentices and older people of the town, then split up within itself to form pockets of rival entertainment – with a juggler or a troubadour

It Begins in York

diverting eyes from the main horror – I cantered clumsily into the middle of this mob.

My large black mount reared up and with its hooves almost clouted one or two menials about the ears or chops. I slid ineptly from the saddle, grabbing the reins, hoping to hold the horse back from greater damage.

"Whoah, whoah Midnight! . . ." I shouted at my mare.

As I was a gentleman the crowd made way. But these people, most of them old, showed blackened teeth and empty gums and mocked my lack of horsemanship.

They had good cause. The puritans snarled. Here was something that smacked of that most corrupt of institutions: Court. Yet I but pretended – or aspired, adopting the outward appurtenances, but quite without credentials.

To the crowd appears a dandy, ladies' man. Large-eyed, with long black curls, earrings in the shape of our saviour's cross, blushing like a modest girl. But I was not young anymore. Oxford, then Cambridge. I had a strong conceit of myself. I had birth, beauty, good shape, discourse, learning, gentleness, virtue, youth, liberality. Not to mention a strong lusty member, able to iron out any wrinkle in a girl or young woman.

"Out with your dainty rapier else I'll prick you with a pin," jeered a puritan.

I fingered the very latest and deadliest of swords but then a jerk from Midnight brought me back to the need to tether this wild and difficult beast if I was ever going to get near enough to witness the execution – or whatever it might turn out to be – let alone enjoy it.

I pulled my unwilling mare over to a nearby sturdy shrub and knotted her reins to its trunk. I had not forgotten the slight on my virility. But where was O'Hearne? I was at our meeting place, but I looked around for him in vain.

The spike-studded door creaked, yawned and gaped ominously open. What had been festive now grew ugly, stained, and dark, so that the sun, no longer a blessing, shrank to a babbling, incoherent intruder.

The York beadle slid out from the black hole first, a shadow emerging into the sunshine, a grim and grisly presence of punishment, a sword dangling from his thigh, a staff of office in his hand.

Several constables followed in the uniform of grey and blue, bearing halberds.

The sight which next the crowd saw cut a path through it like a sword of unearthly light. The butcher's wife – Margaret Clitheroe, in sound coarse and abattoirish – was as far from beef marrow bones and blood puddings as healing power from an Elizabethan surgeon's knife.

She was tall with an elegant bearing, a figure of perfect straightness. She was young, so there was a sudden hush and intake of disbelieving breath. Her hair was dark and abundant, so glossy that it tossed off the sunshine with a gleam. The face was mysterious and attractive, marked by an impressive brow and deep black eyes.

Even the puritans, assembled there to see divine will satisfied, sensed another kind of will about to stir.

Through the lane opened in the crowd of spectators, and preceded by the beadle and constables, Margaret started to walk towards the place where she was to be punished. Soon she arrived at the west side of the market-place before a sort of scaffold, or penal machine, a framework for the assembly of instruments of discipline.

Beside the scaffolding Richard Topcliffe, chief torturer and catcher of recusants, strutted like a grandee. A giant of a man, he was close-shaven. He had blond hair, blue eyes and was dressed meticulously like a gentleman; sometimes he would adopt a weak, regretful pose, as if stirred into cruelty with reluctance. At this time, early in his career, he cultivated the scholarly, impartial approach. He had become a master of the art of wielding suspicion.

Between one- and two-thirds of the people were reckoned to be Catholics, but they no longer had any defence in law, while their whole inherited pattern of life had been dubbed criminal. To trap the priests who tried to minister to them, or to the noble families who were their figureheads, a whole army of spies, blackmailers, informers and law enforcers had been enlisted.

In such a threatened nation no one could afford to have an open mind. Better ten innocents should die than one guilty party escape. Topcliffe understood this well. To apply justice, which was based on an open-minded scrutiny of the evidence, meant that the outcome would be uncertain. This could never be risked. Spies, *agents provocateurs*, torture, backed by public shows of rhetoric and by an endless production of books and pamphlets, these were the tools of the Protestant terror.

Our terror, that is; it became my personal weapon.

Margaret climbed the steps to the platform. Her slender, appealing figure sustained the weight of scores of searching, unrelenting eyes, fastened and concentrated on every move or expression she might make.

"In sight of God and us," began Topcliffe, "your guilt, Margaret Clitheroe, is great. You must receive the full sentence of the law."

"Law, what law? – the law of the Babylon whore and her scoundrels!" shouted a voice from the crowd.

Topcliffe blinked and let the sun warm the lids of his eyes. He had men placed in the crowd. Arrests would swiftly follow.

"This is a scandal to our crown!" shouted another voice.

Topcliffe opened his eyes and looked into the crowd. His gaze fell on me and on the man next to me whom, up to then, I had scarcely noticed.

My neighbour, some ten or more years older than I was, had a shrewd look, and although his face expressed sensuality, he appeared wise in judgement: his black hair was tinged with white, his beard full and virile, his neck strong and brown.

He stood with legs apart, easily, in a posture of worldliness. Immensely tall, he was dressed as a nobleman and wore a lace-edged collar and cuffs but no ruff. He wore no earring, neither was his face painted, like mine. His colours, the richness of the material he wore, proclaimed him to be at the very apex of fashion. I shuddered at his unknown identity, fearing he might be recognised by Topcliffe as a Catholic.

Topcliffe's mouth moved and watered slightly. He had never thought of Mistress Clitheroe as bait, but it now seemed she could serve as such.

"Margaret Clitheroe, you are condemned to be stripped, laid out on the scaffold, your hands bound to posts, with a door placed on top of you, piled to the weight of 800 pounds. For three days you are to be so pressed, and kept alive with a little barley bread and puddle water."

In the front row of the crowd, horse and insult forgotten, I swallowed with pain. I had greeted the stranger casually and without another word stood beside him, but instinctively sheltered in his calm and strength, as if in the shadow of a spreading oak. I had lost my own father when I was small. I knew about grief and pain. The physician whom my mother had married within six months of his death had never much taken my own father's place.

My father had been a powerful City of London figure. A rich ironmonger. A king in iron. My stepfather was a fall from grace.

Campion's Ghost

A tragedy, as Aristotle calls it, when someone topples from a high state to a much lower one.

"Mr Dimmisdale," said Topcliffe, who spoke to a tall, black-bearded, morose young clergyman who drooped near by, "the young woman may acknowledge her fault to you." He turned back to the scaffold. "Woman, make your peace with God."

She would have nothing to do with any Anglican confessor.

I found the response of the condemned woman penetrated my feelings. If it were I who had to meet so horrible a punishment I would have screamed and thrown myself on the ground, stabbed myself, done anything to avoid it being carried out.

"My joy is death," spoke Margaret in a soft and gentle voice. All through her trial she had guarded silence. "Death at whose name I have so often quaked with fear because I wanted this world's eternity. I have done with my robes. I fear no shame of what I am commanded . . ."

Steadily and without passion she began to plead her innocence. I grew nauseated and giddy at the thought of this lovely young woman being sacrificed. Part of me wanted to assume the role of her champion, jump up and pit all my mortal vigour against the cruel system. For I had fallen instantly for her. I tasted perfect love with death and grief as its end. Her loss would be unbearable.

Two hangmen now mounted the steps and began to divest Margaret of her finery. She wore a rich gown, embroidered, and adorned with gold buttons.

"Can't we do anything to stop this?" I whispered to my neighbour. But he said nothing. He had some air about him, alike to that of the young woman. In a way I could not quite put my finger on, they were oddly together. So, too, were others who stood there. I myself felt a mysterious affinity, as between an artist and his model, an inexplicable yet sensual sensation.

Convulsions of horror and outrage continued to pass through the crowd. An old woman hurled herself at Topcliffe. The urbane torturer put a hand to his brow and reeled back shaken. Topcliffe would not tolerate any physical threat, even from an old woman. He drew his sword. The harridan sobbed and screamed as she was carried off by constables.

The puritans smiled as they saw revealed yet again the frailty of woman's flesh. Had not John Knox, the Scotsman, written in his Protestant *Blast against the Monstrous Regiment* that nature had made women weak, impatient, feeble and foolish? From a corrupt and venomed foundation could spring no wholesome water. This was popular stuff among the men in England where – in the reformed spirit, that is – the women lagged well behind the men.

Margaret had lost her girdle. Her breastplate had been unpinned, and she was being unlaced by crooked and coarse fingers. One man stood on each side of her, and from back and shoulders and thighs ripped her gown, her busk support and undergarments, revealing her lovely firm breasts, slender shoulders and naked loins. She fell to her knees. They pushed her on her back and – joined by two others – roped her down to wooden posts by wrist and ankle.

The more ugly, contrary voices in the crowd had swollen to a high and screaming pitch of anger. Margaret's nakedness, far from being a dirty feast to excite jeering and lewd anti-papist celebration, suddenly became a shield and weapon to Topcliffe's enemies.

"She is expectant, you deaf old brute, in her early months," shrieked the old woman at Topcliffe.

"I don't believe it," gasped Topcliffe. "Let her die quickly," he commanded. "Pile on every stone you have!"

"Child-killer! Child-killer! Child-killer!" The crowd picked up the cry. The executioners hastily placed a sharp stone under Margaret's head. They lowered the door over her breast and stomach, and began piling rocks on it. Her ribs snapped and burst forth from her skin.

2

The Lord Keeper

"The Footman Inn," the man observed. "I believe like all good English parlours full of flies and fleas and all variety of vermin for inspection or dissection. You have to drink deep to kill off the bugs."

The death of Margaret Clitheroe had confused me and disturbed me. I was in such sympathy that I was tempted to follow her myself. By the end most of the crowd had been on their knees in prayer. Was this to be the path that God had ordained for me? At this time I was as wax, ready for the imprint of the Pope's design. Or would I choose a different way, which would lead to a different, more comfortable form of ruin?

"Hey, ostler," shouted the stranger at the sight of an inn servant passing the top of the stairs. "Bring us a pot of Canary."

"Coming, good sir."

"Make it Sherris Sack," the stranger changed his order.

"I tied my horse in the yard, but there were no oats, only some dry peas and beans. They say oats are too dear."

"Because of the harvest last year?"

"Because of the fines." The stranger had stopped grinning. "They're serious. Soon this part of the world will be the poorest in England." He laughed again.

"Here's the sherry." I felt uneasy. The sack arrived as more drinkers forged upstairs. The downstairs parlour was full. Judging from the round roof of the old inn, this was a shady place compared with the market outside, and not too dirty despite what my new friend, who seemed not keen to give much away about himself, had said.

"Hhmm, not bad," he commented as he drank from the cup. I picked mine up and swigged some of the fortified wine which vaporised my sullen mood.

"Well, here's to you," he said, raising his cup. "It's not often two people meet in such circumstances – although these executions fall more frequently." His voice was deep, and he could not keep back a rich and irrepressible tendency to laugh.

"It appals me," I grunted, "that they should need to make such brutal shows in order to instil obedience."

"Obedience is not faith," said the man lightly, fixing on me his twinkling brown eyes, which had about them almost a malevolent or devilish air. "Here's to the Sacred College!"

His words sent a tremor through me. I had no doubt Margaret Clitheroe had been harbouring Jesuits; but although the everyday sights of hanged felons, running sores, and myriad deformations never much shocked me, her punishment had been so much greater than the crime, if such it was.

"You cannot terrorise people into belief," I said in a neutral tone of voice.

"Ah, but you see," said my companion, "they're frightened. They're trying out something new, and they don't know whether it will work."

"They?" I asked provokingly, as if to know if he was one of them.

"Well, what do we care?" He stared down at me from his lazy, good-natured eyes and yawned and blinked. His eyes appeared to change to a mischievous blue.

"I don't mind," he went on, "if my dear friend Callow wants to sell a drop of our Saviour's blood for twenty pounds. I'm happy to believe the balance of humours in the body fluctuates with the fullness and leanness of the moon. But I'm not like Bishop Latimer whom Queen Mary burned at the stake. He thought that if he became a friar he could never be damned!" He chuckled.

"Then why didn't Bishop Latimer become a Catholic?" I could see that he was manipulating my feelings.

"Oh, I expect they wouldn't pay him enough. And he could also savour the sexy joys of wedlock. Who in his right mind would be a celibate priest? The Pontifical pudenda are about as useful as vestigial nipples on a man."

Celibacy never tempted me. I had no gift for it. My senses had ached at the sacrifice of Margaret Clitheroe's beauty. The hunger she had awoken had not been altogether spiritual.

At this moment two men, presbyters or puritans who had been in the market square, came charging up the stairs, swords drawn, bucklers pointing towards adversaries as yet unseen.

"There he is!" shouted the first man pointing to the tall and bearded nobleman.

"With Satan's mooncalf!" He meant me.

"Search his pockets. I'm sure he carries the bread."

My companion rose and turned to the window, throwing it open wide, as if we might make our escape from here, although we would risk breaking our necks.

"Come, you beast of disorder, I saw you talking to Lucifer while that witch died!" taunted the second man.

They were close to the table where we sat, but their intended victim, I noticed, had not lost his good humour and composure. Seizing the large pot of Sherris Sack he flung its contents in their faces so they spluttered and backed away. I drew my rapier, a much superior weapon in such a confined space to the unwieldy sword and buckler. I had trained with the best in London, an Italian Protestant refugee who had taught me every devilish Neapolitan thrust and feint.

The puritans had confirmed what I had perceived, which made me none too easy, namely that my drinking friend was publicly known to have Catholic connections. God help me if he was one of the most dangerous sort, a Jesuit! I too might be arrested and disembowelled for sticking up for such a man.

The assailants, seeing my superior armament and my determination to use it – and apparently not noticing my youth or inexperience – made off to the far end of the room where they had counsel of one another. Others had now gathered at the top of the stairs – one or two goodwives, another courtier, dressed much as myself, perhaps from London or the son of a local landed gentleman. Some grooms or tapsters watched avidly.

The first man spat.

"Our say will come," said the second. With murderous looks at myself and the stranger they withdrew, while the onlookers vanished. I, relieved but also swelled in vanity and by the enormity of my success in frightening them off, shouted for more sherry, which arrived almost at once to take the place of that which had soaked and stained the floor rushes. These were gathered up deftly and replaced with a gleaming fresh supply.

"Thank you," said the stranger with his bright, but dark and amused eyes fastened on mine. He extended his hand, which I seized.

"You don't carry a sword," I challenged him.

The Lord Keeper

"I know how to use one."

"But would you?"

He could see the drift of my question, but he chose to avoid it.

"I don't think," he said, "that they will report us. Puritans are not popular in York."

"But Catholics are . . . ?"

The man laughed, sat back, drinking more. "They were right. I am in sympathy with Catholics."

I blushed. When I think of it now I do not know why I could not do anything to stop it, but the blood rose to my ears and set up a powerful buzzing.

"My name is John Donne," I stuttered, "I am a student . . . at er . . . Cambridge. I have . . ." and here I became self-conscious, so that I was almost making a "play" for him, turning on him my large and frank brown eyes to fill the Catholic with complete trust in me, "a family with a blackened history. On my father's side we are descended from Welsh nobility. We were Yorkists during the Wars of the Roses, but my great-grandfather made his peace with Henry VII.

"My father, a younger son of the family, was sent to London and became a tradesman, an ironmonger. We still have the family arms – a leaping or jumping wolf with a crest of snakes bound in a sheaf."

I was aware I was playing a game. If anything could have drawn out intimacy from another, this should have done it. But the reticent stranger was neither interested in me, nor encouraged to talk about himself.

"And your mother – what of her?" he asked in an indifferent tone.

My hand shot to the hilt of my rapier. To talk about my mother stirred ambiguous feelings. I had a distasteful suspicion that this stranger understood about me, had been informed about my mother and our family.

"Who are you?" I demanded in an arrogant way.

The man thumped his fist on the table and roared with laughter. "Who am I? . . . Well answered – you are right to throw out my question! I deceived you. For I know your mother."

"You mean . . ." I was horrified, and again felt my hand reaching towards my weapon. "You have known all along who I am?"

The black thought crossed my mind that my mother had set this stranger to spy on me, yet I knew she would never sink to such an ignoble action, or behave in any underhand way. Yet why – and about this I felt sick and anxious – should I suffer such instinctive suspicion towards her?

"No, no, have no fears, nothing like that. England is a small country. If you have moved, as I have, through the great places of learning you know and hear of those who are expected to make their mark."

I sighed with relief. "I am flattered . . ."

"I believe you are something of a poet."

"I should like to be thought so."

"Some Donnes have suffered for the faith. I need not mention . . ."

He spoke correctly. Our family has, for use of a better word, a "libertine" strain – and a devout one. There would seem to be nothing much in between the rakes and the religious maniacs.

I had at home half of Sir Thomas More's tooth, a holy relic given to me by my grandmother, who had been the niece of Henry VIII's chancellor.

"Have you formed any opinion of your own vocation? Perhaps you have a divine gift?"

I attempted to ignore this question.

"The man to whom Divine Providence vouchsafes a vocation is bound to pursue it."

"So whom have I the honour of addressing?" I again asked.

The man looked down at his fancy buckled shoes. "Sir Jasper Underhill, Gentleman. At your service." Then he laughed.

"Did I hear you correctly, sir?" I asked icily. Again my mother had talked frequently of such a man, a preposterous rake and dandy, and the black sheep of a devout yet divided Catholic family. Everything was devious and crooked. Someone might be impersonating Underhill, either to reap the reward of my surprise and support, or as an agent in the pay of the government, to find out if I myself was a Catholic. Yet this man did not seem as if he was going to touch me for a florin.

"Yes. Yes, you did hear me correctly. We are the Underhills of Presteigne in County Radnor. I am on my way over from Ireland where we have estates; I make for France and Italy to study."

Had not this, I recalled, once been the path followed by Edmund Campion? But surely no one would be watching and following this Underhill that he needed to take a boat from the Humber. Perhaps he, too, was a connoisseur of executions.

"The agents and officers keep contacting me, and watching over me as if they feared I would become a Jesuit and cast devils out of women. They fail to see, poor idiots, that a devil is the last thing I would ever cast from a woman. I prefer them still in!"

I shuddered. This was the choice that had been so often presented to me, between the painful climb to the good, and the icy plunge into the abyss. Were we a sort of demon with predilections for goodness, or saints with an overpowering proclivity towards evil?

I sought to reverse his threat. I insisted on asking, "And you yourself, sir, have not been tempted by the power of priesthood?"

"Become like that poor fool Campion? You must be joking. The finest scholar in Oxford, the favourite of the Queen, he could dispute any subject from astrology to ants and moldwarps. He could have been Bishop of London with huge benefices, a wife – and a mistress!"

Not only had Oxford resounded with stories of Campion's courage and sanctity, but in my own family Campion was the ideal, the perfect man. The Queen and her ministers had tried to woo and bribe him to change his mind. But he would not hedge his beliefs, nor waver in his avowal. "The expense is reckoned, the enterprise is begun; it is of God, it cannot be withstood. So the faith was planted: so it must be restored." His death revived the Catholic cause. Every day my mother would say prayers for him.

"But Ignatius Loyola, the Spaniard," I pleaded, "founded the Jesuits fifty or more years ago under the banner of obedience for that very reason – to resign all intent of wealth, honour and pleasure."

"Why would a modern man like me, with riches and freedom at his beckoning, want to tie himself down with all that mumble-jumble?"

I cannot explain why, but to hear him talk so scathingly unleashed in me anger on the side of Catholics.

"Would you become a machine?" He gave a foolish laugh. "Would you take the vows of poverty, chastity, and obedience *to the death* – *perinde ac cadaver*. Would you embark on ten years of study and spiritual exercises – just to get yourself killed in two."

"I am sure I would not be any good."

"Nothing deflects a Jesuit, not even the rope and the rack!" I was turning into strictures on him my own mother's haranguing of me, for she had always wanted no more or less than for me to become a Jesuit.

"Perhaps only they really know how to stop the devil."

Underhill hooted with laughter. "That's because they are devils themselves. Do you know that they are even allowed to swear an oath in one meaning, and keep it in another?"

"That sounds very wicked," I said coldly.

II

Further talk was cut short as voices and movement up the stairs forced us to become vigilant. I bit my lip and kicked myself for not having had the wit to leave straight after the puritans had gone, for most likely they had run off to plead their case with the authorities. As for Underhill, he seemed in no way bothered. What a prating foolish fop, I thought, more intent on shaking out his cuffs than avoiding purgatory. A man who could become many various men in a revolving moon. Yet why were the puritans after him? They must know something I did not. And why was he at Margaret Clitheroe's execution?

A moment later swarms of armed and liveried men surrounded us. Underhill rose to his feet, so did I, becoming conscious that the *lèse-majesté* and nonchalance of his sleepy good humour offered the best protection.

The retainers swiftly parted for their lord, a cheerful man well into middle age, perhaps thirty or thirty-five, grey-haired, with puckered brow and lines of resolution around a strong and forceful chin. He was a political heavyweight, perhaps a member of our government.

"So here you are!" he bawled at us without rancour. Underhill stood well before me and his appearance impressed the noble. "Why, they are gentlemen."

He came over and peered at us closely. "Who could say their mischief is yet mature? This one – " he meant me " – is hardly capable of growing hairs on his chin. It's true that the other has a little more mischief settled in his face, yet if he was a real Jesuit – " and here the noble laughed, "he certainly would not be so stupid as to dress like an apricot who would only grow on an aristocrat wall!"

The nobleman thought this was a good joke and as no one else laughed I joined in. He glared at me.

"Sir Thomas Egerton – at your service! We've had a complaint by those qualified before law to make denunciations – and on which the law is obliged to act. But puritans!" He spat on to the rush floor.

The Lord Keeper

"Them I hate more roundly than papists. In fact, if pressed about it, I can't say I hate papists that much, I rather admire them, but if they plot then I'll . . ."

I felt my pulse beat terribly fast, while my forehead broke out in a thick and prickly sweat. It was really my duty to tell Egerton, who was Master of the Rolls, or some other high court dignitary, my suspicions about the religion of my friend. But I would keep quiet.

Yet what if Underhill himself offered some reckless comment or other, then I would be implicated. I knew from the airy and heedless behaviour of some of my own family – those that were religiously as opposed to physically debauched, that is – that Jesuits reach a point when they will not hold back; when, to put their moral force into the world as an example to everyone, they will claim defiantly that they are what they are.

What if Underhill had a similar instinct for self-immolation? Where would it leave me, and how could I side-step its damage?

Egerton doffed his feathered hat and helped himself to some Sherris Sack, swallowed a mouthful and surveyed the pair of us. I had a peculiar sense that he knew Underhill, but did not want to acknowledge it. Something about their whole manner and address was similar, yet this could be explained by the conformity of their upbringing and the style of their lives:

"If you are Catholics and don't wish to own to it, that is a matter for your own conscience. I am *not* Topcliffe who, although I have but arrived in York an hour or two ago, has sent out ripples of infamy which hours ago greeted me on the road. I prefer not to let Catholics make bloody martyrs of themselves."

"Far from it," I spoke up boldly, "I am not a Catholic, but I come from a Catholic family. I wish to make my way at Court, and I wonder if I might be able to ask your advice on how to start."

"What's your name, young man?"

"John Donne."

"Are you not the stepson of Dr John Syminges?"

"I am."

"He is my very own physician. Absolutely useless, like all of 'em. The only thing is to post a stout retainer by his front door. If there's a new epidemic, or the daily body count grows out of hand, the doctor'll know about it first and so when he packs his bags to leave London my servant runs to inform me. The only cure for the plague is a lusty pair of legs! Well . . ."

He paused for a moment to wipe the sweat from his brow. "I

know all about you. You're at Cambridge and, as they say, a bit shaky in terms of faith. I'm right, aren't I? Correct me, of course, but they say while at Oxford you escaped taking the Oath by saying you were younger than you were. You are dangerous, John Donne. Watch it, young man!"

I sweated again. It had been my mother who made me swear not to take the oath of allegiance to the Queen, curse on her. It would mean they kept a Star Chamber file on me.

Egerton helped himself to more sack. The man was more than clever. There were some two or three thousand noble families in England and he gave the impression that he knew every one of them.

"Well, young men's oaths and beliefs are for trimming and changing – don't you agree?"

He addressed the last question to Underhill, who hummed, looked away and said nothing, clearly pained by this exchange. He coughed, did his best to radiate a bored and indifferent expression. I wondered why he said nothing – or Egerton nothing to him.

"My Lord," I said, "this is Sir Jasper Underhill. He is on his way to Italy to study."

"Study?" asked the Lord of the Rolls.

"Sculpture," I added quickly. "He has an absolute passion for the nude, isn't that so, Sir Jasper?"

"Especially the naked variety," added Underhill with a twinkle which the nobleman caught.

"Ha ha!" roared the courtier. "That's a good one. Well, he'll find plenty of that in Italy. A big flesh shambles if ever there was one. You know, I myself was begot between unwedded sheets. I wonder if the good priest Edward Billoton, whom I – dressed in the pomp and ceremony of justice – put away at Westminster last week, knew a bastard was accusing him.

"Not only was I born to a married Cheshire squire, who rogered my unwed mother with great, well you know – but I will let you into an even deeper secret . . ."

He waved to Underhill and myself to sit down, and we faced each other across the table. He spoke in a quiet and confidential voice.

"I was summoned by the Star Chamber when I was a law student in London – do you know why? . . . For going to Catholic Mass . . . One goes through these stages!"

Egerton, as slippery as he was genial, watched both of us: those who confess have barbed tongues as ready to catch as to console.

The Lord Keeper

Who knew if his disposition really was kind? I certainly did not. I had never felt so awkward and threatened. Had I given Underhill away I may have saved a thousand souls from the curse of papist belief.

Yet what if Underhill and Egerton were conspiring together to trap me? Again I questioned myself as to why Egerton had not asked Underhill to give an account of himself. The anti-papists in England would sink to any low trick to defeat the papal monster. What held me back? Perhaps there was another presence here with all three of us – besides, I have to add, the presence of my wretched mother which pursued me unforgivingly.

"So you must believe that I am sensitive to the religious predicament of others – especially to one such as you, John Donne. With the mixed fortunes of your family . . ." He let it hang in the air, like a menace.

"I do – I do, I do," I stammered.

Egerton fixed his eye on me. "Then my advice to you, Master Donne, is to make your way quickly . . ."

My nerves faltered. "What should I do?"

"To begin with, you ought to inform on one or two of your friends. Such an action from you, with your clouded background, and one which is so open to" – and he spoke the words slowly and carefully – "misinterpretation and manipulation, would be taken as a sign of change."

I clapped my hand to my head, for a great pain struck there.

The image of Margaret Clitheroe, the soul of beauty, whose naked shame, and the sordid spectacle of whose end had carried my imagination to a fever pitch that I would never have believed possible, overrode every stirring of ambition inside me.

"But I know no recusants!" I cried out in torment.

3

Jezebel

Whore of Babylon Jezebel, the mighty yet confused subcontinent of the mind wrestled with a deeper fable which I had already slightly uncovered. I did not know at that time how Margaret Clitheroe would haunt me like a goddess: who was she?

Atlanta, perhaps, for I, like everyone else, was steeped more in Ovid than in the Gospel of Mark, spun out my fancies of what the real world was on the humming wheels of ancient mythology. It lived.

It sung to me every hour; the filth, the smoke, the oily grating and noise, the sheer beastliness and muddy insignificance of survival were countered by that golden, yet spiteful and unpredictable world which had captured my imagination.

I was frightened. I hesitated, I hovered; at one moment I felt an impulse to evil would master me, at another that its opposite could drive me to equal desperation.

I still have to know why the death of Margaret Clitheroe happened, and why I had been so drawn to it. They say that on that sun-kissed York morning Margaret Clitheroe converted a hundred souls. Did I ever convert anyone? The answer must be no.

Here is the old Dean again, forced to intercede in his early life, trying to detach his true self from his false.

O'Hearne, for a start, I knew to be a recusant. I wondered what had happened to him, because he had taught me strictness about keeping appointments.

Egerton had left and, detaching myself from Sir Jasper Underhill, I followed him out of the inn, collected Midnight from the bush to which I had tied the halter, and crossed over the Minster square to the schoolroom.

O'Hearne was not to be found. The hall seemed like a shop where the keeper had just slipped out for five minutes or so; I sat down in the hope that O'Hearne would soon be back, thinking, for a bachelor, how a schoolmaster's life could be ideal.

Jezebel

Here, in reaction to the fatigue of my mind, I fell into a dream of my own childhood. When I was ten the Queen made a visit to our poor house, and we put on a masque and pageant for her. We had a river in our park, and where she was seated on the bank the bushes were opened and Father Neptune appeared with nymphs in attendance. He recited a long poem hailing her as Queen of the Seas; we then had a pageant with Venus, who handed over her sceptre of beauty to Elizabeth. The Queen wore a suit of blue velvet whose train was borne by no fewer than four ladies. Invited into our house, she called for a wooden staff to help her upstairs.

This memory lasted but a moment. By the lectern I noticed a piece of paper on which I found a note:

"They have come for me. Please arrange bail."

The writing was O'Hearne's. I felt damned for eternity by my own last words to Egerton. I was caught. To ignore O'Hearne's plea was treachery to an old friend, but to meddle with the guardians of the law was to declare my family's allegiance to the old faith.

II

At this moment the door bursts open behind me and a young Scot enters. He must have been one of those on his way to find his future in London. He is in a height of fashion. An olive-coloured suit of the type that clings to his limbs, a pair of unscoured stockings. His neck cuffs come from Edinburgh, his wrist cuffs from London – and both are strangers to his shirt. He has a barren half-acre of face where an eminent nose advances itself. He is tended by one or two creepy fellows who make way for their master, the young Laird.

"What a grand schoolroom," he said in an arrogant tone. "We have nothing as canny as this in Scotland. Don't tell me they made you master?"

"No," I answered evenly, "its master, my friend, is away on business."

"It is he, I am told, who serves the Antichrist, and conjures small people's minds with witchcraft."

So he was trying to trick me.

"Who told you this?"

"Friends, man, who are not in league with the Devil, and seductive painted whores like Margaret Clitheroe. I saw your face when she died. I was watching you, mon."

I stepped back, hand on the hilt of my sword. This peascot wrangler made me think of that wretched scribbler about martyrs, not the Scottish Antichrist John Knox but John Foxe, so beloved of the puritans and Protestants for his feats of arguing with the devil. His followers went about the countryside in gangs, and when they found a house where they thought the Catholic host was being celebrated, they attacked it with staves, broke down the windows, saying, "Jesus, we have come to drive you away!" They believed he was there.

"A look is the gate of the mind – yours was a Pape!" He was determined not to let me escape.

Here indeed was a very young and impetuous man, possibly younger than myself, who was deliberately trapping himself through pride and puritan arrogance into a situation where he could not withdraw.

"Catholic or Protestant, what does it matter?" I said as gently as I could.

"What does it matter?" the young Scot replied: "I'll choke in hell sooner than swallow such Vatican garbage!"

The boy was still in the stage of his extravagant passion. "I suppose you are one of these Londoners," he said to me, "attracted by the filth of lewdness in the theatre. I shouldn't wonder if you would go to a play on a Sunday . . ."

"On a Sunday, a Monday or whenever I want," I replied, but no longer trying to keep back my temper.

"An excuse for immorality. With boys as women. I wouldn't be surprised if you hadn't played the orange-wanton yourself," sneered the young Scot.

"Come outside, mon!" I mocked him. My heart was pounding with joy at the prospect of fighting this supercilious Lutheran or Calvinist puggy, or whatever he was. No doubt he would have loved to take his argument forward by stages. How they loved to dispute, these puritans.

"We'll be all right here," he answered, as his servants took up positions around the hall.

"The advantage is on your side," I said. "And the light is dying."

"Men," he said to his servants. "Light the torches and lay

down your swords so that our friend may see there is no advantage."

Suddenly Underhill swaggered into the school hall, attended by a servant. Seeing what was about to happen he took me by the arm. "Resist temptation," he said. "Don't take any notice."

"I can't back off," I hissed.

"I can see him playing in the 'Creation to the Crucifix'," sneered one of the young Scot's companions. They laughed, although I saw no reason why they should. Puritans had all but stamped out the miracle and mystery plays which once were so popular. I loved them – above all the lives of the saints in Latin.

I shook myself free of Underhill. There seemed to be no restraining the young Scot. I glanced again at Underhill who sighed and signalled the inevitability of the clash. I knew enough of the ways of the world to see what was expected of me. Underhill had indicated to me to take up the challenge; now we had some indefinable sense of likeness.

"If I could avoid fighting, I would," I said to my adversary.

He gave me the petted lip and lifted his head derisively. "Yes, because the coward metropolitan papist knows he would lose."

"Enough," I said. I drew my sword.

The torches were lit. The seconds took up their posts. I was a swordsman skilled well beyond my years; I was very calm, no feigned strike or punto reverso, hardly a retaliatory cut, only a prepared blade, but very careful in my placing. I kept my distance and proportion, ready for every twist and turn in my opponent's play.

The young Scot was impetuous and excited: he threw himself into each foin as if it was his last. *Stoccata. Stramazoun.* I would downthrust his blow. *Stoccata* again. *Stoccata*! These made me place more and more soberness and reserve behind my warding off. It needed but a few moments for my opponent to uncover himself with a degree more carelessness than was prudent. An overreaching "hay!" put him at my mercy. He was disarmed while Underhill and the Scottish second pressed forward to draw the duel to its end.

But something in me seemed to provoke and inflame the young Scot even further, although I studiously avoided giving any kind of sign or word that I exulted in my win, or that I wanted recognition of my superior prowess.

"That was just the beginning," said the Scot, wiping the sweat from his brow, and straightening his cuff. "You think we don't want to go the whole way. I'm not setting out to sea just to make me sick."

I tried to ignore these words but they were to stick in my memory. "You have fought well," I said. "What other satisfaction do you need?"

"You shall renounce your joy of stage pleasures and give up sin, or you shall pay. God is on my side."

"You are mad," I answered with a gesture of benevolent outrage. "Is it not for God to decide whom he is to punish?"

"Beg forgiveness – here in front of these people. On your knees –"

The boy, seized with mad zeal, had become more and more extreme in his demands. I felt sorry for him, for I knew only too well, from arguments with my own brothers, how he simply needed some face-saving formula to release him from the public spectacle he was intent on making of himself. But in the surroundings of the schoolroom and in front of his family retinue, what way out was there? Here was a child's passion suddenly projected in the public arena, and given the gravity of life and death.

"Pig-faced papist! Pig-faced papist!" he shouted over and over again.

Even his uncouth companion tried to intervene on the side of reason, but he fought him off. He would heed no other being. He hated me with the deadliest venom and with, to add to this, all the resentment and failure of the uncivilised North for the suave and sophisticated ease of the South.

The atmosphere grew even more charged as it became apparent to those who surrounded the Scot that the quarrel must have only one issue – else they would turn themselves loose to string me up themselves.

"*Pardonnez-moi*, but I shall renew the challenge," I said in a loud and presumptuous voice, because by now I too had lost my patience. "Our young adherent of Mr Foxe desires a further prick in his bosom from his Lord Lucifer. Have at you, sir!"

The others quickly drew back. The space cleared miraculously as the swords flashed once more in the bright glow of the torches and in the last rays of sunlight pouring through the windows.

It might, up to now, have been a knockabout farce such as I loved. But from now on the drama was serious. This time there was no doubt as to who was the master of the play.

I commanded the action from the first clash, for the Scot threw himself about in the most reckless way possible, worse than before, supplying vulnerability, unguarded moments – opportunities galore.

Jezebel

Until it seemed to the tormented spirit in me that I was being offered the opportunity a dozen times over to end the conflict with a fatal thrust.

I knew later I should never have taken such an opportunity: I should have skilfully resisted all the chances given me. But, then, perhaps it would have spelt out my own death, for at a certain point when relaxing my guard I would no doubt have left some vital part unguarded, slackening my eternal, restless ability to cover myself.

There was a moment when the Scot seemed almost to impale himself upon my sword and while my instinct was to recoil, there came to me again the image of Margaret Clitheroe.

No doubt the young Scot had been in the front rank of those who wanted her death. I allowed myself this one emotion of revenge; this was for her. This was against the ever-rising tide of barbarism that swept the land in the name of purity.

And this time there was no deception. Without a sound the boy fell, while the sword dropped from my hand and I caught the dying boy in my arms. There was nothing more to be done.

I turned to defend myself against the followers of the Scot, but they had no thought of avenging their leader's death, for Egerton then arrived at the top of the stairs with the local magistrates. Underhill explained in civilised tones that I had attacked in legitimate self-defence, and although the Scot's major-domo and his hacks were trying to spread the lie that I had, unwarrantedly, assaulted their master, Egerton frowned and nodded as if he believed Underhill.

While this went on I shivered and stood drenched with sweat as I clasped the boy to my chest with a mad and abandoned sense of grief. It was as if he had been my brother.

4

The Citadel

I showed Underhill the note from O'Hearne.

"It may be a trick," I said.

Underhill did not answer for a moment. "Come," he said, "there's only one place for him to be. There is little time. Topcliffe, when he had O'Hearne arrested, lacked knowledge of the conditions. Especially of York Castle."

"We're not going to try and get him out?"

"My dear fellow, it will be easily done and just as soon believed."

I was not so sure. His impudence was untried; it was easier to flourish than to fight.

"But we need more men."

He shook his head. "Your friend is not rich, is he?"

"His father was a furniture maker. My mother employed him as our tutor."

"The corruption by which the authorities pay their way singles out the richest catch. He would not be placed under lock and key in the King's Manor, for to stay there would have cost him his whole year's pay."

"Then he will be at the Castle."

"Exactly," said Sir Jasper. "Topcliffe has left York. I heard that he was furious at some old Catholic woman and that she threw holy water at him as he was leaving so that his horse flung him to the ground."

I burst out laughing at the thought of Topcliffe's discomfort. "But surely he would not have believed in its effect?"

"He did. He then railed at her for putting a charm on him and making his horse 'lay' him – as he said – on the ground."

"Providence . . ."

"I thought you Protestants didn't believe in it."

We exchanged looks. Underhill was not serious. It made me uncomfortable, for such debates were no light matter. Underhill laughed.

The Citadel

"But we must be quick, or they might send him to the notorious blockhouse in Hull."

"How will we get him out?"

"I have a plan."

Collecting Midnight, I set off after Underhill who had already mounted and was chafing at how slow I was. He had tied his steed to the iron rails near the scaffold; no doubt he had just vaulted into the saddle. I clambered up on Midnight with my usual clumsiness, twisting stirrups and tugging the reins so hard that now, as we trotted, I clung to a lopsided pommel.

But my blood was up. I felt I was equal to any dangerous proposal Jasper might make, and I would be more than a match for any swordsman. But if there were twenty, armed with staves and clubs? What if O'Hearne was locked in a guarded cell?

"Don't think you're going to get into another fight," said Underhill laconically. "We'll be laying the yellow trail."

What did he mean? The ride was short. The drawbridge across the outer moat had still not been raised for the night. Sir Jasper rode straight into the towered gatehouse, and in the name of the Queen asked to see the commander of the watch. Beyond and behind the gatehouse the rest of the crumbling citadel was strung out, a rambling and confused mass of stone buildings in poor repair, a maze of rooms and lean-to erections of wood and straw. As the dark began to settle a ragged army of torches began to flare and burn in the clearings and in the windows.

The captain of the guard swaggered in with his hat askew, his breastplate loose. He blew out smoke: he hardly listened to Sir Jasper's demand that by the order of Her Majesty's privy council he had come to collect the prisoner Richard O'Hearne for further questioning. He merely examined the purse Underhill dangled in front of his eyes, and with a gesture demanded to check its contents.

The scoundrel had the naked cheek to bribe his way openly! Underhill tossed the bag down to him. Duly satisfied, the keeper never gave back the purse but beckoned for Underhill and me to follow him.

We trotted through the gatehouse into the compound. It was crowded with prisoners. For the most part they seemed well fed and contented, although they must have lived the lives of primitives. There were numerous priests in soutanes, some of them old men, dating back to the days of Mary.

Campion's Ghost

I rode along beside Underhill easily. His presence in fine clothes and bright colours gave me confidence, it absolved me from the horror I had just suffered. He drew me after him like a magnet. Yet what if the Scot's kinsmen or friends were preparing their revenge or even now seeking me out?

We were led to O'Hearne and I dismounted to embrace him. I turned to Underhill.

"Do you mean to say now that we just walk out?"

Underhill nodded. "When money goes before, all ways lie open."

O'Hearne was keen to escape. "I myself was thinking of trying tonight. But once you have been arrested you are a marked man and your neighbours inform on you. They corrupt children to do it. Even your own class – " he added mournfully. "And I would have nowhere to hide. Most prisoners stay because they have nowhere else to go. It is convenient for those who are pious."

Underhill laughed cynically. "So this is how the monastic rule is kept alive! I reckon it is more of a Catholic gentleman's club than anything else. And it's about the only place in England you can receive the Devil's sacraments without fear."

"Are you sure we won't be pursued?" asked O'Hearne.

Underhill became more serious. "Not at first. Later, yes. We must look as if we are the gentry. O'Hearne, jump up behind me. Put on this hat."

He gave him a hat of murrey red that he kept tied to his saddle.

We rode out of York Castle.

5

Margaret in Arcadia

I used to escape into stories of how bodies change and take on different shapes. Most of all I loved to assume the role of Jupiter, the ruling male force and eye of heaven.

Imagine my surprise. One day, on a visit to Arcadia, I am caught by the sight of a girl of extraordinary beauty who forces my dead passion to cough and explode into new life. Is she Margaret Clitheroe? Does she carry the name of someone else? Kate, perhaps. But Kate's for later in my account, except that she must already have been there, if only in another form.

I follow her towards evening. She has been hunting. Her route brings her through virgin woods and into a grove where she lies down on the turf near to a river, unstringing her bow and resting her head on her embroidered quiver as on a pillow.

Here is a little escapade which Juno, my jealous wife, will never know about (if she does, it will be worth every bit of her rage).

I change my self and assume the form and dress of Diana, the goddess this girl worships above the others. "Best of my followers," I say to her, "where have you been tracking?"

She raises herself from the grass. "Hail, divine one," she answers. "Greater in my sight are you than Jupiter himself, though he may hear." I laugh to hear this and, in enjoyment of the flattery, I kiss her but with more warmth than is proper for Diana.

I then catch hold of her wrist and gently pull it to one side. She is sprawled out on her back away from the stream on the sloping shelf of a bank. Her tunic, gathered loosely around her and held by a buckle, slides open beneath the belt, and exposes her thighs. I press my mouth against hers. She resists as far as she is able (how can a mere girl resist Jupiter, although if Juno were watching she would not be so angry).

She turns her head away. My hand gently travels down her thigh.

"No, no, please don't," Callisto (this is the nymph's name)

attempts to say, but her exertions pull the dress from her breasts and they are uncovered.

My lips find her once more and this time she does not refuse; her kiss begins to match mine while her arms draw me tight. The fastening buckle tumbles, the dress falls more open, the belt snaps.

Callisto gasps, her breathing tightens, her hips rising from the bank as she impels me with a sharp cry to have my way. I return to the upper air.

She falls back sobbing and shuddering, loathing the woods and plants that have been witness to the loss of her chaste innocence.

The huntress Diana, proud of her kills, now arrives at the stream's edge. As soon as the nymph recognises her friends she is persuaded to join them. Diana finds a delightful, sandy-floored cove by the river and bids her nymphs undress and swim. They are only too happy to obey; but the lovely, abused nymph delays and seeks to hide herself.

The others give chase. Catching up with her they pull the tunic from her body, so that at one and the same time they reveal her naked loveliness, and the cause of shame welling between her thighs. Diana is outraged that she has stained their pure spring and sends her away.

In the course of time Callisto gives birth to a son. Having long since discovered the truth of this, Juno flings her rival to the ground. She spreads coarse fur over her lovely imploring arms, stretches her hands into claws, while those lips so loved by Jupiter she prises into a gaping hole from which there issues endless growling and misery.

This is what I, John Donne, must confess. Watching Margaret Clitheroe die I lost my innocence. Now, like the bear roped to the stake for the pleasure of an audience, I bait myself to reawaken that sense of shock. With pink eyes I leer at the approach of the dogs, my flesh about to be ripped into a pillar of running blood and slaver.

I become haunted with executions, fearing that one day I will be attending my own.

II

That night we rode south together. Underhill, O'Hearne and I. After the lovely day the heavens suddenly opened. The skies teemed with water, as if to try and soothe the gaping wound in nature wrenched open by the death of Margaret Clitheroe. As our mounts grew tired and sluggish after some four or five hours of riding we reined in, and, on a sign from Underhill, we followed him off the pitted and uneven main highway down a leafy passage roofed over by giant chestnut.

Our hair and faces streamed with water, but I cannot say I felt any the worse for the fury of the elements, or for the naked-headed and unprepared way in which we rode.

The night suddenly became warm. Although I felt my head loll forward and my eyelids sink, I was alert. I suspected something was up. I saw pursuivants, impostors with gaping pockets, waiting at every halt we made.

It was dark. There was still no sign of dawn. Perhaps two score people sat on the earthen floor of a mud and wattle barn into which Underhill led us when we stopped and dismounted from our steaming horses. But I could hardly make out faces in the meagre light: smoking dips lay about on rough tables, while one or two lanterns hung glowing from rafters.

The door was hastily locked, and the pig grease smell and rushlight smoke filled the barn. A young man of fair countenance intoned Latin before a crucifix: on the table in front of him, on which all eyes were focused, stood a pyx, with a corporal to one side used for covering over and hiding the contents.

Some thirty or more white hosts sat in the basket, gleaming almost with an unearthly light, as only a divine banquet could. My heart almost stopped. What if I should be called upon, be watched over until I took into my own mouth one of these supernatural essences which even then, in perhaps five or ten minutes, would actually become changed into the flesh of Jesus?

Would I not be swallowing something that never again would I be able to throw back from me: would I not be, for the rest of my life, marked and inwardly converted to what I feared most inside me? That to which my whole soul cried out in appalling alarm.

"We suck honey from the rock," the boylike priest was saying. "And oil from the hard stones. Every drop of gall must be drained to the point of intoxication . . ."

He glanced gently over at a huge, red-faced man who only too clearly betrayed the debauchery of the flesh. As a slight rustle of laughter greeted these words he went on hurriedly, "We renew with communion our joy in the beloved – "

I felt only shame and unworthiness. All through the desperate ride when the wind buffeted my face, buzzing in my nostrils, I had thought only of the pleasure of love and the perils of sex.

When the rain pringled upon my skin and hissed past my ears I had imagined concupiscent joys, ecstasies of flesh beyond belief, tearing the clothes from one like Margaret Clitheroe. My eyes were damp and had glistened with imagination of another forbidden fruit. I dreamed of a dark space where a woman and I could both do all we could ask of each other and all we could think of doing.

A wind outside banged the shutters close. Suddenly the Scot I had run through with my sword presented himself to my vision, not as I had known him, an awful parody of a puritan, a figment, even, of my mind, but as a real person, who had a father and mother, sister and brothers.

Had I not acted rashly? Should I not have sought every means to escape from the horrific predicament? Had I not blood on my hands which I would have to pay for? Surely communion with my God would be the answer. I had wasted so much time.

Here were children and unlettered people taking part in worship, pressing before me into the Kingdom.

I fastened my eyes on Underhill who stood beside me.

Would I never learn? But what? I gulped down that black bitterness in my throat. Hot, melted animal fat added overpoweringly to the heat while the packed congregation shifted in the shadowy, rudimentary space. The young man cried out, "Your beloved is here. See where he marches with giant strides from one end of heaven to the other."

"Don't take too much notice of what he is saying, dear boy," Underhill whispered flippantly in my ear. "He is expressing the extreme view!"

"Suspense, loneliness, fear – all these are verses in the hymns of night. The informers and guard watching you, the beadles gathering the taxes, the pox and the plague, fever, hunger, the rows and fights you have – it is all God's work. We must look beyond the shadows."

The door of the barn opened and a man passed through into the shadows: beyond the sagging and dissolving light I could hear whispering.

Underhill gripped me by the arm. He said, close to my ear so that I could smell his costly perfume, "Come on. We must go." We collected O'Hearne. The priest was accelerating the Mass to its climax – "This is my blood of the Covenant, which is shed for many."

I have to admit that outside the hut my huge physical dread of becoming implicated in the Eucharist abated at once. But I was still caught between two poles of mortal sin: the first for those sins that I would never relieve, as I believed, even with full confession, until I consumed the proper Catholic body and blood of Christ.

But the second — perhaps worse by far than the first — was the mortal sin I would contract if I took the body and blood in the proper spirit. I would be damning my material soul to persecution by that which I still held in a high state of fervour and love — my own country.

The poor people in the barn before I left were on their knees, their hearts reaching out in the shape of the cross, inert, immobile there, as if they would hold that position for ever, until the zealous noble Catholic-catcher arrived with his posse of armed men, rounded them up and fined them to within an inch of their possible life.

I felt humbled by their taut and hunger-drawn faces when they could live in plenty and enjoy the rewards of this life.

For even the indolent and lace-laden Underhill and his likes it was something different: he would never be caught while God still wanted him free — his moment would be chosen.

And what of myself: did I not in my crisis feel the most numbing and inconsolable pang, denying even then the presence of God in my body for the first time with an adult sense of choice. The forbidden but not impossible fruit of which I always dreamed?

We avoided the forces of the law and rode fiercely the next day, stopping only to feed and water our horses, until by seven or eight o'clock Underhill brought me to a different kind of experience.

6

Underhill Shows Some Force

This was a manor somewhere, I guess, on the borders of Leicestershire and Northamptonshire, belonging to a well-favoured knight and his attractive wife whose names, even now – even with applause during this terminal fit of sympathy towards the old faith – I will not mention. Even in easier times the tide can suddenly turn to fill with blood the inner chambers of dread.

The owners of this house, where builders and carpenters openly hammered and plastered holes for the concealment of priests, welcomed Underhill as an old and honoured friend, and O'Hearne and myself no less. The house had a small Gothic hall with a strange hooded fireplace at one end, a mysterious stone staircase leading off to little hidden rooms with cheerful and bucolic painted ceilings, and intricate chimney pieces of alabaster and marble.

Here, compared to the darkness of our previous night, everything was mirth and merriment. Our clothes, filthy and mud-covered although dried in the hot sun, were removed by watchful and obliging attendants, and new ones supplied. Baths of warm water were prepared, and then a delicious banquet with the lord and his family laid out.

O'Hearne surprised me with news – for I had not yet heard it – of his projected visit to the English College in Douai. Here, he declared, he would become a priest and then travel to Rome to enter the Jesuit order.

Underhill made a wry face and opened the palms of his hands as if to say "You cannot stop wilful madness, can you?" His worldliness and cruel mockery still reassured me.

"But to what end – merely to return to England, become hunted down, die a martyr's death?" I injudiciously echoed Underhill.

My host and his lady looked askance at my impudent question. But Underhill turned on me his mocking face, and smiled on me with those serene and secretly curved lips, which, for me, a man, held more than a hint of sensual charm.

Underhill Shows Some Force

"What others do to us is not what we do to ourselves."

"It would be a waste," I maintained.

"If we behave ourselves," said our host, "then the Queen will grow to trust her English Catholics."

I could see, from the expression on his face, that there was duplicity in his words. He was deep into plots.

"Unfortunately," said his wife, "there are too many hotheads and fools about."

The host must have caught an odd glint in my eye. "Have you made up *your* mind?" he asked pointedly.

"Of course he hasn't," O'Hearne entered the conversation with gusto, offering me a lifeline. "You're thinking of coming over to Douai, aren't you, Donne, if only to have a look?"

I shuddered, showing as little of this as I could, for even then there was something to me unappealing, temperamentally, about Englishmen who remained Catholics – I make O'Hearne the great exception.

"I have only just left Hart Hall, where I managed to avoid Anglican services because the college lacked a chapel. The horror stories of those who attend such polluted sanctuaries make your hair stand on end." I reddened and bristled with irritation.

The conversation at the dinner table went on and on: of which personality in Douai had been to which Oxford college.

I tried to eat heartily but the food stuck in my throat. The spectre of my unintended victim tormented me. I tried to unravel the event and play it differently. I needed to understand. Had I not been too proud? Could I not simply have ducked out of the school hall, or thrust a little more quietly? A minor wound would have satisfied to finish the duel.

Underhill caught my arm as we were leaving the table. "At the table just now you seemed unwell. Do you believe in ghosts?" he asked me and without giving me a chance to reply, then commanded, "Follow me, for I want a book to read before I sleep."

We proceeded up the stairs and through several rooms which had no doors but openings in their centre, to a room where I detected a faint glow. This was a library, where an ebbing lamp burned on a table.

He motioned me to sit down.

"What's happening, John? You now look as if you have the fever."

I explained to this sparkish fellow, who still, I felt, wanted no more than to be considered a wit, my remorse over the easy slaughter of the Scot.

"But you were provoked beyond reason! Quieten your conscience."

I gulped, and asked the question which was really troubling me: "Do you think I should seek a Roman priest?"

Had there been light enough, Underhill would have seen my cheeks engorge to a high colour.

"Seek ghostly counsel? I suppose it may help many a melancholy man burdened with a problem. I should not wonder if the increase in suicides and bastards has not something to do with the lack of priests to hear our faults. The gallows is no answer to the departure of the confessional."

I was irritated by his half-hearted, blasé approach. I was agitated and fearful, the sense of my sin grew and grew.

"Can you find me someone to absolve me?"

I blurted this out. But he did not answer. He rose and squeezed between thumb and finger the sputtering and smoky flame of the lamp, and as the light died I saw him go over to the tall, heavily stacked bookcase in front of which rested a ladder.

"I will protect you when the moment comes, but you must put your trust in me."

He had now become a shadowy figure, etched in the faint spill from the crescent moon.

"I am not sure, John, if you have any idea of the spirit's real power."

"Well, you may teach me."

As a cloud covered the moon we were plunged into darkness. I do not know why, but anxious and cautious as I was, I moved to a new place in the room. Underhill's disembodied voice came to me.

"Does this darkness affect you, John Donne?"

I did not answer where I was.

"Perhaps you would like to reflect what is being hidden in it. You know this room has nothing except a table. You saw when the lamp was lit. But now you are not so sure. Because you cannot see anything. So your own mind invents for you."

Then I heard that insolent laughter.

"My voice tells you of my presence, doesn't it? I wish to pick a book before I sleep. I am on the ladder which was set by the shelves. But if I touch you . . ."

I felt a light touch of fingers on my cheek.

"Now that scares you, doesn't it? Because your mind tells you it doesn't make sense."

I quickly moved to a different position and listened as my own feet scuffed over the boards.

A harder finger prodded my neck.

I moved again, all the time keeping in motion, reaching out for the wall, fingering it as something solid by which to keep my bearings. Then my stretched fingers stumbled upon a face. I recoiled in horror. A dazzling light forced my eyes shut. When I opened them Underhill was holding a lamp to my face.

"You were helpless, John."

"What were you trying to teach me?"

"A tiny lesson about how the real can also be unreal. If *I* can do this, think what the Devil can do."

They say the mouths of the statues in Rome ran with blood when Caesar died. I could believe it.

II

O'Hearne and I had to share a spacious and comfortable bed in a warm chamber hung about with tapestries of hunting scenes. We had a midnight taper burning in the room. I was tired and began to doze, but my mind was confused.

O'Hearne, sensing me awake and unable to settle, said quietly, "I am sorry, John, that I annoyed you when I suggested you might be coming over to Douai, but I felt our host was growing angry with you. He is one of the belligerent kind who would as soon bury his blade in a Protestant groin as adhere to the dictum of Jesus to love his neighbour. The Catholic Church is full of such people, and they – I do not mean my host – are sometimes as much our enemies as those who want to murder us."

"I suspect," I said, contemplating O'Hearne's deep-socketed eyes that seemed even more secure and craggy-browed than ever as he lay back on the bed and massaged his forehead, "that were I to become a Catholic, I might also be scathingly critical and belligerent."

O'Hearne shrugged. "Your mind is wavering," he said non-committally.

"My mind is clear. My emotions and spirit are unsatisfied."

I tried to take comfort from the meeting that Underhill had

arranged for me at the first light of dawn. But I felt a resistance building up inside me.

"You are wise for a young man of your years. Many could not see so clearly the issues at stake."

Since I had attempted to sleep, furtive noises had besieged my imagination. I heard whispers of command, of people arriving or departing. Once I fancied my ear caught the sound of a man running and panting.

Now it was O'Hearne who wanted to distract me. What exactly was going on?

"To see clearly is not to be able to choose wisely," I answered.

I needed to impress my old teacher with my rational side, but was not I as primitive in emotion as the most dirty-minded schemer?

"You don't have to be a saint," O'Hearne continued. "Many of us just have to earn our living: you don't have to be involved at all in religious schism, John."

"I don't see how, with my background, I can avoid it," I said gloomily.

"Of course you can. You may write about anything. Trees, plants, herbs, travel, gambling, sport. You can, as never before, become completely realised outside these schisms and conflicts."

"You mean," I said, my eyes lighting up, "forget the rituals and myths of Catholics? Turn to the meticulous study of plants or creatures?"

"Certainly. You may write of the fair sex; or collect and edit the ancients or moderns – there is nothing you need, or are impelled, to do. There are freedoms abroad of which our ancestors had not dreamed . . ."

So here was a third way that had not occurred to me.

"Yet in order to write I am still forced to find a patron, a great lord or noble to take me on as his secretary . . ."

"You can keep silent about your political or religious opinions."

"I wonder. But if you believe all this, why do you not choose it for yourself?"

"Because I am so bad, so deeply false and wicked, that I have to make up for it by being good!" He laughed. He pointed to his head: "I have a criminal in here!"

A puzzling reply.

"Is it up to you to judge how good or bad you are? Aren't you being proud to pass judgement on yourself?"

Underhill Shows Some Force

He shifted and turned over to me where I lay in that hushed and warm enclosure.

"I am sure that you are right. *I don't know*. But I go on searching."

"You are a scholar. Why can't you place your gifts at the service of your country? The search for you will soon die down. No one will be looking for you in London or the South."

"What you say saddens me, although I know it to be true. But my country has erred; it has strayed from its true path. This glorious age so beloved of our poets is a golden bubble which one day will burst."

I could feel the heat of irritation rising again. I broke into sudden fury: "Even our host would not like us to be controlled by some Italian priest or be a vassal to Spain. Isn't independence the most precious quality we have?"

O'Hearne answered quietly. "Yes, yes, I know all that. But can you be a Christian and be a nationalist? Like an angry little dog, fighting to keep your territory and urinating over it at the same time?"

"Tell that," I said, sitting up sharply, feeling the juices of my sumptuous dinner rising biliously to my throat, "to your continental friends the Catholics!"

I do not know why I spoke quite so harshly, except that I was still suspicious of some conspiracy taking its shadowy form around me.

There were mysterious echoes outside; champing of bits, the pawing of soft ground, the tossing and snorting of animals. Were these sounds just shaping themselves in my head? Had Underhill placed a spell on me? Were he and O'Hearne working together?

"You will make," said O'Hearne softly, "an excellent anti-papist propagandist . . ."

I bit my tongue. I hated O'Hearne for the truth he uttered.

"But I hurt you, and did not mean to do so, John. Come, tired though we are, let us rise and smoke some of the excellent new weed that Sir Walter Raleigh has brought from the New World."

We sat by the ebbing fire in armchairs, sharing a pipe and inhaling the fumes of the intoxicant from the colony that later we would call Virginia.

"Tell me, Master O'Hearne, if you become a priest how will you manage, you know, the . . . chaste bit. I mean, men and women are irreducibly sexual beings and a constant source of temptation to each other."

45

"I will try not to allow my sex drives to escape from the control of my will. I will make sex my servant rather than my master."

"Easier said than done!"

"Sex is a symptom of the frailty inherited by mankind from Adam's first act of disobedience."

"Eve's first act, surely. She thrust us out of paradise. She sinned first."

"I don't believe she had more fault than Adam."

"But she did. She picked the apple. Alas that we should fall for those whose fault in the first place yokes us to painful love."

"I shall try to avoid such dangers."

"But think of the nuns you will meet! They will provide the greatest temptation. Pious women are sexually alarming."

"John," answered my tutor slowly. "Your imagination is too alive. Sex separates us from God's spirit. Such longings divide your face from your heart."

"Without them I should fear extinction."

"Then you are wrong."

"Well, if I was you I would celebrate the beauty of my resolve. I would seek fellowship and good companions."

Our conversation suddenly halted. "What are you listening for?" O'Hearne asked me.

I had an intense vision of men closing round the house, cutting off escape. I foresaw the bursting in of armed men, my capture, a ride to the Tower . . . constant questioning faces of interrogators . . . the end.

I knew O'Hearne would have answered any examination of him I might make, but then I understood that I did not want to know too much.

"If God did not want this new spirit to be in the world, why has he put it so prominently in evidence?"

Now I could clearly identify the sounds of departure. Undoubtedly a small party of men was moving off, for then everything grew calm and still, the silence became absolute – so that my own vague and nameless fears, no longer attached to something outside myself, began once more to plague me with a vengeance.

He turned on me a mild and loving gaze. "We understand one another only too well. But I must try to look for a more searching form of self-knowledge and love God in a closer way."

Underhill Shows Some Force

I could only feel emptiness. I tried absolutely to believe in my God. To trust him unconditionally. Serve the servants of God, they say, and you will learn to love God. But who were his true servants?

7

To Lie in Oblivion

I could not sleep but lay like one awake in a heavy dream. I had made my choice to confess. Underhill had told me that there would be a priest in the stable at dawn. Even so, my soul was not quiet and I could not prepare myself.

I rose from bed when I heard the crowing of cocks and the barking of dogs. O'Hearne slept soundly. I could not believe he was still under threat of bodily extinction from Topcliffe.

As I approached the horse's stall a trembling overcame me. Yet my urgency was great. Midnight greeted me with an affectionate nodding head, squinting her dark velvet eyes to the approaching dawn, and with an impatient champing of feet, for the mare believed I had brought her food.

I found the priest in the empty box next to Midnight. He was old and wore a tattered black gown. His white hair and long beard, and the raw darkness of the ugly dawn disguised from me any clear idea of his features, except that I had the sense that they were rough. Yet the priest radiated grace and the power of God. I thought of my earlier talk with O'Hearne, and of how well a man can feel when he abstains.

As soon as I saw him I became overwhelmed with remorse. Confused by my sleepless night, my conflicts and fears, I burst into a flood of tears and asked him to hear my confession.

The old man's voice was high and clear. Sing-songy, with a sharp staccato resonance. It made Midnight start next door, and she neighed.

"Have you prepared?" he asked, motioning me to sit on the straw, but never looking directly in my eyes.

I stared up at the tangled nests of pigeons and doves in the rafters. I could hear the padding of their feet and low cooing to their broody mates.

He was a fierce priest: to my answer "yes", he asked, "How often do you come to the sacraments?"

"Two or three times a year." Or so I had in obedience to my mother, before these last few months.

"It would be better," he continued, "if you came more often. As things are, I advise that you spend time making a good and exact examination of conscience. Then, when you come to confession, you will get more benefit from it, and we will both be satisfied."

I said, "I will do willingly what you say the next time. But this time it is quite impossible for me to put off confession."

"Why?"

"Because I believe I might be arrested and fear I might be in a state of mortal sin."

"What do you mean?" he asked.

"Two days ago on my travels I was insulted by a Scottish gentleman. I could not overlook it and honour obliged me to challenge him to a duel. We fought, during which he fell on my blade and died."

"Heavens," said the priest angrily, "and now you come and offer me your confession! You should have thought beforehand and not made up your mind to take revenge. What you have done is not merely a sin. It involves you in excommunication. There must have been some other way to defend your good name."

I was trembling with obvious agitation and shame for what I had done.

"I beseech you, Father, pray for me, and if you possibly can, hear my confession."

I believed I would lose my mind if he could not help me.

"I don't know if I can," the priest said slowly and evenly, although slightly more kindly. "You were under no necessity to defend your honour. You could have called a magistrate, or put yourself under the protection of others. You persisted in an evil enterprise."

"I have paid dearly for it, Father, with regret and self-punishment."

"And what if you had died?" he said sternly.

"I don't understand," I answered.

"If you had died, you would have fallen into everlasting shame and eternal punishment. You should have forgiven your adversary before your fight, and never engaged him."

"I was afraid of what others would say if I showed myself to be a coward."

"And what will happen to you now? Will you be arrested? Perhaps you will now receive your death at the hands of the Queen."

"I think it is unlikely. By the code of honour, it was I who was provoked. But I do not wish to die unshriven."

The priest was silent. He wanted to help me, but something was clearly holding him back.

"I am anxious about you, my son," he pronounced after lengthy consideration. "Your name means too much to you."

"I will never do it again."

"You are in mortal danger," he said. "But not from the Queen and the Court. I see you wandering blindly on the rim of a great and dark void. I see you confiding in those whom you had best mistrust."

The priest was frowning.

"Is Sir Jasper Underhill one of those I should mistrust?" I asked, my heart aching with anxiety.

The old priest caught the sharp early air in his throat and shook his head to cough briskly, or even laugh – I was not sure which.

"I will hear your confession," he said unexpectedly.

At last my confused brain could clear itself of its dark obstruction.

After he had absolved me from my sin, he said, "Go and conceive in your heart the true sorrow for having offended so good a God."

Earlier, in front of the fire, I had been trying to trace the finger of God, wondering how it would here consume, here ignore, leap across unlikely gaps, or fail to ignite the wood.

Like an over-zealous boy consigned to keep a fire burning I sought to squeeze and poke the bellows on my flame.

I had one hand raised with a big flat stone ready to squash it for ever.

He had finished. "May I know your name?" I asked.

"You may call me Father Edmund."

The name sent an uncontrollable tremor through me like an earthquake: some part of my brain froze in the perpetual cold of mystery. I hardly dared to question the priest further.

The notion crossed my mind that the ghost of Edmund Campion had returned to earth, making me a special target for his ministry.

The figure's body had substance. Yet what if he had been the Devil who, with his supreme artistry, had assumed a form to tempt me to self-destruction?

PART TWO

The Marriage Temple

8

Sex and Sovereignty

"This is the biggest lie I have ever heard!" boomed a magnificent voice.

"I do defy you and spit at you!" from another noble throat.

"What does my Earl of Burghley say?" asked a woman whose regal timbre I could identify at once. Then there was silence as they conferred.

Submerged as I was in bizarre ranks of common petitioners, who themselves were arrayed in expensive finery, I could not make out the other speakers. I was at Court, an unattached bachelor jostling like any other young and aspiring writer for advancement. Outwardly I flaunted myself, a braggadocio in style and appearance – if not in inward feeling – who dressed, with black velvet doublet and open white blouse, to show as much naked skin of my chest as I could to both sexes; who also wore, for the same reason, tight, suggestive breeches and silk hose and discreetly fortifying codpiece, cut in choice leather by the best glove-maker I knew. The town promised such a variety of dainties that I was impatient for the rustle of a skirt, a glimpse of bosom or thigh.

I also cultivated egoism, paganism and the habits of an epicure. I affected – if not in practice, at least in powerful suggestion – the Italian vices, above all that of self-love, with a suggestion of sexual ambiguity, and with an ill-concealed delight in the large-scale consumption of the new pornography that flooded our native land.

Although there were some who held that Italy is the Circe's court of Europe, and that everyone who comes under her spell is turned to an ass or pig – or, as they put more precisely, "the body of a swine, the head of an ass, and the womb of a wolf" – yet I felt as impervious to the bad effects of her magic as a master-magician who knew how to weave charms to his own self-pleasing.

(I cannot say that in those years I did not suffer many disasters, for like a shipmaster who learns his vocation by many wrecks I foundered, or near-foundered, on many perilous entanglements.)

So picture me, now a fully graduated sophisticate, with earring provocatively in the shape of a cross, with cut-down moustache close to my lip, with *inamorata* scissored beard, with hair short and round, frounced with curling irons to resemble a half moon in a mist, standing, jostling for closeness to the divine majesty. How I sweated and suffered in this mingle-mangle, near-suffocated by the stink of so many forms of public petitioner! Every butcher or shoemaker with his legal suit, every clown's son in purple pantoufle, had squirted himself in civet, musk, oil of tartar, lac virginis or camphor dissolved in perfume. So amazed am I to see everything and everyone that I lose sight of the world's main intention, as well as my own – that of being seen.

"Close the hall!"

The Queen's gentleman pensioners, with their pikes as staves, swept away the common crowd of petitioners. The popinjay blue, the pease-porridge and goose-turd green miraculously dissolved before me.

I showed my letter and was told to remain.

"Now," said the woman in a crisp and satisfied tone. "Ourselves will hear the accuser and the accused speak freely."

Two courtiers stepped forward from their line. Both quivered with anger, each had a gloved hand on the jewelled hilt of his weapon. They could not keep still; they strutted and lowered their heads, like gaming cocks.

"My Lord of Oxford . . ."

The tall, fair but sharp-featured man stopped his pacing and haughtily drew himself up.

"I am afraid I have seen enough of you these days, Edward. You will stir up everyone so! You do so aggravate us!"

This was greeted by laughter, but the tension in the air hardly lessened. Oxford stamped his foot and drew his sword. He had curly hair, and I was excited by the sight of so nimble and fiery a horseman, for such was his reputation. He was everything that I was not.

"By the sword which my Highness laid on my shoulder, either you drop this foul deception . . ."

"To what deception do you refer, my Lord of Pembroke?"

Old Burghley whispered in her ear. She smiled. She seemed to be enjoying herself.

"Is that all?"

The Earl of Pembroke grew even more angry. His face became crimson. He was stout and swarthy, and had, so they said, an unyielding character, but strong moral fibre. More than they said about Oxford.

"All good men should hate such a foul liar!"

Sex and Sovereignty

"My body shall make good what I say upon this earth. My soul shall answer for it to heaven."

"Dear, dear," said Elizabeth. "How shall we resolve this without a duel? Go and fetch William Shakespeare."

"You will never find him," said Burghley in an exceedingly tired voice. "We have sent for him before. No one ever finds him."

"Exactly! No one ever finds him. Because *I* am *he*!" shouted Oxford exultantly.

"Edward, restrain your rage. You've always wanted to be someone else. Before it was Sir Philip Sidney. That's why you kept trying to kill him. But you would not have liked to die like poor Sidney on a lonely foreign field. You should marry and beget children. I'll have to banish you to Italy once again. Now out of my sight."

She swung round quickly. She was wary and watchful; she held me in a regard of unselfconscious intensity.

"Here's a new poet come to Court."

"What is his name?" inquired the sullen Oxford, giving me a cold and louche stare.

"John Donne," I answered boldly.

"Or undone," quipped the Earl of Pembroke, which provoked an explosion of mirth.

"I expect you'll be claiming next that you are Donne," said the Queen to the Earl of Oxford.

The previous night I had been unable to sleep at the thought of my audience and this morning had arrived at Westminster two hours before it was due. How would she respond to my verses? I had written songs and sonnets of airy and metaphysical conceit; or with elegies and satires I had addressed myself to imaginary mistresses and courtiers, embellishing my verses with cynical or obscene comment. Like my master Ovid in his *Amores* I sought to show that, behind the boiling expressions of passion, there lurked, invariably, a desire for unbridled voluptuousness. I played to a pit composed of like-minded young gentlemen of questionable or libidinous taste.

In short, I took myself very seriously and, at the Inns of Court where I had resided for the past year, I gained a small reputation. My friends considered me to be a writer of fiery imagination who shone in dark places.

With a hissing intake of breath Oxford accepted his punishment and left the Queen's presence. She sighed.

"William Cecil, have you a spare daughter to tame that peevish boy? I believe it's all that's left within our power."

"My liege," Burghley answered. "I have only one remaining daughter. Surely it would be a waste?"

She made a sweep of the hand to show that I should follow her, and with several of her attendants departed from the petitions hall. Tall and slender, she walked impatiently. Indeed, her more natural rhythm was fast, but she had a second, cultivated Court tempo: slow, measured, commanding. She was, as soon became apparent to me, at least two people if not more, but these were held together with beaten and cunningly softened joins of gold.

Burghley, her impresario, her master of forbearance, trotted along beside her, trying hard to keep up. Obediently I followed them into a withdrawing room. Burghley remained, guarding over her with his pale blue eyes, and while only thirteen years her senior, fathering her in his constant careworn expression.

Elizabeth wore white silk, bordered with pearls the size of beans, and over this a mantle of black with silver threads. Her train was long, its lace held up by a lady-in-waiting and she had an oblong collar of gold and jewels. She stood with her bosom uncovered.

I made to her the usual reverence.

"Well, young man?" she questioned me. "Your courtesy seems strangely timed."

No regular beauty could be seen in her features. No serenity. She was pale. She had high cheekbones, a luminous complexion and a thin face. Yet there was something irresistibly engaging in the burning look she gave me.

She held a paper on which my regular, neat hand had transcribed the fair copy of a poem.

"The fashion is not to my taste," the Queen grumbled. "I do not like un-regular rhythm and unusual beats."

"Some may see them as more adventurous, Your Grace."

"I prefer my own sonneteers and their honeyed tones."

"Although I have much admiration for our good, much loved and lamented poets Sidney and Spenser, their rhythms are predictable. Our age needs more of the baroque. If Your Grace will permit me . . ."

I launched into one of the decadent Italian sonnets of the year, translated by myself, which had a surfeit of lewd conceits and double meanings. The old faith of the Italians had been injected with a worldliness which had failed to influence Catholicism as practised in my country, but had inflamed the more extreme Protestant zealots with its descriptions of love and villainy. We assimilate what we hate as much as, if not more than what we love.

I expected a frown and greater anger than before; she smiled on me indulgently, replying, "At least yours has more pleasant a mood, and more healthy an expression!"

Thank God, I silently prayed, for having given mankind a dirty mind.

"But beware," went on our Queen, "of the vice of literary men. Many are fickle popinjays. This violence and filth they spread will turn my kingdom to a sewer . . . but I see from your expression you do not think that it is violence and filth."

I had noticed already her morbid, nervous, incessant restlessness. The soul of this woman was never at peace. It was well known that she made scenes with everyone. I could feel my own alarm rising at her provocation.

"Muck spread over the soil will swell a good crop."

"Know, young man, that I am the English soil!" she answered unexpectedly. And then added, "And the soil does not much enjoy it."

"The soil, Your Grace, deadens the excrement to make it release its goodness."

I confess that since the moment I had been ushered into her presence, every feeling of fear or uncertainty had left me. I gazed with unrepentant wonder on those unconquered maiden breasts. Any Englishman's hand would have smoked with pride to make its stand on those blue veins.

"Yet they tell me, Mr Donne, that in spite of your attempts to write elegies and satires and be a purveyor of attitudes of love and sex, you also delight in delicacy and treat of angels."

"I have tried something of the kind," I answered.

"You seem diffident to praise."

"Everyone prefers the rich armour of satire, Your Majesty."

"Yet one's naked . . ." She paused " . . . innocence is more attractive."

"You think so, my liege?"

"I know so, Mr Donne. Now entertain me with some tender subject."

"Angels come in many forms. Which would Your Majesty prefer, the sacred or the profane kind?"

"I leave that to you, Mr Donne."

"Twice or thrice had I loved thee," I began, "Before I knew thy face or name; – "

I had stopped.

"Do go on," she commanded.

"It becomes more difficult."
"Try."

> "So in a voice, so in a shapeless flame,
> Angels affect us oft, and worshipped be;
> Still when, to where thou wert, I came,
> Some lovely glorious nothing I did see."

I looked to Cecil for reassurance but he gave me a hard nod. I curtailed the rest:

> "Love must not be, but take a body too,
> And therefore what thou wert, and who,
> I bid love ask, and now
> That it assume thy body, I allow,
> And fix itself in thy lip, eye, and brow."

My heart was pounding. My lips were dry. It could so easily be misconstrued. There followed a terrifying silence. And what if she thought I was trying to make her look stupid? I peered cautiously into her face. Her expression changed.

"Bravo!"

She clapped her hands softly.

"I like your conceit. You tell the lady to whom you speak that she is an angel and yet a woman of bodily allure. Such is the sovereignty that all our sex desire! But you must tell me who the lady is."

"She is . . ." I was about to say "no one" for she was a fantasy. I blushed and kept silent.

The Queen laughed. "You shall finish this sonnet another time. And you shall be rewarded."

She smiled once more. She filled me with an incredible glow. Her Court was a blaze of enormity, a share in which she was offering to me, her newest acolyte.

Could not this smile also be construed as the salivating joy of the female spider, the Mantis, which poses its forelegs in an attitude of hands folded in prayer; which entices its mate to sexual intercourse, and then bites off his head?

"You shall arrange and write a masque, Mr Donne – and take part in it yourself."

II

A masque! God help me that I should be forced to take up the hack trade of playwright! But I would do it just this once, for – the great honour of such an undertaking apart – it would put me in touch with further patrons and through them I might earn good sums of money by writing verses for births, betrothals, marriages and deaths.

It was time again for Jupiter. I chose as subject the god and the twelve nymphs he seduced or raped. I am sure no one would have to look far for the reasons of my choice. Here was *carte blanche* granted for my research into the nature of woman's heart. I had already reckoned, with good cause, that the duller half of mankind was man.

Yet the subject was incredibly flattering – to man. For this half of mankind to which I belong is so dull, insecure and frail, it needs constant reassurance of its power and virility. Nothing does this better than the account I would give of Jupiter under the constant jealous eye of his powerful wife, Juno.

Her punishment never stopped him disguising himself and philandering over the face of the earth – and applying some godlike pressure when he was not getting his way.

We would have many transformations to achieve. There was even the beautiful cow that he seduced. We found an old headpiece in Clerkenwell for this. They were a deceitful bunch, these Olympians; we worshipped them alongside Jesus.

But if half the nymphs and earthlings Jupiter had for his pleasure ended by being turned into plants, trees or animals – bringing the planet alive with mythical reality – so also did Jupiter take many forms. Imagine a silvery pink Europa carried on an azure sea by a beautiful white bull, while plump nymphs and muscular tritons sported in the waves. A riot of tricks and effects. The royal workshops and wardrobes would love it.

"This masque will be dear, far too dear," said the Lord Keeper to whom I was directed for an advance of twenty pounds, for I had to find a better appointed lodging nearer to the choking thoroughfare of the Strand.

"Good day to you, Lord Thomas." I do not think at first he recognised me, but I had recognised him, not without fear. I had last spoken to Egerton in York.

"Well, well, well – hearing of your exploits at Court I expected I should bump into you."

I blushed, for I had an immediate and painful memory of that day and hour when I had spitted the imbecile Scot upon my sword.

"Should I come to you, sir, or should I ask the Revels Office?"

"Here young man." He handed me ten pounds in gold, a sum greater than I had ever earned before. "Give a good account of yourself with Jupiter, and you shall be my secretary."

There was little work to be had in the courts or at Court, and hundreds of young men, with lawyers' and masters' degrees of logic or doctorates of philosophy, clogged the chambers around Whitehall, sleeping sometimes twenty to a room.

Flies, gnats, lice and punaises plagued these lettered hopefuls. Not to mention the mice and the rats. The sheets were filthy, while as for the communal bedfellows assigned by Court, honestly it was better to sleep with pigs than end up with the foul, scabby, hard-pimpled and crusty dried sores of some future "Justice" rubbing against you.

Farting, stinking breath, babbling and drunken raving kept you awake all night; pissing and spewing were the order of the day; no sexual behaviour was too beastly. You dined on tablecloths black with grease, feeding from a common bowl in which had been dipped fatty lips and slimy beards. A country idiot's life was bliss compared to this.

So the offer of a secure position sent my hopes racing.

"You are shortly, as I see from such text as you have shown, to be a privileged man among virtuous ladies! Be sure you make your reputation."

A wink formed itself in his jovial eye. What kind of reputation could he mean?

"But what of your soul, John Donne? Are you still friendly with the likes of Sir Jasper Underhill?"

The question robbed me of my breath, as if my least favourite horse had hoofed me in the diaphragm. I had dismissed knowledge of this man. Since the time Jasper had, in contradiction to his flippant and foppish manner, arranged the escape of O'Hearne I had hidden further report of him in my darkest and inmost self.

And yet that buried self would haunt my dreams and give me nightmares.

Sometimes I would be addressed by the most dreaded beast of all, the Manticore, who had the body of a lion, the head of a man, the quills of the porcupine, and the sting of the scorpion. I still did not know who in that dark dawn had confessed me of my crime.

"I have not seen or heard of him since I was in York some eight or more years ago." I exaggerated, for I wanted to make the gap between myself and the past seem wider.

"Is that so, is that so?" replied Egerton lightly. "Well if you do, Mr Donne, let us know. Our Grace would love to have a talk with him."

Egerton was prying and imputing to me more than I knew.

"Well, here is someone who might help you to know more." Egerton wrote down a name and an address. "I visited him myself. He's a doctor who has had success with the plague: even survived those swellings on the groin and in the armpits. Not like Doctor Syminges."

I laughed. I read the name. Simon Forman, a magician and astrologer much given to seduction of the women who sought to consult him. I was surprised to hear that Egerton had gone to see him.

I dismissed it. Nothing would come between me and the flagship of my new enterprise, sex, codenamed "Jupiter and the Nymphs".

Casting the right women as Juno, Callisto, Europa and their peers was the key to the success of the venture. While others set out on a costly and dangerous exploration of the seas, I also would sail to a new world, a Newfoundland of sensation and expression.

It would drive me to expect more of myself, for no one had made discoveries in the regions that I would explore. Not even Ovid. I would not become a pirate like Sir Francis Drake, an inveterate circumnavigator of the globe like Frobisher, who showered his sovereign with precious metals and stolen spices. Instead, in the *terra incognita* of my mistress's drawing-room and of her bed, I would begin a great new English tradition, that of the sexual adventurer.

Don Juan was the Catholic seducer who went down to hell. I would become the Protestant version; the Don Juan who ends in the heaven of his own devising. I would become subtlety itself. The rake and libertine, who after his seductions of sainted novices and unstained virgins – and far from being roasted alive – wins universal admiration.

I would become a new invention.

9

My Brother Henry

It often seemed to me at the time as if I was crushed between two mighty feminine forces. On the one hand the Queen, but on the other hand my mother. It was hardly very surprising that, so threatening as they both were, I should have to carve out my own space, then fill it with something that existed uniquely for me.

My mother was the same age as Elizabeth, yet there was a world of difference between them. A mother first of all, her brittle sexual or emotional availability no longer applied to the opposite sex. Her four sons had the first call upon her heart and feelings, their stepfather limped a poor fifth.

I disappointed her most sorely of all. Especially by my ambition, with which she quarrelled constantly. She also submitted me without pause to a blistering commentary on my private life, the truth about which I did my best to keep from her.

I would have loved her to adopt a more relaxed attitude about her faith, as so many of the older and well-connected families were doing. In fact such people were generally agreed that God had sent England the Armada and its subsequent destruction to save English Catholics from the horrors of Spanish torture.

It is likely that destiny reflects our parents in us in ways that we may never understand, and that we pass on to our children those features we are blind to in ourselves until, perhaps, the moment of death. Her rebellion against the Protestant rule may be likened, then, to my rebellion against her.

My brother, Henry, had unfortunately none of the scholarly attributes of a priest, yet he had become a lay helper. He had been serving a priest who had been active in Shoreditch, just outside the limits of the city, when the priest, Father Anthony, had been captured by a party of Sheriff's men who had each been given one pound reward for their zeal.

Both men had been taken to the Clink in Southwark, which, next to the Marshalsea, was a thriving papist community. Unfortunately they were captured at a bad time. While they awaited torture and formal trial, persecution grew and grew: a witch-hunting panic, a dark, combative and threatening mood seized hold of the people. More Catholic priests landed, more wooden boxes full of wax *Agni Dei* blessed by the Pope were discovered by the customs men, more printing presses spewed out their papist tracts.

I went to visit Henry and found him in a wretched state of squalor and filth. He had been kept in a small room where he could not stand up properly – although he could sit down – while other prisoners had their privy adjoining his cell, so the smell was foul and intentionally contrived to break his will.

Henry had put on ten years in as many days, the time it had taken for us to track him down. When I saw his torn but unshaven face on which the hair barely grew – he did not wear a beard – and the sores that covered his hands, and heard the pitiful cough that shook his thin ribs, I wanted to entreat him to renounce his Catholicism, or at least, like so many thousands, to become a schismatic, attend Protestant church – but keep his private thoughts to himself.

But I dared not offend our mother, or even shake Henry's own unconquerable resolution. I was – or much of me still was – on Henry's side.

"Have you heard how Father Anthony is?" asked Henry.

I could see he was determined to be pure in his resistance: he had no anger against his captors; he did not care for his own perilous trials.

"No more than that he refuses to admit he is a priest. Yet the chalice and wafers were caught on him . . ."

Henry looked at me eagerly. As I was his older brother, he sought my approval for his actions. He knew he had his mother's. Yet a great and unexpected sigh was torn from my heart.

"You don't really approve, do you, John?"

What could I say? I loved Henry more than my other brothers. In my mind Henry was committing suicide.

"They say the Queen is in a forgiving mood. Father Anthony, if he confesses, may be expected to be put on a boat to France."

Henry threw a piece of stone at a rat which pushed aside the straw at an unofficial entrance low down the cell wall. It scurried off.

"John, my dear brother," said Henry in his most gentle tone. "Father Anthony is Christ's representative. He stands in for Jesus. He aspires to the life that Jesus led on earth. If he is rewarded with death and martyrdom he will have fulfilled his life in a way infinitely stronger and more rewarding than ever I could."

"Yet you are content to die beside him?"

"I am."

It was on the tip of my tongue to call my brother mad. But I held back. I did not believe Henry could be persuaded – not by me, that is.

"Where is our devoted mater?" I asked Henry.

Henry knew what I was thinking. That I might persuade my mother to argue him into compromise.

I had begun to frequent the pale and naked cathedrals of Protestantism. With guilt, as if they were stews or bordellos. Something, a sweet mustiness in the air, roused me in these empty shells of a departed faith. They smelt of death.

"It is no good trying with her: she would willingly take my place – and that of Father Anthony. But since the death of Margaret Clitheroe many years ago now, Our Grace will not permit the spectacle of a woman dying publicly for the faith.

"The Queen believes women have a higher moral authority than men. That there is something ultimately comic about cutting off a man's prick and balls in public. Moreover, it terrifies those who perform the action more than those who suffer it."

I shivered when I thought that what we uttered was no doubt being publicly transcribed by some creature on the other side of the grimy stone wall.

"And if she commands you to be tortured, Henry? What will you do? Will you resist the rack?"

"I will be joyful. I will be only a heartbeat away from Jesus."

He shone on me an expression from which all pain and suffering had gone. "John," he went on, "don't do it! Don't give in. Protestants take their stand by the Gospel, by a dead memorial . . . Our Christ is alive."

"You mean he is a miracle," I answered. "I don't think I believe any more in miracles, Henry. But I still believe Jesus was a man."

"You will lose your soul, John," said Henry gently and with great and respectful warmth. "You will never be happy."

"At least I won't have to become someone else. I will be myself. I will be alive. I will never be satisfied with myself, that is true. I will be restless and searching, I will be tired, but I will be moving forward. I will be the world's first literary egotist. I will possess 'self-knowledge', be 'self-sufficient', and become 'self-made'!"

My Brother Henry

"John, I have no notion what your words mean."

"They are new. I have just minted them, Henry."

Henry frowned. "It is not good which admits of no compromise, John. It is evil."

I spoke without considering the full implications of what Henry had said.

"Or just nature, Henry. The natural spirit of the universe."

I could not resist in my voice the slight feeling of triumph.

A buried thought, like a buried body, will rot; and through the moral being that is its grave or its jailer it will spread pestilence.

10

Kate Ferrars

The Queen was rebuking one of her younger ladies-in-waiting for the treatment of a husband whom she married against her will but in accordance with the wishes of her family.

"I command you to love him! God told us all to love Himself and one another. You will find that as you apply yourself to knowing another person, learning his mood – that love will grow."

"Love will grow," echoed the old Cecil at her elbow, snigging the wind of her mood. From him I learned that with Elizabeth you had to become like a clever child approaching a dangerous wild beast or a ferocious dog. You reached out a hand to see if the animal would bark or bite; made a small motion with your eyes, trying, with life – or death – precision, to detect the shadow of a stare, or a smile which you could nurse or suck.

". . . By discovering the needs of your husband and being obedient to his honest will, you may find that you awaken in him a similar response to your own needs.

"But beware. All men are the same: their emotions are ice. They are touchy, sticky, they are brittle. They break easily. They melt when exposed to sudden heat – and become a watery patch on the floor!"

She turned to her listeners for laughter which, duly received, flattered her, so she preened herself.

The young woman in her service, foolishly, saw fit to challenge her.

"But, Your Grace," she complained, "only yesterday you told me that I should put myself first; that I should leave a man if he did not respect my independence; that you could not coerce love, that it could only grow if nurtured, if given room!"

Elizabeth frowned. She would not be criticised.

What she might have said – or done – yesterday, was yesterday's stale meat.

The fox gently firmed his slender old fingers around the plump and white forearm of the young woman, leaned over her bosom as if inhaling from its pale blue veins, and managed with incredible sleight of hand and magnetism of personality to make her vanish from the presence of his mistress.

It was as if he had hidden her in a cloud, like some creature protected by a deity.

But as she was leaving she and I brushed against one another. I ran my eye quickly over her. She was a sweet but determined-looking creature of about twenty, dark-haired, with blue eyes and a slightly tip-tilted nose, dazzling white teeth and a clear, almost transparent delicacy of skin. If not a lady of more special rank, she was every bit the equal of one. She looked frail, shy, yet made of steel.

Seeing me she started.

"So you are Mr Donne," she whispered quickly.

I marvelled at her beauty. She gave me such a stare, a hard and taunting, yet soft, beckoning and provocative look, that I was pierced.

Here was the one I would cast as Juno. Her motivation would be revenge against Jupiter for his infidelities.

"Master Donne," the Queen declared, "you are here at last! I have just suffered the greatest humiliation known to woman. I have been pulled. I think I am dying!"

I was overpowered. I was dazed at the apparition which had just left. I tried in vain to shock myself into reality.

"What is her name?" I murmured almost inaudibly.

"I mean," said the Queen in a harsh, impatient whisper, "I have had a tooth pulled from my head!"

II

One day the Queen commanded me to walk with her in her garden in Greenwich, asking me for my arm in support where we moved from terrace to terrace up flights of steps.

It was almost midsummer, and the sun shone hot and cheerfully.

She had given her ladies-in-waiting the nod (among them the one I had cast as Juno, the delectable Kate Ferrars), for they stood off from our conversation, although they remained within sight and call, like pinnaces commanded by their admiral not to sail too near.

At this time I was playing many roles. I became each role I assumed better than I played my self. The role demanded by this situation seemed to be that of a chaste and brisk young man who yet was capable of romantic gallantry.

Yet a strange new knowledge lay at my heart. I had a secret. A wonderful feeling of well-being flowed through me. I was in love.

I opened my game, "Your Majesty is looking especially youthful today. Can you tell me the secret?"

She had a strong, masculine presence, a tall brooding power, yet was tantalisingly feminine in not submitting to any rationality or logic of procedure. She could, as I had already discovered in her treatment of her gentlewomen, advance one day one reason for doing something, the next day flatly contradict it. Near to me she seemed often to bend, and even to adopt a mien of indecision and tenderness.

She thanked me. She would never see through a compliment or view it cynically and it always afforded some time in which to breathe.

She considered me with a shrewd look. "To be simple and natural . . . to live in the moment!"

"And of course – to be in love," I added rashly, not meaning it to be personal. Too late I saw I had committed the most foolish of gaffes. I tried to extricate myself. "It makes all of us possessors of eternal youth."

"In love – whoever said I was in love?" she demanded scornfully, her voice plummeting to a manly rebuke. "If you found a good enough man, then perhaps I would be in love! As far as I am concerned they are all trash."

"Far be it from me to defend my sex, Your Grace," I answered, "but I expressed myself foolishly. I meant, to have someone in love with you. This surely keeps us young."

Her expression changed. It was common knowledge at this time that Our Grace was being wooed by the Duc de Houpeville, hot and impetuous grandson of Catherine de Medici, whose wizard Nostradamus foretold the doom of England. Years ago the Queen, although severely blemished by an open ulcer on her leg, had negotiated with the Duc d'Anjou, de Houpeville's uncle and Catherine's son.

Parallels are curious, are they not? Here was a sinister echo of her father's life. The old syphilitic reprobate Henry ended his days with the hugest, most painful open ulcer of the knee ever recorded in mankind's diseased history, howling like an infant on the lap of his last wife Catherine Parr.

At the time of the Frenchman's wooing of our Queen, Anjou was a mere peascod of twenty-five or so, indulging Elizabeth's penchant for frivolity. He was a master of the art of wasting time – an art which the Queen put above most others in her "youth" – that period of her life which lasted until the final years of her reign when fantasy, severely held in check, at last gained the upper hand.

While Catherine de Medici was pressing for the marriage with all the power and cunning she could put behind it, her son, a papistical mule with an obstinacy which was only surpassed by his vanity, refused to let himself be drawn into such a match. He would never, he said, marry an old woman with a sore leg.

Elizabeth got wind of his description. She raged and she would never forget. She sent letters demanding of her courtiers whether Anjou had received proper appraisal of her parts.

"Let it be known," she thundered, "that my body is a temple, a palladium, as well as a citadel of corporeal certainty on which the safety of my nation rests entirely. Have you told him of my beautiful feet, or other more personal and private zones?"

The marriage faltered on the question of whether Anjou would be allowed the liberty of attending Mass in public. The French would never waive this, the English who surrounded Elizabeth never concede it.

Even this might have been negotiated to a satisfactory end had not the Spanish then cleverly backed a plot engineered by a completely absurd Italian, Ridolpho, to assassinate the Queen. The plot was uncovered and the English once again became united in hatred of all foreigners.

But now the younger Frenchman was on the scene – or at least panting in the wings. The joy – or spectre – of Elizabeth with a full womb, and therefore with a half-foreign heir, had revived spectacularly. Everyone began again to hope the virgin queen would at last put herself to the test. She herself was convinced that she could still have a child.

There had arisen great feeling against the marriage, and this had been richly orchestrated. The increasingly deranged Lord Essex – jealous and violent because he of all her suitors had come physically the closest to intimacy – put it about that foreign agents had tumbled the Queen's mind with intoxicating liquors and magic – with chemical potions, and with the use of deep and hidden knowledge – in favour of the marriage.

III

"How would you woo me if you were de Houpeville?" she asked.

We had stopped before two wondrous sculptures of boys riding on racehorses.

"Stormily, I think. Imposingly."

"You think the man should be master?"

"Unless a man has true command he will never respect himself. Also the sexual urge for children (I meant the sexual urge *tout court* but knew the Queen's delicacy in such matters) operates much with the man's sense of domination. Men who give in to women make poor lovers."

I was risking my neck by such loose talk. But they say she had scared the *"couillons"* off the young ape Anjou because she would not "shew" herself to be compliant to his desire. Men of the cocky nation of France hate above all to have their coxcombs upset by a woman who knows her mind. As I calculated, the Queen was amused.

"I must tell that to my dear fox when we next speak of such matters. Whatever I say to him he always gives in! I play this little game: 'I think we'll withdraw our garrison from Flushing', I say.

"'Yes, My Grace', he answers. Then he goes to search for the ambassador of the United Netherlands. Before he reaches the door to the ante-chamber, I change my mind. 'I think we'll keep the garrison in Flushing'."

I kept silent.

"Some would find it virile in a man who knows how to give in to you, and yet keep his price," said the Queen.

Her eyes sank – in the demure game she played – to regard the ground, a blush came into her cheek, then her eyes moistened. "And there could be other ways of taming me . . ."

I paused to let her say more, but she would not. She appeared, now, grown and enhanced in attractiveness beyond what I could have hoped. The years peeled away, a youthful unspoilt girl stood in front of me, my own age and rank. She was possessed of a skin of glowing paleness: her father's complexion more than her mother's seductive *oli-vaste* tint. One is attracted to the darkness in the blond woman. Just as one is drawn to fairness in the dark.

Her faint reddish eyebrows had a peculiarly soft moulding at each side. She began to glow with an inner light and strength. Here was the most virile member of our race advocating another way of taming than the wanton male mastery to which we were bred.

"Fiery passion, you mean, Your Grace. The self-punishment of the lover starving and penitent for his loved one? Hurting himself, accusing her of neglecting him, pining away in unrequited sorrow – or wearing ill-matching hose."

"Is that how you love?" asked Elizabeth, whose eyes had widened even more.

We were now sitting on a bench, side by side, hardly daring – at least I did not dare – to meet each other's eyes. But her posture towards me was not that of imperial haughtiness. She was reminding me more and more of Pump, my skittish mare, who on a spring day would "up" her young hind parts and even with the whiff of my useless old gelding in the same field, open the quiver of her haunches in the hope of a love-bolt.

In my mind's eye I pictured the young and married lady-in-waiting I had seen barely once yet had already built into an obsession. The memory of her poignant face refused to die. It called to my nerves instead of my brain, plucking on these with a compelling fertility of resource. I had moaned out my unrequited passion to God – and the Roman gods.

"I believe I would sink under a great love – and crush the person I most wanted to please."

"Ha –" said the Queen in a rather cruel and wicked tone of pleasure. "Everyone passes through that phase. If love weighs on you like grief, be rough with it – hit it back; beat it for beating you."

She was provoking me to go on. As I conjured up Kate, I grew bewitched. Yet there was another side of me that would have been happier enjoying, in rank, itchy lust, the bareness of a plump muddy whore.

"Her face would become a shrine . . ." I looked up and saw the Queen's dangerously vulnerable face close to my own. She had, by proxy, participated in my extremity of feeling.

So near was her face that it seemed naked like another part of her: strangely informed, too, with beauty. Was she really affected? I averted my gaze, and far from meeting earth or darkness my eyes slipped down into the bodice of her pale blue silk dress, and unravelled the lace that encircled her breasts in a loose skein.

"Yet love built on beauty dies as soon as beauty."

Give me even a cheap drab, I thought, worn by as many different men in sin as black feathers or musk-coloured hose.

I prayed for the custodians of the Queen, some ten or twenty yards off, to protect their sovereign.

"And what is the name of this so attractive member of our sex?" asked the red-headed woman softly. I recalled that no one in England bathed herself so much, or lavished such care over her cleanliness, as did the Queen. We grappled so often with the singular unpleasant delights of unwashed quims and stinking armpits even in young beauties – or of poor breath, breasts caked with cracks and lard. This care over becoming clean added to my intoxication. I leaned towards her.

She had worked her spell. But at this moment I was aware, just over the short box hedge that reared up behind us, of a statue I had not noticed there before. Earlier I had registered the alabaster column on which it stood with a fountain at its foot.

The statue was clothed in a flimsy green and nymph-like attire which drew my heart towards the centre of its being: the dress rustled. Pale, perfectly motionless, this was my guardian spirit. This was Kate.

IV

Neither the Queen nor I could be angry with Kate for the intrusion. Elizabeth saw the beautiful and mute figure at the same moment.

"It's Kate – to remind me the little frog has requested an audience and I promised to attend." She slapped her hands together with delight. "Well done, Kate!"

It was my turn to stand and bathe my loved one in adoration. If only she knew how much I sought to express every nuance and softness of love, and how, in that sighting of her, I understood her. For in her cheeks spoke a pure and eloquent blood; so distinctly formed and shaped was her body, one might say that her body *thought*.

"No, Mr Donne," said Elizabeth, "I must be the mother of my people. Other ties that make an ordinary girl happy must be denied to me. Were I to be free to seek my own happiness . . . but I am not."

"I hope my arguments have not offended Your Grace." I did not mean arguments, of course, but other less delicate business.

"No. I already have a husband."

11

The Golden Needle

Leda performs a dance. There is a special quality about her, an intensity, that projects from behind dark burning eyes and penetrates those who watch it.

We rehearsed at night in a great chamber in Clerkenwell, in the old priory of St John's now lit by dozens of torches and candles. In daytime we live in a wild confusion of properties and costumes and people, with the smell of paint and glue and the sounds of hammering rising from and above everything else.

Leda dances playfully, flirtatiously, clad in silk fleshings, her hair of hip-length cotton streamers dyed the shades of lawn to look like seaweed. She spins transparent veils of dark undersea green around her head and arms. Yet she is the embodiment of innocence, the purest form of chastity. Her face is the kind of face most men would like to have beside them in bed. She stamps her feet in a change of rhythm.

Venus appears, leading Jupiter disguised as a swan. Venus brings wrath and urges fear. Her lace gown exposes her lovely bosom and arms. But her robe is scarlet. Her head's attire is black. Streams of fire shine from her naked breasts. She carries a wreath of yew. She owes Jupiter a favour, but she hates to be a partner in deception.

I appear as the white, but black-eyed, swan, proining my fair plumes, as if seeing myself in a mirror. I am supposed to make everyone laugh. I pretend to be wounded. Leda takes me gently by the wing, wraps her arms around me, while with a spare white and downy neck (held by my right hand) I start to nuzzle her breasts and legs, and dispose her to yielding.

This is the way to convince the Queen that cold virginity is the gentle queen of love's sole enemy. Making women into temptresses so that, as well as mastering them, we can turn them into misty-eyed beauties that will torture us into greater and greater creativity and achievement.

How meekly woman submits herself to the golden band of the

beauty contest. Only the winner, she knows, can prescribe her own laws. And even the winner will destroy herself.

The rewards of adultery were sweet. Soon I had both fair and brown. The playful ones, the ones who wept with spongy eyes, and those who were dry cork and never cried.

I liked them as I liked the many different aspects of a subject. I could always find virtue in one feature of their character, beauty in some quality of nature. A pair of outstanding legs, a cleft of a bosom that sent me wild, a strange slanting intimation of desire in the eyes. The wives in my cast were greedy and eager.

I enjoyed no less planting horns on the foreheads of their husbands. Cuckolding is excellent sport. Beasts change when they please, so why should women – who are hot, wily, wilder than beasts – be bound to one man? Waters soon stink if they bide in one place: while it is captivity to live always in the same land. Change is the nursery of music, joy, life, and eternity. All this and more I wrote into poems in some of which I sublimated the baser instincts by teasing and refining them into spiritual wit.

Love's mysteries in souls do grow, but yet the body is his book.

There were many small storage rooms in the old priory cleaned out with long-handled brushes, fitted with piles of taffeta, velvet and damask and cloth-of-gold, where we could close the door and fall into our pleasures.

And so I made my leaps and turns with delicate dark chestnuts, fine lean heads, large foreheads, round eyes, even, smooth mouths; with deep sides, short fillets and full flanks, with round bellies, plump buttocks, large thighs, knit knees and short pasterns.

But the unique, the heavenly and beautiful Kate was difficult and I knew that, as Juno, I had cast her perfectly. She permitted no liberties at all. Even though her husband was now engaged in war, campaigning in the Low Countries for his Queen.

That she would not respond to me outweighed by far the many unclothed bodies and minds of pleasing doubleness that I could suck, smack, and embrace. Her soul was close and secret. Her body no less sheathed.

12

Division

"I want this woman to fall in love with me."
"The person you are missing will be with you very shortly."
I smiled uncomfortably.
"But I am not missing any person."
"Wait a minute. You have a tooth?"
"I have all my teeth."

I had not wanted to fly to bawds, panders, magical philters and the like. But I was desperate. This Simon Forman, the necromancer whose name Egerton had supplied, prescribed depressants for my Lord Southampton to keep him away from the molly houses where the new breed of he-whores frigged among themselves.

Forman's shop, in Lambeth, had been accused of having many a lewd picture on display. They even said he had materials for the manufacture of men and women: indeed later than at this time – for he lived to compound his mischief well into old age – Forman became alchemist at Court and made obscene creatures to perform in "anti-masques" as prolifically as King James coined new lords and ladies.

I had expected half-dressed sluts and a crew of pimps, but Forman himself had greeted me at the door. He was alone. He was a tall man, squint-eyed, with a shock of flaxen hair and with large buck teeth. His eyes were red and sullen: I could not imagine why women found him attractive, yet they say he had well over a thousand visits from them each year, many leading to more than consultations.

His rooms were clean and light. He had encouraged me to come quickly to the point and explain my difficulty.

"You can do as Jesuits do, put on a solitary and fasting meditation to alter your mind. Improve yourself beyond yourself, make yourself mad. Ravish yourself!"

He spoke thus and often at a tangent.

Did he have someone in the next room eavesdropping through a hole in the wall? I wished I had been innocently browsing near by in the shop of my friend Emery Molyneux, the compass-maker.

"What should I do, Mr Forman?"

"Like kill a queen?"

I looked blankly at him, but then he added rather quickly, "Or the like. There are many ways to the truth. I can put you in a melancholy chamber where for many days you will see no light. Nor anyone. Little meat. Ghostly pictures of devils. In you I can see the shadow of the great Antichrist, the Pope himself."

At last here was the reason for all this. "Someone who might help you to know more," Egerton had said to me about Forman. Had Egerton imparted his suspicions about me to the man? I pumped my mind dry.

"But I come about a woman," I repeated firmly.

The necromancer shook himself. "What do you offer?"

"I am but a poor scholar and poet."

"Pythagoras offered a hundred oxen to solve a mathematical problem; Venus her dove, Vulcan his fire."

"I crave only for my loved one to like me."

He rose from the stool on which he sat bolt upright.

"Let us find whether you are destined to marry."

"This sounds more like it."

"I must examine you both." He went on in Latin: "*Si dominus septimae in septima vel secunda nobilem decernit uxorem . . .*" He coughed and then continued, "That is to say, by the examination of the seventh house, the almutens and planets, we must examine the man and woman's geniture."

"How can I know if this is true?"

"The stars incline but do not enforce," he said peevishly, his face beginning to twist.

"So how will you change her feelings towards me? Can you not cast a spell?

"I had much rather you conjured up some spirits to help me. I've brought along," I added, "this piece of Sir Thomas More's tooth. It's miraculous. If you succeed I shall give it you."

"All right," he answered somewhat grumpily, "I suppose I had better try magic." He became furtive and haggard in look, like an old Franciscan friar. But he read my doubt about his occupation. "It's not what you think. I seek nothing for myself." He sighed. "Yet even Saint Francis had to strip himself naked before his bishops to show he posed no threat to the women who came to confess to him . . ."

Division

He stood up and waved his arms. Heaven forbid that he should remove his clothes.

"*Ignei, aerii, aquatani spiritus, salvete* . . . She whom your eyes shall like, your heart will have . . ."

No sooner had he begun when his spell grew potent and I began to feel an eerie presence. What if this servant of hell's monarch could summon Kate and force her to submit to diabolical ravishment?

"I've had enough!" I cried out. "Stop it."

"Too late," answered the wizard, "we cannot go back. The machinery has been set in motion."

One of the walls of the room, at a height of about five feet, had a portion the size of a buckler or large plate set in relief. This began faintly to glimmer. At the same time gentle unearthly sounds crept over my ears, not exactly of music, but not untuneful.

"What do you know of the gore of a snake crushed by the weight of a dying elephant?" asked Forman. "We call it dragon's blood or cinnabar . . ."

"I . . ." I stuttered.

"Wait," he cautioned. "You shall see! True cinnabar is extracted from the sand found in silver mines. Then it is mixed with goat's blood or crushed service-berries. I cannot make it stay . . ."

An image began to form. I now firmly believed that Kate was starting to be conjured up before my eyes. If she knew, she would never speak to me again. Faint lines of red began to run and form in the wall.

"It will not last," said Forman. "A surface painted with cinnabar is damaged by the action of sunlight and moonlight. I would ask you to put on a loose mask of bladderskin to prevent your inhaling . . ."

"Ah!" I gasped with horror.

Here was a face. Lips and eyes were emerging. "But whose face is it?" I called out as Forman slapped some foul-smelling organ over my mouth and nose.

"Whose but the one you love?"

I watched in greater horror as the face digested more and more of its red-lead contours.

"I think you have the wrong person," I blurted through the mask. "This is not Kate at all."

Forman rose and uttered a string of obscenities. The music ceased as suddenly. He paced up and down in front of me. The face quickly dissolved.

"Magic often does not work. I have to explain this frequently. It is not the magic which is at fault, it is me. Come another time . . ."

Forman seemed ill and confused. I left him. I dared not say the truth, for he had worked up a face I knew. Shrouded in a dark red Jesuit hood. I could not give his name.

Riding over London Bridge on my way back to my lodging I threw the broken tooth of Thomas More with all my might into the Thames.

II

One afternoon I ask her to join me at the Blackfriars playhouse to watch a play of humours about five men in love with the same young woman who has a miserly father and who has been deprived of her birthright. She has but a few lines to say. She has, or so I joke, also been deprived of her tongue.

Mostly the matter is full of low comedy and horse manure, which is spread everywhere from a scuttle.

It was late June and the weather was still fine and warm at six o'clock.

"Shall we walk through London?" I asked Kate afterwards as we came into the open town.

"No, I must hurry to my house."

"Where are you going tonight?"

"I keep my chamber."

"But where?"

"In my house. No other."

"Can I call?"

"I forbid you to. I am in mourning. I am made wretched by the death of my young lord Alex."

"You don't wear mourning. Why did you not tell me earlier of his death? I hope the play did not distress you."

"No. I only heard the news this morning. I did not want to cancel."

"How did your husband die?"

She shook her head sorrowfully. "In bloody fight, or in fever or of the plague. I have not yet heard."

"And yet you did not love him very much?" I suggested gently.

I thought she would spit at me.

"You, Mr Donne, should go and vent yourself in a Pimlico brothel among the bawds and brokers!"

Division

She had a low and gentle voice. How much in that moment, in her extreme hate of me, I longed to have her.

"But I heard the Queen advising you to value him. I merely touch you on the quick."

"My husband was mild and virtuous. You are a treacherous, evil man who seeks to exploit a private moment which had nothing to do with you. You seek advantage of everyone."

"I only do what everyone does."

"One minute you swear one thing, the next its opposite. One day you praise the virtues of constancy. Next day fickleness is your champion. You disgust me when you write,

> Women are made for men, not him, nor me.

Yet you are also capable of

> She is all states and all Princes, I,
> Nothing else is:

and

> Perfection is in unity.

You claim to seek the truth. You have no allegiance to anything but your last clever thought."

"I agree. The word is a weathercock for every wind. It bears a different sense to each interpreter. This is why poets are so admired."

"They flatter the sick and the rich, but not the honest."

"I would become dull." There was silence. Her meaning was plain. "It is the wives who cheat their husbands, not me."

"Your dullness would be preferable to the life you lead."

"I will stop if you love me."

Her blue eyes were as cold as rain-soaked slate. "You are a blackmailer. I wish you were dead."

I drew my sword, seized the blade which scotched my hand so that blood ran freely, and offered her the hilt.

"Put your sword away."

"I love you."

"You are merely rubbed the wrong way because I will not love you."

"Then you shall be my executioner."
"That's not good enough!"
I then saw a tear which wet her eye. This intimate and delicate sign, so much at odds with her anger, shouted at me to change.

13

The Fox in his Lair

But I could not. I wished I had been capable of it. I would have saved myself a thousand trials – and perhaps gained eternity too. In practice I continued to pursue Kate savagely, and even more savagely in my imagination. I seized every slight occasion that gave me sight of her. I fashioned jewels of verse out of the experience of failure. I also paid dearly for the failure.

In a month or two I believed I merited more than I received and gradually came to meet the tempest of her provocation with a calm and godlike mastery. I gained confidence that my love for her would prevail in the end. My passion itself grew calm.

It happened once in my life that I was in the Azores on an expedition with Lord Essex. We were at sea waiting off Flores. The wind would not bear the sails before the masts, while at night the sea was so breathless that the lanterns remained unlit, the dust and feathers from one day to the next undisturbed. I again thought of that unnatural calm that settled over my love for Kate.

Waiting for her brought me to the conviction that ultimately I would win the glory of forcing her to love me. I could not believe that the unreasonable extent to which she withheld her affection would not lead to victory. I could gain the hearts of others so easily, that to turn them away I had to advise them to be inconstant.

This did not impress her. She believed I sought only to capture her for her money, for she now had the rule of her husband's purse, some hundreds a year. She told me again and again that she did not love me, could not love me, was sure that she would never love me.

II

I was staggered at what developed next in my relations with the Queen. One day I was in Whitehall engaged on some legal business when I was taken to one side by Lord Burghley under a corona which dropped great goblets of oily wax upon our heads. He was remarkably long-suffering, with great pouches of tiredness under his eyes as if, to himself and when on his own, he wept too much. Yet this old fox, now enfeebled in appearance but expanded in wisdom and experience, had bright humorous brown windows, which, unlike those of his animal counterpart, could see in every direction.

Only a few weeks had passed since my meeting with the Queen in Greenwich. The Earl of Essex, in his opposition to the marriage of the Duc de Houpeville to the Queen, had been neatly foiled by the agent of de Houpeville, Jean de Bouvier, who discovered his secret correspondence with the Scottish King James and told the Queen. She confined Essex to his London house, and would have had him committed to the Tower, then his head cut off on the Hill, had not the wise old councillor Sussex spoken and persuaded the Queen that in so acting she would be her own worst enemy.

It was Jean de Bouvier who again demonstrated that wooing can be entrusted to a seductive intermediary. Our Grace loved handsome, well-built men, but Bouvier was no such marvel, quite the reverse, a pox-pitted, puny dwarf with a nose so great and fiery red that it would have lit an army to its camp.

Such a shrunken carcass had an eloquent command of words, while his ardour made up for it even more, for he would picture his master's youth and dash in such a way that it caught the Queen's imagination. Everyone at Court had nicknames. Bouvier called himself, to Our Grace, "Your little monkey". His master used the epithet of our marsh inhabitant, "Grenouille" – the cold and volatile frog, but in Roman mythology a figure of constancy.

The frog had visited once and been a great success. She had dipped herself in the public spectacle of his homage. But what did she feel? Elizabeth's inner feelings were her biggest traitors, servants that would plot and then betray her, and could never be counted on to carry out their duties or obligations.

But now the timbers were being driven home for the construction of a diabolically subtle stratagem, rising below and behind the dazzling façade of Elizabeth's wooing by the Duc de Houpeville. It was on this inner, hidden, and secret platform of the Queen's passion that I became destined to be thrust as player. I was given a part and my cues, but allowed to perceive nothing of the larger

The Fox in his Lair

design. I entertained little suspicion for, this apart, I was concerned only to catch further sight of the face and form that haunted me.

What did Burghley want now?

I asked him as tactfully as I could if the Queen would like to hear more of my poetry.

His answer surprised me and terrified me. I saw myself surrounded at once by members of her inner guard.

"Read her anything; go to it, my boy, while the time is hot. Take your chance. She is sizing you up."

A sweat broke out on my brow: to cover my confusion I bent to tie my lace, only just restraining a great fart, and then I felt on the back of my neck the searing heat of a black and smoky droplet of grease.

"A wise head keeps close." The old fox smiled. "Know that *you* are her latest suitor. She seeks to heal the state of her soul."

I threw aside all caution.

"I may be suggesting the most treasonable sentiment that a man might be driven to utter, but surely I should never believe that I could entertain a hope of becoming the Queen's consort?" I was as padded in speech as in Court costume.

The old fox laughed. I expected my arms to be pinioned, an attack of invisible thought pensioners to flatten and obliterate me.

"Well asked!" He pulled me over to a side of the hall and scribbled a pass. "Come tonight to my house to supper. I will advise you further."

Would I ever be the right person to heal the state of anyone's soul?

Burghley House, famous for its cloth of gold patterns laid over walls of grisaille, was full of revels that night: the strolling players had been invited – I forget which group – but they made lively sounds. The summer air was thick and heavy, weighted with the oppression of heat and conspiracy.

The hall resounded to the thumps of the players' tumbling and their gigs, while the watchers, the wife of the fox, his daughter and Robert, his hump-backed son, greeted me on arrival. Robert surveyed me coldly from head to toe with his bulging hare eyes, noting down my every detail in the book of his memory.

The fox would not let me tarry but led me to an upstairs chamber, a timber-framed and book-lined study where he ushered me to an easy chair, drew up another for himself and offered me a pipe, while lighting one himself.

"I have studied that woman for over thirty years. I believe I know her backwards and forwards" – he saw the darkness of "know" cross my brow. "Oh, do not misunderstand me, Mr Donne. I have ever been her dutiful servant, for which perhaps uniquely she has rewarded me with great wealth and position . . ."

"I think she must love and honour you more than anyone," I said. I was still mortally terrified.

The piping, hermaphrodite voice of the old man warbled on, "For Our gracious Sovereign men divide into two kinds. Those that serve her, and those that interest her. I do not interest her in the slightest, not in the sense that you do. But she relies on me, she depends on me utterly.

"I serve her emotions as, in my role as minister, I ceremoniously carve her meat at table and hand her her plate. In such capacity, I have long watched and studied her. She is – in no sinister or sexual sense you must understand – a devourer of men. She has an eye, she has an instinct. She is voracious: she has enjoyed, in her own way, every eligible man in this kingdom."

"It is not for nothing," I laughed, "that the poets call her the Queen of Love."

"She is not only Queen of England, but Venus," said the fox sternly. "She is the Queen of heaven; the Queen of hell, the Queen of the witches, the goddess of the underworld. She is all nature; the mother of the gods."

"You would have done well as a poet, my Lord."

He signalled at me menacingly. "I warn you not to speak to anyone of what I say. She has no love of women, no friends among her sex; they are sisters, mothers, slaves, all to be commanded, even the half-sister she once had. She cares for women as a lover of nature might care for the gentle defenceless birds of the hedgerow and the sea-margin.

"There is no woman in England who comes near her in decisiveness of word, range, power, amorous delay, or uncertainty. There is even a tenderness in her . . ."

"But why do you come to me?" He was growing excessively long-winded.

He cast glances about him to make sure we were not being watched or overheard.

"Men have always been the object of her obsession. She recalls every detail of every one – those, that is, she has not put to one side. For example, last night she mentioned the papist Campion, and a treatise he delivered, oh years ago, on an abstruse, astronomical subject – something to do with the way inferior bodies, in the distribution of astral forces, look up to superior ones."

There was suddenly in the air an exact state, a condition of sound and stillness, which I recalled from that time long before, when Underhill had played that trick on me in another library.

"What of Campion?"

The fox looked over at me sharply. "Did you know the man?"

I feared some encounter, some light brush of a hand. I transferred my eyes from my Lord Cecil to the ceiling. Yes there, there among the classical emblems of the golden age we so loved to emulate, the face again came into view.

His handsome face. There was, in the smile that beamed down on me, a challenge. He was, or was not, there. I felt like a creature about to be hurled over the abyss. I caught myself, I recovered as I caught myself in my fall.

"I met him once. I was only ten years old."

I bit my tongue. Cecil had praised me for my taciturnity, and here I was dribbling my interior doubt and my family secret like the phlegm which the fox's tobacco soothed and dried up.

The fox sighed. "He, too, was a suitor. She takes a fancy to the dangerous ones. I fear for their lives." His eyes lingered on me and he noted me trembling. My thoughts were still stampeding.

"I do not think you are dangerous, John Donne."

"What do you want me to do?"

"This is the last chance I will have to marry off the Queen."

I was still trussed fast in my nightmare. I had to escape the pounding uncertainty the name of Edmund Campion exerted over me. I felt trapped by the morbid religious insecurity which was deep inside me.

"What in the name of goodness is the matter?"

I summoned all the force I could to contradict the bad impression I was making on Burghley.

"But you are not suggesting that I myself . . . ?"

"No, no, the Duc de Houpeville will be at Hatfield House watching the masque. I want you to make it so persuasive of married love that the Queen will become inflamed and intoxicated."

"And then?"

"As Jupiter, I want you to seduce her and lure her to bed . . . de Houpeville will be waiting."

I was flushed and out of breath. I coughed with embarrassment. I could not countenance such an affable and bashful old man working up such a depraved plan. Was there no intimacy too sacred that he would not use it or pry into it? Even so I had to ask, "But how, my Lord, can you know that she will be ready to be made pregnant?"

"I *know*," said Burghley. "I calculate her days."

His meaning was plain. He computed her courses. The old fox passionately believed that the hot French blood could make a detour round the well-noted blockages in Elizabeth's womb.

"I plot single-mindedly for a child," said Burghley. "I read magic books on how to make sperm vanquish barrenness. We have negotiated all this."

Miraculous and mysterious events swelled up and were born daily, but none more enormous than Burghley's proposition. My forehead was drenched. I was baffled. Perhaps my visitation *had* been the Devil.

I drew a deep breath. I was chafed with sweat.

"I will do what I can."

My answer was rewarded with an echoing crack of thunder.

"Good." The old fox shifted. He seemed to relax.

"What about my secretaryship with Lord Egerton?" I inquired.

"You shall have five secretaryships."

I nodded. "And what do the players present tonight?"

"Ah," said Burghley, "Marlowe's unfinished 'Massacre at Paris'. I think it will flatter the Queen, for at the end of the play the dying King of France swears to ruinate the wicked church of Rome, and protests eternal love to the Royal Lady of England."

"Doesn't it also show the Duc de Houpeville's grandmother, Catherine de Medici, as an accomplice murderess of Protestants?"

"I know, I know," answered Burghley. "But it's fitting for this occasion."

His old veins, pale from exertion, vividly anatomised themselves on the side of his brow.

"You cannot please all of the people all of the time. I am trying tonight to assuage the feelings of my Lord of Essex, who has been hurt by the Queen's rough treatment of him. We need also to stiffen the Court's attitude towards Catholics. The 'Massacre at Paris' is short, bloody, and full of butchered heads."

Burghley, signifying he had little time, brusquely instructed me how I should present my masque at Hatfield House, telling me of certain extra things to be said and done. Then he led me out of his study and down the stairs.

The Fox in his Lair

Stylish women had appeared everywhere, in blond wigs and with their faces painted, thrusting their exposed breasts freely and fiercely to the greedy, naked eye in the manner of Venetian courtesans. I saw Kate Ferrars alone on a landing. I asked permission to leave the Secretary.

"Beware that girl," warned Burghley. "She is Scottish, a puritan, and some say she spies for King James. I abhor that griping and weak-kneed Scot! Her mother ran off and her father went mad – her only brother died young. They say she holds a grudge against the world. She is her whole family alone."

I quickly but courteously withdrew from the old fox, believing he spoke trumpery. Kate had little by way of a Scots accent; she had married early and taken on her husband's manners and speech. But it was hard work to corner her, for she would not answer when I called, and walked quickly away from me, as if seeking escape. It grew into something of a chase.

Outside the storm had reached its climax of thunder and lightning.

"If you still wear black you must continue to feel great sadness and weakness," I said when I had caught up with her.

"I really wouldn't bother your head over me," she answered crossly. "I am not worth it."

"Stop giving me that awful look."

She turned away and stamped her foot. "Leave me alone!"

"Why are you so impatient in my company?"

With these words of mine she gave a gesture – not a very polite one – that I should leave her. The consort of instruments struck up a dance. The thunder sounded again and again.

"Do you not want to be loved?"

I can see now that in her I found reflected my own incapacity to love.

"I don't believe there is anyone in the world who does not want to be loved – by the right person. But do you love yourself, Mr Donne?"

"Too much," I answered. "I suffer an excess of it. Yet I also despise myself and I live in a seraglio of self-slaughter."

"Words, words, words," she said mockingly.

She brought from behind her back a small, snarling skull which was chalked vividly on to a background of black card, and clapped it over her face.

She seized my hand. "Come," she said to me, "let's join the dance."

I danced wildly, desperate always to follow Kate who showed her wobbly snarling head. A group of masks suddenly surrounded us. Kate was trying to push me away. The boisterous merry dancers seemed to be suffering from a collective fit. Everyone was jumping, stepping out, chasing each other, gathering, dispersing.

Then there was a blast on the trumpet. The play was about to begin.

Kate threw off her mask, grasped my hand again and we climbed the small staircase from which, above the hall, we could watch. We were high above the players' heads while, far below, the fictional Court of France assembled in the well: only the front row of the audience was visible.

We were on an empty, tenebrous landing; Kate was leaning against the banister at the top of the stair. The staircase and landing were full, at every heavily carved turn, of eyes of naked cupids, lions and other heraldic clusters which surveyed us. The drop below made me dizzy.

"Look," I said, reaching inside my jacket, "what Lord Burghley gave me. You are to wear it for the masque round your middle. For as Juno you are to embody bashfulness and shamefacedness, as well as chastity."

"Why?" she asked. Her face was drawn, as if ravaged by a feverish passion. I could see, close to, that she was made up like some provincial prostitute; unusually, for her, she had not resisted the temptation to paint her face, like a violent mask, with a cloudy, threatening severity.

"Jupiter and Juno are to become reconciled at the end of the masque. After all his faithlessness Jupiter is to dedicate himself once again to marriage."

"And then?"

"You and I are to be tied like lovers at the waist with silks as a token that we must bind one another's minds in a self-sacred knot."

Kate laughed harshly.

I produced the small red sphere of silk that Burghley had given me and showed it to her.

"What's that for?" she cried out, startled.

"This is what you have to wear next to your naked skin – inside your most intimate garment."

I could feel Kate tauten with excitement.

"It is meant to be freed by the bridegroom on the night of marriage. Dissolved with ceremonies of delight. But not for you and me! You are to take yours off and give it to the Queen. Or, rather, I take it off as a token of Jupiter's submission to you."

"Shall we put it on now?"

Her intention, or rather invitation, was clear. In the meantime, below in the hall, against a curtain of searing green and scarlet satin inlaid with flashing spangles of silver, the Duc de Guise had commenced his massacring of Protestants – under the dispensation of the Pope.

> "Give me a look, that when I bend the brows,
> Pale death may walk in furrows of my face."

The murderer was acted by the bull-throated Edward Alleyn.

"Where shall we go?" I said in a dry-throated whisper.

"We don't need to go anywhere," she replied in an even voice which provoked my state even more. I peered down into the well of the staircase at the zodiac painted on the stone flags.

"Here!"

She took my hand and placed it under the skirt of her dress. The other hand she guided through the back of her dress, which was fastened. I was pressing against her. While my left hand found and stroked her breasts, my right gently climbed to the top of her thigh where, I realised, she wore no guard or dessous. I could not pay attention to the play.

Down below, the play momentarily ceased. The Queen had arrived. A trumpet fanfare greeted her. The Queen stopped at the bottom of the stairs. She stared up eagerly and greeted Kate and myself. Or Kate, anyway, for I believe that from below I could not be seen. I stopped my investigations, and made to retreat; but using her thighs like shears Kate imprisoned my hand and would not let me go.

"God save Queen Elizabeth!" Kate called down as she forced her stomach against my hand, wriggling and writhing so hard that for the first time my fingers unceremoniously entered her. She trembled.

Elizabeth moved below in a jewelled head-dress and marvellous yellow gown embroidered with mouths, with eyes, and with ears. All those she passed fell to their knees.

But she was in a towering rage. Her fingers twitched and clenched. She was shouting madly. She had had enough of it. That day a good Catholic priest had been executed and the outcry had been huge.

"Dangerous or not, Catholics must be stroked and coaxed. I'll have no more murder! Send money to the priest's family."

Kate trembled more and strove to impale herself harder and more firmly upon my fingers, plunging and turning herself round.

"These are dangerous days, good mistress," I could hear Burghley saying to her soothingly. The Queen was not calmed.

"I'll not be forced to persecute holy men and women!"

I was now aware how wet Kate was, and of a Medusa ornament with snakes whose eyes drilled into mine. I was pitched beyond the wildest coastline. Kate threw her skirt over her waist and her cule or buttocks showed like pale ivory in the dim and fluctuating candlelight.

She stiffened for a moment or two. She came. There was a wonderful prettiness and play of feature in her face.

But no echo of my own. No relief from my own anguish of arousal. Would I be rewarded?

No. She completely ignored me. I was at her mercy. I was enthralled. I would have said or done anything for relief. I could think only of words.

14

Mother and Son

My stepfather Syminges was now over sixty, but my mother Elizabeth, known as Sylvia, was ten years younger and she drew on his energies in such a way that he hardly seemed any longer to have a presence of his own. He gave, to me at least, the feeling that he did not have many years to go.

Sylvia devoured husbands with the single-minded zeal of her faith: he was out of his depth, drowning by trying to live up to her expectations. His physical presence, however, was weak: if you sat in a room with him and my mother, he would hover in the background, taking a sip or two of claret.

I had just beaten my hand down upon the oaken table.

"Henry must be freed from that dreadful jail!" I insisted.

Henry was now lodged in Newgate, the most disturbing and shameful of London's prisons, where mainly common criminals were kept. There you could be hanged for rape, or abduction; for buggery of your servant, for cutting a purse, for stealing hawks' eggs, or for just letting out a pond. In the meantime, while they deliberated upon the enormity of Henry's crime, he was kept waiting.

"If you were to use your friends at Court to ensure this could be done without any loss of his dignity and courage . . ." Sylvia let the implication grow in the unfinished nature of her sentence.

"You know that is impossible," I replied. "If we were Norfolks or Southamptons, we would be left at peace with our faith. But conformity is necessity for the solid middle – even if the brain is unsteady and the feet clogged in mud."

My mother would not listen. "I have provided well for Henry. I spent seven shillings and sixpence for food; and today a five shilling tip for his keeper. I trust you had no problem in being admitted."

"None at all. Neither did the rats!"

Most of all I feared the Hole, where those without money of both sexes were packed, stinking, prior to a pressing to death in the pressing yard, or being boiled alive in water or lead.

"John Donne," said Sylvia very severely, "you are becoming very worldly."

"Oh yes," I answered, "I suppose it is more important to you that Henry earns a proper place in heaven than a life on earth that might afford him satisfaction!"

I could feel my heart quickening its beat in defiance of my mother.

"John," said Sylvia again in a tone which escalated the seriousness of her warning. "Don't tell me you are on their side? . . ."

I blushed. "Their side – our side, what exactly does it mean?" I said in that careless kind of suppressed angry mood, when I failed to realise how deep my emotions went about such an issue.

But Sylvia had not missed seeing how profound the difference between us ran.

"Do you mean to say you value Henry's stand at naught?"

By now my neck prickled. Then in a vision I saw Henry dangling by the neck in a place of public execution. I almost cried out, but I pushed down the feeling so hard it came out only as a bitter question.

"So you want him to die . . . ?"

She was too clever to respond to my anger, but she turned it round on me.

"What do you want – for yourself?" she questioned.

I ignored this. I determined to drop my bombshell.

"I request formal permission from you – from you both – "

This I added almost ironically, because I was sure the second earthly father I had – if one could extend to him that name (for he was about as interested in me as the horse in the fly that settles on its nose, to be twitched and scratched at) – "to persuade Henry to ask the Queen's pardon."

Sylvia dropped the glasses which she had lately, and with great self-consciousness, started holding up to her eyes, which even so still sparkled with youthful zest. As she bent down to retrieve them from under the table she showed her breasts still had in them an attractive resilience and pinkness.

Seeing my eyes fixed on these tender parts in an unfilial stare she grew confused, suddenly flushed, sat bolt upright and said nothing. I remained in the confusion of our collision. Then she started talking again, completely forgetting the previous incident. She spoke proudly and firmly.

"I have noticed in you of late, John," she said, "great restlessness and a tendency to peculiar moods. Such division as you propose within a family might well drive you to – " She left the ominous and dark remainder of her thought unsaid, but the threat was specific.

Old slobberbreech, who had done well from this second marriage without lifting a finger to help his wife and her children, now offered a suggestion. His skin was unhealthily yellow. I felt a wild impulse to spring at his throat and strangle him.

"I believe we should arrange an escape," he quavered. He must have noticed my change of expression and the sudden light of anger in my eyes. "They are not uncommon. There are hundreds of supporters who could be called on. It won't even pose a great risk."

Not for you, I thought, knowing my dear stepfather would not even chance his oldest citizen of London cap for Henry – but would push forward others if he could. Every wrinkle on his ancient schismatic face denoted shiftiness.

Sylvia was frosty to this suggestion. I at least sympathised with her there. She wanted the full martyrdom. Nothing less would satisfy her. I hated her so much for it. I loathed her – and I defied her.

II

Father Anthony died one afternoon in July and we put him straight on a cart to take him down to the burial ground. At the last minute we had to change the plan as a new servant of mine was suspected of being an informer and he left that morning, never to be seen again. So we buried the priest in the vegetable garden. At least no charge had been brought against him to raise a fine on the Donne family.

Sylvia organised Mass in the room she had furnished for this, but I refused to go, for my disgust had grown so great by then at the meaningless waste of this priest's life. Sylvia was no doubt consoled by the thought that he had died for his faith.

It was Father Anthony's death that set me even more seriously thinking about becoming a Protestant. Kate, too, had a hand in it. I feared at that time that she was sent to convert me by the Queen – or at least by some of the toadies around her.

The following weekend in my Surrey home I found Sylvia even more sharp with me. Since Henry's move to Newgate, and since my continuing encounters both with the Queen and with Kate, my mind had been working fiercely and intently. On the Friday night, after my hard ride, Sylvia and my stepfather had been silent at supper, but I knew they wanted to challenge me. I kept them at bay with how I had coaxed the utmost speed out of Pump, and regaled them with tales of her skittish and temperamental peculiarities. The old man had been unusually abrupt and distant, scarcely looking me once in the face.

I believed I knew the reason. All during Saturday no word was spoken to me: even the members of our deeply loved and trusted household – all Catholics, and this was probably the reason – treated me distantly.

Sylvia looked displeased when she came in. She had been riding. The summer had been a disaster and mud covered all the tracks. She wore breeches like a man, and these were now splashed above the knees. She stayed over by the fire even after her boots had been drawn off by my stepfather, and she had put on her soft, leather shoes.

She settled in her chair without a word and commanded supper. At first, while our servants brought us in soup and meat the meal proceeded in a dark and ominous silence. They had found out my secret, of that I was now sure.

Sylvia intoned grace in Latin without devotion or sensitivity to the words, and when supper was over, my stepfather made himself scarce. I followed my mother into the parlour behind the dining-room. She always poured wine for her sons, but this time she made an exception. She served herself from the glass decanter into one of our fine silver goblets – and left me the decanter to help myself.

"I have heard grave things about you which I hope are not true," she began. Her head was very straight. She had always been an excellent horsewoman, and retained great pride in her carriage of head and her posture.

". . . I have no means of redress. I cannot cut you off. Moreover I had a plan for the future of our family – " She stopped and quavered emotionally on the word "family" as if the severity gave way before some maternal feeling.

I found myself – up to then bristling and ready to engage in argument – silent and tongue-tied.

Her decline into gentleness compelled me to look at her. I gazed over at her once or twice, sipped my wine thoughtfully. Even now I thought irreverently of her in bed with Syminges. Although she had acted with every due decorum after my poor father's death she had married against my wishes, for I had much need of her, and possibly we could have consoled each other.

I had always felt she had been exacting towards my father,

could never allow him any faults or weaknesses, while she did not understand how he was often only weak on the surface, out of petty self-defence or fatigue, and because, unlike Sylvia or myself, he could never think up quick extempore replies to gain for himself – in this superficial age of quick retorts – a reputation for his wit.

Sylvia, impatient of him, would never give him scope for his true strength and qualities to emerge. With her clear precise delivery of words and with her sharp tongue, she would jump on him and criticise him. He would turn the other cheek or walk out of the room, never offering defence. Self-awareness was never my mother's strong virtue: she had a strong vertical presence, but no sympathetic embrace towards those close to her. She could never see sideways. She was Catholic to the core.

But my father had never tried to dominate her, and she had seized the power he had taken the trouble never to assert over her and used it as her own. I did not believe that she respected him much for never standing up to her, for her high expectations seemed with age to grow rather than to diminish.

But when Father died, unexpectedly, on a trip to Italy when a holy house in which he stayed was visited by the plague, she made the ultimate progression of a strong woman, and married a complete cipher, a galliarding nincompoop who was little better than a glorified house-servant, or perhaps just about deserving of the title of steward. It was since my father's death, I realised, when my mother had been both father and mother to me, that she had taken on many of the qualities of a man.

I suspected – and for this reason my jealousy quickly abated – that little by way of bed-work went on between them, and that Sylvia's high expectation in every other department was offset by, between the sheets, her almost total lack of excitement. Perhaps, who knows, they had taken a vow of chastity.

If this were true, then he gave her a complete free hand in virtue. She had of late concentrated very much on "form" but having the moral strength of ten ordinary women and to my mind always behaving like one of those Roman matrons of old, her Catholicism – although generally known – was overlooked.

"What are your intentions?" she snapped at me.

"What are yours, Mother?"

"Answer me first."

"I will try. But I am torn, Mother. I am rent. My heart is riven in two."

"So you mean to thwart and disobey me – and your dead father –"

"Now wait a minute, Mother . . ." I always had the feeling that my father might himself have been about to move along the dangerous path that I had emboldened myself to follow. But I let this drop.

"I have no desire in any way to cross you – except in a matter of the deepest conscience . . ."

"Conscience – dear John, what can you mean by the word conscience in such a connection?"

I knew to her it seemed like cynical commodity, narrow accommodation instead of conscience. But she should not have been so intolerant.

"Have you no sense of honour?"

Now she touched my pedantic soul to the quick.

I licked my lips carefully and thought over what to say. How I wished at that moment to be employing them in some other occupation. I sat up a little straighter in my chair, still sore from having ridden so far the day before.

"Mass is to be said in the morning at six o'clock at Chippenham Hall by Mr Owen."

"I do not wish to know."

"It is not your intention to attend?"

I said nothing.

"I trust it is not your purpose to tell the justices?"

At this I flew into a rage. "Who do you think I am?" I shouted at Sylvia in spite of my resolution not to shout. "A Judas that would betray my own flesh and blood?" I could feel froth forming at the corners of my mouth, as if I were a wild animal. A kind of despair surged through me. Why did we have to quarrel?

"I have heard, John, of your attendance at Westminster Abbey. What do you think it makes me feel?"

So it was out in the open. I felt at once calmer. I tried to become more reasonable in tone.

"Mother, I must turn the changes I feel inside me into persuasive words, so that your heart may perhaps understand why."

"Do you believe, John, that I do not know all the arguments?"

"My son," she went on, "I am torn in my loyalty: between God and my loyalty to you."

"I disappoint you, Madam, I know. I am not made of the stuff of martyrs and exiles."

"You would dilute or turn to water the substance of our faith."

"I would still in some spirit be a Catholic."

"A Catholic, sir, to my mind," said Sylvia steadily, "is one who holds to the Catholic Church of Rome and no other. I mean nothing offensive. It is not for me to condemn you."

"Mother," I replied, "you are not being just to me. You have taught me too much. I need time. Maybe then I will see the validity of what you say. Just now it hurts me beyond measure to have suffered the death of Father Anthony and to see Henry threatened with a similar end."

"Henry regrets above all," interrupted Sylvia, "that he has not a good enough mind to become a priest . . ."

Here Sylvia caught me unawares. I too had felt the desire for Catholic priesthood. I choked with what I spurned.

"Mother," I cried out stupidly, "I am in love!"

"Who on earth have you fallen in love with?"

I could see her take, in metaphor at least, a step backwards. But neither of us would yield. I could have submitted to her feelings and her aspirations, and then gone my own way . . . "With Kate Ferrars – one of Our Grace's ladies of the chamber."

Then Sylvia started laughing. It was laughter that was at once hearty and bitter; it concealed a sneer, but also a dead passion that caused pain.

The fact that my love was for a Protestant minion of the Queen stirred up scorn and contempt. She was not just merely angry, or robustly furious. She closed an open door in my heart.

15

Venus and Mars

By the light of one sick taper I lie on the canvas of my pallet.

For my head I have a bolster of straw, but not yet a pillow of feathers. These are thought only for women in childbed. Luxurious counterpanes of swan's down are for later. I will use my rough quilt, but I am still dressed. My chamber is like the husk of my days as a student, my physic books and written rolls of moral counsel strewn everywhere, some with their strings all untied.

Relics of an even earlier self are preserved from childhood like emblems or chastisements. They hang from racks, or rest on shelves let in the walls.

My childhood hunting guns and birdbolts, my snares, my nets and sleave-silk flies for fishing. My collections in boxes of small birds and insects. Do they not know I once removed and counted five hundred fleas off a young hedgehog?

But who is the real me? The provisional self I am at Court. I have hundreds, literally hundreds of conflicting thoughts. Like a chameleon I take my colouring from what lies round me. The thoughts turn me over and over like clotted butter in a churn. I am on a turning wheel of the self . . .

Kate, my love for her; my wooing of the Queen; my despair over my mother; my dead father whose presence haunts me like a ghost saying, "Change – be ambitious – do all the things that I never dared because your mother always preached self-effacing virtue, which was good philosophy for those without talent or individuality, but lethally destructive to the gifted."

Then Henry's pained and tortured face preys on my mind – as if I am murdering him myself, denying his soul its resting place and then crushing the virtue of his gesture. Then Burghley's plan to involve me with the Queen on the night I am to present the masque – in which I join because I know it is sanctioned. Am I conspiring with all that is evil in my kingdom?

Shame increases. The wicked, forward way I have answered. I

Venus and Mars

have never wanted to hurt my mother, above all not to wound her in the area in which she is sensitive, namely faith.

Has she not had enough pain and grief to contend with, especially with the unending persecution of all those around her who are her friends and cling to similar beliefs? Is she not the most courageous person I know? If I defy her, will I not be like that medieval and wicked magician Faust who figures in the plays, selling his soul to the devil for the rewards of earthly reputation and glory?

She hates all vanity, all self-regarding praise which eats itself in the very act of self-puffery. But I am attracted to this.

Does not my very occupation draw its life-blood from the daring praise of oneself?

Lost as I am in the search for myself I find I am drawn to images of my mysterious Kate, and enchanted with the thought that on the afternoon of Monday I will be back at Court. Superlative Kate: all that my mother is not. I love my mother. Yet there is something hard-boiled about her, although she looks very young.

Yet Kate: her blue and steady eyes, her sleek dark hair as brilliant as the new lacquer from the east, her skin white as a camellia. Her legs are lyrical. She wears unusual clothes. Dresses without tops and without backs. Will she let me again feel her soft and springy nipples?

Coupling and erotic foreplay are basic to the security of these two selves who fight each other. Chastity is a devil, an alien cold side of an isolated being. Between the poles of sex runs the electricity that joins the two sides of being.

I have bought for Kate a picture I found in a dusty shop in Maiden Lane. It lay wrapped in parchment by the door. I had not time to admire it in the shop which had been dark and unlit. So now I go and unwrap the paper from it and set it on my table. I can commune with Kate.

II

The subject is that of Mars and Venus fastened in Vulcan's net of slender bronze chains, threads and snares which he has set around the bed. The sun has informed on the passion of Venus and Mars to the husband of Venus, who, as blacksmith of the gods, has fashioned his trap to humiliate his wife and her lover. The gods are in uproar, but at least one prays that he too might be so humiliated!

Venus does not forget. Her revenge smoulders on until it is fulfilled. She punishes the informer. The picture shows the sun slinking off at one corner, with the naked Venus impaled on the weapon of the god of war, but promising the most murderous of retributions.

This is the Birth of Night: the banishment of the sun for half a day from the earth. The painting is exquisitely executed, the flesh tints perfectly lifelike. It does not reveal the underneath parts – as some of our more recent Court painters have done. It captures the sinuous interweave of limbs, the mixture of abandon and resentment on the face of Venus – and Mars as a well-muscled machine of war.

The door behind me opens softly. I do not notice Sylvia enter, but, sensing her presence, I turn to her, just in time to catch the mood of conciliation, the tender forgiving mood of a mother who, above all in a time of danger, needs the support of those close to her.

Her arms and hands are slightly extended as if she would even be prepared to embrace her eldest son and cry in his arms for comfort. In a word she would forgo pride.

Her eyes fall on the object of my rapture. In the circles in which I move such depictions of gods are commonplace. But to Sylvia this is what she would expect to find in Beelzebub's cave. There surges over me a wave of grief and shame. My face goes scarlet; my eyes fill with tears.

"John!" she cries out, her already pale face blanking even to chalkiness. "What have you come to now?"

"Mother, this is my private bedchamber."

"This is *my* house!" she retorts.

She strikes me across the face.

I drop on my knees.

III

Later, Kate and myself. Kate was not in a good mood.

"You ought to see how many dresses she has got . . ."

"I know. Three thousand and more, so it is said."

"If you saw her stripped naked and in her bath you would not be so interested." I remained silent, which provoked her more.

"John, you are lying."

"She commanded me with a look . . . I mean, she made me give her attention. She would have had me arrested by her pikemen."

Venus and Mars

Kate said: "You were about to be arrested on your own pike. I spared you. Well, an ugly old woman – bah, she is hardly better than a witch."

In spite of Kate's temper, the Queen's attention which I received had emboldened Kate's love towards me. I could feel that because of my sovereign she was becoming more and more impelled to give herself to me.

I fumbled with the buttons of her dress. I perceived that it would not be long before she noticed one of her breasts was uncovered. I hurriedly pulled the edges of her chemise over it and closed up the buttons. I owe this gentle approach to my sovereign. Kate liked to convince herself that she was still resisting.

Next day, the Queen was called away to Rycote; I was taken by Kate into the private bedchamber. We entered the royal apartments by way of a barred oak door that gleamed with polish. I was so scared at my first sight of the awesome hall – with its inside gallery for musicians – through which I was led into the bedroom, that it needed Kate to give me confidence.

Part of the far end of the hall gave way to a tiny chapel on the wall of which hung a huge crucifix. This surprised me, for I believed the Queen's puritan advisers would not allow such blasphemy and superstition. I could not help fingering the priceless ornaments I saw everywhere – gold, silver, wood, marble, copper and bronze. Although we were accounted well-off, our own possessions were modest by comparison.

Kate loved the trophies of the royal household. But as a lady of the wardrobe she was taking big risks. I was amazed at the change which had come over her: royal preferment of me had acted on her like a love potion. As we entered the royal bedroom, she put an arm around me and kissed me on the mouth.

Up to then she had been greedy in receiving but backward and demure in repaying. She placed her mouth on mine, not even waiting for me to respond, and reached down a hand for my codpiece. The kiss was an endless one.

"But if someone comes in . . ." I fought to say between gasps.

"Do you know what the Queen does if she finds a speck of dust in some corner? She calls her lady of the chamber, makes her go down on her knees and lick it up with her tongue – as you might try to train a cur."

I now did not want to stop. I was swept away by a fury of possession, and wanted to embrace violently, kissing, biting,

101

crushing her in my arms. But I was deadly afraid to take three or four steps back to that Royal Bed which lay beyond the precipice edge like a drop net.

"Kate, I think we must leave . . . Now, at once . . ."

"It will be all right, I promise. Watch me." I stepped forward to help her. "No. I will do it myself. I want you to see that I am not only much more beautiful than my Queen, but than all the other rich women in the world."

I gazed on her. Soon she was completely naked. Was she really offering for me to take her? This was the moment that for months I had treasured in hope and with an ever mounting delirium of anticipation. But not in this place. I was paralysed.

"Juno will have her revenge on Jupiter," she said coldly. "You may use your mouth but no more."

As she arched over me I could see her writhing in ecstasy in the light of one candle that burned. I could see the large lips and the regular layers of her opening, a quick bright pink shining with wholesomeness and happy urgency.

She wore, still, the red silk disc around her middle. Was I to be so tortured until death?

At last, but only as an exception – as she made plain – she took pity on me, turning to me, unfastening my points.

IV

The weeks of rehearsal passed in an intoxicated haze. On the one hand I rode, literally, a wave of female faithlessness. My fancies multiplied as thick and fast as their expression. But my eyes remained firmly on the conquest of Kate. She enslaved me by the delay, the indifference, she imposed on me. By the end I wanted no less from her than a promise of marriage.

Widowhood was teaching her the discipline of grief. And this, translated into the region of sex, had made her mistress of hints and caprice, opacity and wicked skill. Nothing could be taken for granted.

Nothing was more urgent than our next meeting, nothing more effective a stimulus than the last. In the charge of excessive energy, between desire and delay, like a current caused by friction, lay the twists and turns, the purified mind and desire of my songs and sonnets. While I sweated for her, I could see she well understood

Venus and Mars

the delicious admixture of fear, shame, honour and arousal. Only perilously short of becoming obsessed did I stop. I idolatrised her. But sometimes I was bitter:

> When by thy scorn, O murdress, I am dead . . .
> Then shall my ghost come to thy bed,
> And thee, fained vestal, in worse arms shall see . . .

For on me she gratified herself, and openly too. She played with danger. She fed me always with more delay. The irony of Juno in my masque is that she wants Jupiter to prove his love to her by becoming chaste. This rapidly became the situation between us. Kate would go much of the way, but she would never allow herself the final act.

Little did I know what she was really thinking. Little did I know that all she wanted was to trust me; but this, above all, was what she could not do.

Piping to me an enticing and irresistible tune, she was luring me nearer and nearer to my own destruction.

16

The Turning

Sylvia was leaving England. Syminges had dropped dead and within a year she had found Robert Rainsford, another Catholic admirer. He wooed her ardently and they planned to flee to Antwerp and marry there. She had several more sessions of trying to proselytise me to the Catholic cause. She then made her intentions plain. She would cut me out of the family estate, or out of my part of it, unless I joined her cause.

"Eternal damnation is no myth to me," I still protested. "I walk over a furnace, separated by a thin crust which might crack at any moment and drop me in the flames. The sudden flash of horror is real to me . . ."

"It's not!" insisted my mother. "It's all lies."

She was in Syminges' main parlour in Drury Lane, and she looked exhausted. I had just come from an hour spent love-making with Europa. My boots were soiled with mud as I had ridden Pump hard, my little member was moist and sticky with its exertions in the dark and intricate grotto of Europa's perfections.

What I said to Sylvia was all too true, but in a different sense. The horror of my immorality being found out by the Queen or her servants was barely hidden by the thin crust. Woman's crack was the prize for which I kept on this hazardous way. I was besotted by it. By my own possession of it.

How could I, while all my feelings were invested in Kate, make love to someone else? Well this was simple. I feared her betrayal of me.

It was at this time I first thought seriously of taking holy orders in the Anglican Church.

II

But she liked the danger too much, did Juno. She would not go into the open fields, or find a quiet bank by the river where at our leisure

The Turning

we could fish and frolic in the sun. She had to have pressure, the possibility of discovery, on the deed that would not materialise. I felt myself a marked man.

So it was a different furnace I was walking over from the one I told my mother about. An actual furnace, presided over by the Queen's torturer, Topcliffe. I was a chivalric knight whose quest for the maidenhead of my love dared him to continuous and impossible risk.

"The persecution of Catholics is getting worse!" thundered my mother, attempting to bring me back to a sense of reality. "We are being accused of everything from kidnapping children to killing livestock to stir up war."

I rounded on my mother. "The king of Spain compliments Elizabeth and yet through his ambassador foments civil war – the Spanish contact thousands of Catholics like you and give them money to plot treachery."

I felt unsure of my facts, yet they issued from my mouth with command. "There is unprecedented evil at large: never has man been so wicked. Perverse, obstinate, malicious, hypocritical, covetous, untrue, proud – and –" I added this for good measure – "carnal." I amazed myself that I could get away with it. I sounded so strong. I felt so forceful and authoritative.

My mother started to cry. "John," she said appealingly, "now you are talking like all that I fear most and despise in myself. I may have been strict and stern, but I am not a puritan."

I stepped back. She caught me unawares; I had never, even faintly, thought as a puritan, and even in my wildest anti-Catholic excesses, later, when I claimed that Popes, dressed as women, sodomised prostitute boys or raped their bishops I never – I insist on this – believed in the salvation of the world for only a few. Calvin's Geneva was abhorrent to me.

"Nor am I, Mother. I am not a crusader. I don't believe in Luther or justification by faith alone."

"My dear boy," my mother appealed, "all that is contrary to the Catholic faith is heresy. For centuries the Church has stood as God's intermediary between heaven and earth. It has brought stability, security, love, honour, and all that is good for mankind.

"Now comes the Protestant, insisting on the intensely inner nature of sin – that cannot be dislodged or exorcised by prayer, by book, by the ritual of the Church. What are you doing, John, but murdering your poor old mother's soul – and that of your dead father, too!"

This was an unfair jibe. I was still angry with my father for dying on me. But I liked the new potency and immediacy of the Devil; we were in the strange murky world of change which Sylvia did not comprehend.

"The Devil confuses with exceptions," I tried to explain, "he clouds the truth with intellectual argument. No longer is he a capering clown, pulling faces and stabbing men with sins of anger and lechery. He has acquired subtlety. He has become interiorised."

My mother laughed. "And soon he won't even exist! What a fool you are, my son."

"Why?"

"Have you talked recently to any Catholics? The Church is up to all the tricks of Satan. What about Edmund Campion? Surely you do not believe that what Campion stands for lives in the past."

Campion. The name recalled me to my true self. I could see all the fallacy and hypocrisy of my argument with my mother, yet my pride would not concede that she was right.

"Look at what England has become," I said. I was off on another tack, trying to muddle and confuse the issue, win victory out of foggy ambiguity. I ignored her reference to Campion: "It's coarse-grained, narrow-minded and ponderous burghers with stinking feet, bad breath and swollen bellies. All they know how to do is to stuff themselves with more rich food, cram themselves into enveloping and creaking armchairs, belch and snore away their evenings. We *need* a spiritual revolution, Mother."

I thought my zeal might divert her from hitting the target of what really preoccupied me.

"I've read your poetry, John. Your Achilles' heel is lust."

It hadn't.

"You turn these lumbering freaks that you hate so much into cuckolds and pretend to cheat on them with their pretty wives. Your poems reduce women into objects of lust. You are worse than John Knox. All because of my unwavering loyalty to faith.

"Go and live in your narrow dark alleys with your horny and impoverished outcasts, and celebrate your male conquests. Circulate your erotic sex lyrics among the Inns of Court. There you will find your worshippers!"

Then for the second time she rejected me.

"Words or acts might be strange or incomprehensible, John. Yet the virtues themselves always remain beyond doubt."

She left me. A crowd of questions and judgements rushed in on me.

I trembled. My shame and grief grew. I had answered everything so wickedly.

Her Parthian shot was a letter which she left upon the table.

This was from O'Hearne, who wrote that Sir Jasper Underhill was in England and could easily arrange the escape of Henry from Newgate.

I suddenly thought of Underhill's face. Did we have a drawing of Edmund Campion anywhere in the house? When a man left this world, even a famous man like Campion, his face became common property and everyone could design him in what image they wished, for there was nothing to check it by.

This is why I have always grasped any opportunity to have myself drawn or painted.

"Please tell John that we need his help and that we count on him, knowing him of old, that he will not fail to help us in every way we should expect of him."

So they counted on me, did they? I reacted angrily; they did not know what I had been going through just in order to survive.

III

In the meantime the execution of priests – we now used the term "clergymen" for our own ministers – continued to provide open-air entertainment for Londoners. Sometimes I could not resist such gory spectacles. I had a distinctive face. The London of this time was small compared to now, containing no more than several hundred thousand souls. I would disguise myself and come to Tyburn by a devious route so that I would not be seen or known.

So I would hide among the rabble. This was my mandragora. All the way from the Tower to the scaffold on Tyburn field the air hung black with poison.

I would listen to the conversation. For instance, two officials from the Court in Whitehall. The crowd's masters. Elegant and cultivated with precisely matched gowns and hose, identically cut beards and manicured nails, both sniffed at oranges. The eddying swill of human refuse, inflamed with drink, sucked and pulled around them.

"One body and head . . ." mused one gentleman.

"Artistically carved to make a day's event – savoured . . . !" mused the other with a light and tinkling laugh.

"Yes," sighed the first, "how relieved I am that the day of miracles is over."

A giant of a man whose breeches were urine-soiled, whose breath smelled of garlic and ale, peered blankly into their faces.

"Catholics the bastards!" he bawled, "whipping and hanging's too good for 'em!"

The crowd, I among them, would press on the scaffold. A special platform holding it had been built so that even those far away could see. The hour would be reached for the climax of the day's outing. The speeches were made. The priest would be lifeless as he was cut down from Tyburn tree.

As one priest lay on the platform I watched the torn robe, which covered him when he was dragged on the hurdle to this place, slipping away. With his back arched over a joist, his legs now fell open and those privy parts which the Lord Chief Justice had decreed should be cut off were raised as if they were an offering.

For the moment the mob was tamed. It contemplated his manhood with a mixture of awe, derision and embarrassment. The smooth pinkish stem radiated power and innocence.

"What a waste," some appeared to think. One muttered, "Wasn't he made for a wife and children?"

The women averted their eyes from this as if the light it shone into them hurt. The men, more guarded, were more curious. Touchy, bitchy, competitive, they concealed their emotions in a consideration of the statistics. They could not believe that a papist priest, an emissary of Satan, died a virgin.

The hangman tore aside the remaining cloth and with his knife cut into the pale and prone flesh. The mob regained its ferocity and roared its approval. Such were the means by which our great nation kept its spirit in order.

17

Hatfield Follies

The suspense was at fever pitch.

The Queen was in excellent mood.

"Remember, William," she said to Burghley, "This is where we held our first council meeting when I became Queen. I love this house but my memories are mixed. As a little girl of three, I was one day a princess, the next a commoner. I was in terror for my life many times."

"And now? . . ." hinted her senior courtier.

"Yes, the possibility that it will usher in a new stage; the end, also, to this most tedious question of the succession."

With its lofty gold and red-painted vaulted ceiling, its carved friezes of heraldic beasts and its mouldings of lions and naked cupids, the hall at Hatfield had embellishments which were unsurpassed in England. Decked out in thousands of late summer lilies to honour the French guest it was lit to give an enhancing glow even to Lord Robert, William's son, who as usual glowered not only on me, but on everyone.

Everything was sumptuous and extravagant. The House spread out upwards and outwards from its centre like a voluptuous waterplant, expanding into a bewildering series of changes and reverses like the most complicated plot of a five-act tragedy.

Much was degenerate and, like a rich and spoiling Gothic cake, enriched with classical cherries. The phantom of the perfect home, with its massive endless ornamentation, pursued the Cecil family as it did most Tudor lords and ladies.

In their own image they had made the overbearing palaces, quarrelled over the masons, and sunk themselves in a continuous chaos of debt and improvement. Upon the slightest whim they would frame and re-erect, pull down one part to enlarge it by just a few feet or even inches; knock out a wall here, put up a massive screen of decorative carvings there, muster a regiment of absurd brick chimney shafts. They competed with marble, wood and painted stone, so that from every point of view their piles teemed with incident and surprise.

I stood and took my instructions.

First there was to be the banquet, while the minstrels played. Then my masque. But so excited was everyone over the preparations that my twelve ladies were already masked and ready, the Queen had adopted her own disguise as the Goddess of Love – for it was unseemly to be barefaced – while the courtiers were already filling their seats at the tables.

A room upstairs and to one side of the hall was set aside for the ladies to dress in. Tempted as I was to see them at their transformations – even spurred with desire to offer them last-minute advice – I kept studiously away.

A tall, upright man, dressed in the latest finery of Paris, caught my eye, and I was astonished to find, when he turned in my direction, that he was none other than Sir Jasper Underhill. All my feelings about this man which I had tried to bury alive, but which had lain at the base of my nature as an unheard protest, came screaming to the surface.

I sought to gather courage by walking over to him and presenting myself, for I could see no possible danger from him in view. No one, surely, would risk exposure of himself at such a function without the proper invitation and authority?

But then I spotted the rangy and imposing figure of Topcliffe, also in court dress, and with his blond benign goodness, which he exhibited like the most specious of masks. I recalled him vividly from that day in York when he wore his everyday official dress. But he, compared to Underhill, had aged. The tortures he had inflicted had turned him into a hoary old devil. I hesitated before going over to Underhill.

If these important figures had a conjunction, there must be a death or execution about to fall. For this was what had happened last time.

My speculation and self-doubt were cut short, for I was summonsed by Burghley, who bubbled with joy and humour at all that was about to happen under his roof. He told me that the Queen wanted to speak with me in private.

II

"What is your view of Lady Ferrars?"

Hatfield Follies

I did not like the Queen's expression. In the tautening of her forehead, a stretching of that freckly softness of skin between her brows, and a slight widening of her eyes, I saw signs that she would lose her temper. I needed to be alert, treat every question she posed as a riddle, the wrong answer spelling death.

"Lady Ferrars is a most promising player. I must request Your Grace to listen to . . ."

"I have intercepted," said the Queen, ignoring my mumbled words, "letters between de Houpeville and Kate, in which he proposes that he wait in Hatfield for her, after these celebrations, and she agrees!"

She was quite emphatic. For once no beating about the bush. I went pale with jealousy and anger. So Kate, who had dangled and swayed me before her like a puppet, had accepted in cold blood – and almost in front of her Queen's eyes – to become the Duc de Houpeville's mistress.

"But how could she?"

I examined the Queen, who said nothing but now had a slightly guilty expression, by which I understood that she had encouraged the liaison. For no other good reason, I suspected, but that she saw Kate as a fair hook to keep the Duc interested in their courtship.

"I will tell you later."

"No, tell me now."

"I can't."

I was making such abrupt and impertinent replies to the Queen I wonder that she suffered me to continue in her presence. I was even striding up and down angrily. But she laughed heartily. I was out of step again, like someone with a hectic raging in the blood.

"So, I was right. Mr Donne *is* smitten by his Juno. Well, this is all to the good. You can serve your Queen, and you may marry Kate, since this is so clearly what you would like – with my blessing, too."

Now I blushed. I was bobbing like an empty nutshell in choppy waters. Here were too many changes of the fickle, inconstant female mind even for me.

I steadied myself. Here was my ambition, to obtain as complete a knowledge of Venus, the most dominating of goddesses in whose likeness the Queen was made. To crack the enigmatic inconsistency of my sovereign I had to master the many sides of myself. I would learn.

"I see it confuses you. But it is easy. No one said you should not be a Machiavel in goodness. I set up that Kate should have a midnight rendezvous with de Houpeville. Why? I will tell you."

I shifted uneasily. I felt in my boots the quicksand suck and trickle of intrigue.

"Yes?"

"So that *I* should take her place. Masked, of course."

My knees gave way and I almost fell. Not with shock, but with relief. The very recklessness of the idea began to weaken some of my total and unreasoning jealousy at the thought of Kate's divine and torturing nakedness placed so easily at the disposal of another.

"But for what end?" I inquired.

She answered me so strangely and as if she had rehearsed it that I became breathless with wonder.

"We know the time. De Houpeville will make his amour pregnant. England will have an heir. The country will be saved from Spain. And Catholics will live in comfort and be able to practise their faith."

"Kate has agreed to this?"

"She needs surveillance, Mr Donne. The plan must not go wrong. Which is where you come in. I want her married – to you."

"No small matter. Have you mentioned this to her?"

"Indirectly. To be frank she would not seem too keen on you. Have you two had a quarrel?"

"Not too keen on me?" I thought of what she had done with me in private and what she continued to do, and decided that this was but her way to conceal that we had been seeing one another.

"I will mention – at the very latest possible moment – this plan to her." She stopped for reflection. "But you will not. Do we understand one another?"

"And if she refuses to go along with it?"

"Then she will not instruct you where to be at a certain time and place . . ."

I was by now in ecstasy at the whole prospect. That for which I had prayed continually was at last happening. Yet who could ever approve of the covert means and deception involved?

At the time it seemed perfectly normal. That we would give our bodies in lust while our faces and identities remained hidden was such an everyday occurrence at Court that it was almost part of the rules. To enjoy, to "know" – but not to be known. A naked face was much more compromising than a naked inner thigh; but a naked heart was never vulnerable if the name of its owner was a secret.

"And what about the most noble Duc de Houpeville?"

Hatfield Follies

The words were out before I had the chance to ponder their implications, which were detrimental to the Queen. I did not like the man, anyway. Why should he have the pick of womankind just from an accident of blood, which was increasingly becoming discounted as a measure of strength and virility?

Elizabeth was surprisingly mild in her reply. Either she was too naïve to take my remark as a possible reflection that he might be angry when deprived of such an appetite-whetting bedfellow as Kate – and having a joint of old mutton substituted in its place. Or she was too carried away by the virtue of such a plan in its resolution of her maiden difficulty in life: the one of providing an heir for England.

"Monsieur will never know until it is too late. And will he then care? He will be crowned immediately after our marriage. He receives sixty thousand a year. He will share with me the power to grant benefices, lands and offices. How would you like that, John Donne?"

Now I saw why there were so many men here in their full court finery. They were hunters of benefices.

"What do your ministers want?"

"Seven were for it, ten against. But they leave it to me. If I am determined on the marriage, they will support it."

I thought to ask what would make her determined. But I knew, for that moment at least, and probably for the safety of my neck, prudence had got the better of me.

But now the minstrelsy began, some lively airs permeated the palace and shot a vigour into our Queen's face so that she forgot our talk at once.

"By your leave, Your Grace. The masque must be ready. I must attend the players."

So I excused myself to spend time in the actresses' tiring room arranging the final details of the costumes, especially the delicate yet provocative abandon of the dress of the nymphs so that a breast was revealed here, a buttock or thigh there, of course all very modestly and unselfconsciously so that no one could charge me with calculation.

Such are the best effects in nature, apparently not intended but acting at a deeper level over feelings and desires. This way wantonness is kindled naturally.

So too did my Io, my Europa, my Atlanta, my Callisto, have the most tempting part of their shapes offered from behind a floating diaphanous veil.

As I darted here and there in the bustle and noise of the changing suite – I would have time to prepare myself during the prologue – I could see lovely Kate painting her face, so that it sharpened but did not change the existing features.

We had decided that of all the women she alone should not wear a mask. For Juno, being the touchstone of duty, of wifely fidelity and therefore of virtuous and righteous anger, could only speak as herself.

I wondered whether to ask her about the meeting later on. I had already a most acute anticipation of it, and I knew that to impose or force any of my expectation on her would remove a sense of spontaneity and happiness. So I regarded her from a distance, allowing her to be the first to make the move. But all the time my nerves raced. What if she said nothing? Where would that leave me?

Everywhere torches burned in great sockets. Even the huge palace of Hatfield had the air of being crowded. It had been the country home for Henry VIII's children, and like a college had a quadrangle, a chapel and a banqueting hall. With table and sumptuous dishes spread by scores of attendants, and with the ascetic Lady Burghley presiding over the last-minute disposition of the guests, some courtiers were beginning to unbutton themselves with oaths, with drink, and with argument.

This would not only be the most costly social function of the year, it would be the critical moment of the reign – and, as with everything else, the Cecils were spinning the silken web of cause and effect.

Leaving my room of chattering and excited goddesses I went to survey, over the shoulders of the minstrels, the arrival of the nobles and their wives. Not only the flower of English nobility, but distinguished men and lovely women from every foreign country exchanged elaborate bows and curtsies with Lady Burghley and then were presented to the Queen. In an upstairs gallery the dancing had begun.

I knew that none of these arrivals would mean anything compared with that of the Duc and his entourage who were travelling from Gravesend. He would be journeying incognito, making a wide detour to the east of London where he might be recognised and abused by puritans. Even now I spotted the French ambassador, M. Bouvier, dressed in black, flattering the old fox.

Having been dazzled by the fashions which made their first

appearance that evening I made my way back quickly to the chapel where our masque was to be presented.

Here I arrived by a side door by which hung – for so it amused me to find – a painting of Juno berating her husband's last mistress, when in the vestry I heard soft voices. I pushed the door open slightly, enough to see inside but not be heard. I was riveted by what I found.

It was Kate. She was deep in conversation with a man. Made up for the masque, and lit by a battery of chapel candles, I had never seen her shine more exquisitely.

It was not my intention to intrude on her privacy – and I knew she had plenty to seek counsel about. Nothing would provoke her anger more than to be discovered. But as I was making myself scarce I heard the tones of the man with whom she was intimately engaged in talk. He uttered six words.

"The decision must be your own."

I can now see that the decision which she debated with the hidden man could have been one of a dozen, but at the time it seemed it could only refer to one thing, namely whether she would meet me later. I redoubled my resolution to ask her to marry me. I also determined that I would now begin, for the first time in my life, to practise chastity, and even were Kate prepared to go the whole way, defer the full nuptial enjoyment until we were wedded.

But the owner of the voice upset my profoundest expectations. It was Underhill.

So he was here on a special errand.

"I warn you," I swore to Underhill my silent vow, "I will betray you if I learn what your mission is and I do not like it."

My speculation was sharply brought to an end because as I crept away from the chapel door I found myself face to face with two of Topcliffe's best-known henchmen.

"The master wants to see you, Mr Donne," said one of these murderers.

I was taken with an impulse to rebel, but I obeyed and walked between them to a private chamber upstairs on the way back to the hall. Here Topcliffe sat at a table waiting for me and he quickly motioned me to occupy the chair opposite him. I was not encouraged to note that he sat before a sensational portrait of John the Baptist's head, severed from his body and ready on its silver platter for delivery to Herod. I had a premonition of Kate as Salome.

"I have heard, Master Donne, that as well as having a taste for beautiful women, you are often seen at the executions of Catholic martyrs."

"You called them martyrs, Master Topcliffe. I believe they are better known as traitors."

He covered his annoyance well. But he would use the anger I had awoken within him. I knew that he could not arrest me at this moment, for I was of crucial importance to the Queen and Burghley. But Topcliffe, who was noted for losing his temper quickly so that he would consume himself and tie himself up in knots, provoking mirth in those who beheld him, was not to be touched on the raw lightly.

"There are many people in this kingdom who do not want to see it joined with France. Are you one of those, Mr Donne?"

"No," I answered. "I serve Her Majesty dutifully, which is more than can be said for you, Mr Topcliffe, for it is well known that you will do anything in your power to stop the Queen marrying the Duc."

He ignored this for the present.

"We are more concerned to hunt down papists and stop them betraying us to Spain."

"France and Spain are hardly the best of friends," I declared scornfully.

"I will come to the point," said Topcliffe. "I have one hundred men posted inside and outside the hall. The Duc de Houpeville arrives soon. It is not his marriage that bothers me personally: others make this their first concern."

I could see the threat he implied. What had they planned that would happen later?

"But I know that a special envoy from the Pope is here, and that he will be giving a sign to de Houpeville so that he can be recognised. De Houpeville, for his part, insists on tolerance of papists as the first condition of his marriage to our Queen."

We had been through all this before when Mary married Philip of Spain. But nothing much happened, people went on in their same old ways.

"What has this to do with me, who acts and presents the masque for the royal guests?"

"It has a great deal to do with you," answered Topcliffe with a more sinister chill of doom in his voice. For he then went on, "Your brother Henry's life hangs by a thread. If you do not follow

Hatfield Follies

my instruction, he will – within the next day or two – be found dead in his cell."

"That would be better than killing him, as you are doing, by inches."

"So you will not give your help?"

"What do you want me to do? Although I don't want to see him die, I have no great sympathy for Henry. I have argued with him a hundred times to change his faith. He will tell you himself."

Topcliffe believed me at once, or so it seemed.

"I have news from Paris that de Houpeville is to meet an Englishman tonight who brings terms from Rome for an accord between the Pope and the Queen. This nobleman has aided the departure of hundreds from this country to Europe."

"And you have no idea who it is?"

"I have no idea," said Topcliffe. "His rank could be as high as an Earl. It could be Southampton, it could be Oxford. It could be Derby."

I let him go on without checking him. But I knew that Oxford was far too stupid for anyone to entrust him with such a mission.

"Make no mistake, Mr Donne, your brother shall . . . have an accident."

"I don't know what you expect of me."

"I want you to make yourself known to this envoy. Become his friend and sympathiser. I want you to help him, gather the names of those he visits . . ."

"How will I know him?"

"He will declare himself to the Duc at the end of your masque. The French ambassador asked the Office of the Revels for a script, and they marked a passage." He had a script of my masque open before him and pointed out some of my text.

"Only you will be able to see from the stage who it is, and what token passes between them."

"You mean to say, you will not be watching?"

Topcliffe smiled. "I think we will all see." He brought out from his coat a small vendetta pistol whose handle was inlaid with mother-of-pearl and bone, and put it down on the table.

Topcliffe had me trapped. For if I chose not to register the sign, or in some way to confuse the issue, he could always claim that it was I who was in league with my brother and with the Jesuits. And had I not perceived that Our Grace's plan had another aspect to it, no less than the possible reconversion of England? Where would the Queen's allegiance lie?

When I left Topcliffe the whole aspect of Hatfield wore a different expression. I waded in my brother's blood. The love affairs of Jupiter may have covered the ceilings, but there were guards everywhere now, with swords drawn and watchful eyes alert for hunter and prey. Even in the murky passages that led off the cloister itself, caught in the feeble, flickering lamps and next to the guests' white faces, I sighted glints of naked steel.

Jealous Juno, crowned in gold and dressed in red, held her sceptre over us to give us all a drubbing. She had her chariot outside, or so the painting I had seen depicted, with a pair of well-trained peacocks to pull it. The naked mistress bawled, her mouth as open now as her legs had been before.

I went down to the floor of the hall to take my place at the banquet. The food was a blaze of colour, for they served fish and vegetable terrines with an artificial admixture of vermilion, verdigris, and white lead dyes. Jupiter's loves had put long flowing blue gowns over their costumes and sat at the tables dotted among the other guests.

III

I knew my seat was opposite to where Kate had been placed and that therefore we would be able to hold some conversation. But two places on the other side of the table were still empty. Although in the hall there was an atmosphere of carnival, with the circulation of hobby-horses, morris dancers, giants, minstrels, men in armour (the Queen's guards), and standard bearers, as well as the Devil – and a puppet show – the assembly excitedly awaited the appearance of the little frog prince.

Everyone belonged to one faction or another. Everyone betrayed in his or her face a watchful sense of strain. At least I was to be spared the role of male decoy. It was up to the Queen to make sure her use of Kate did not misfire. Could I trust her? Imagine her anger if de Houpeville failed to arrive. Burghley, even, could lose his head.

Two missing diners approach the table. Topcliffe is one: he has his arm round Kate who is divinely elegant and even petite with her long and slim, boyish figure. The evil giant towers over her, and with a tall apish grin released like a miscreant from his usually overguarded features, teases her. They stare at me, nod, and laugh together.

Hatfield Follies

Swallowing my humiliation, outwardly seeming to take no notice, I rise from the table and seek a friend – anyone to lift my mood. Earlier everything confirmed my virtue and good intentions. The Queen's plan, if successful, would bring me at the least a modest estate and ten servants. I would, in a month or two, be able to intercede for Henry in Newgate. I would have Kate as my wife.

I try to ignore the diminished prospects of all this, but on all sides I am bounded by spies, presided over by the monster who, I hate to remind myself, is the Queen's servant. With mounting confusion I can see that if the plans fail there will be pointed at me not just one but three accusing fingers.

Egerton spied me ranging up and down like a wolf. But maybe even he had an interest in the plans of Elizabeth not working.

"Nervous about the show?" he challenged me good-humouredly. His eye was like a sharp weapon which was half drawn in its soft sheath.

O that, I thought, that was the least of my worries. One could always act a role. It was why the English are such superb actors. A man who loses his soul has to do something to make up for it.

Some look about Egerton told me that he understood the nature of my raw terror. But also whom I sought. But had Egerton aged in wisdom as well as the ability to conceal in affection and affability his true thoughts? Would I risk my most dangerous impulse, which, like a good poem, I caught from my unconscious on the wing, before I had time to choke it in doubt.

"I am looking for Sir Jasper Underhill."

I swallowed with pain as I suspected he would ask me why. He did not, even though it was clear to him that I was entirely in his power and it would be logical for him to do so. But at that moment I would have enrolled the dead in my fight to outwit Topcliffe.

Egerton relaxed, put down the piece of meat he was chewing, laughed and scratched his ear which shone like a ruby with the nourishment and wine.

"But do you know, so am I. What a coincidence! I saw him earlier. But the damned fellow has completely disappeared. Can't trace him anywhere."

Why was Egerton seeking Underhill?

I had remarked on the similarity of Egerton and Underhill when I first met both of them in York. It was not until we were at the point of death that I could answer that question.

As I sank into my seat opposite Kate she looked at me discreetly from under lowered lids. Topcliffe had turned to his neighbour, Lady Penelope Horner, whom we all knew as a fast lady, inflamed by anyone with loose and dirty talk. Just now Topcliffe was boasting of seeing the Queen in a short dress, so that he viewed her ankle, and of having put his hand in her bosom.

What an ugly brute! The drink had begun to force its way through his deceptive blandness. I realised with disgust that he painted himself and that underneath the paint his skin was pitted and cratered with pox scars. His long ungainly legs and lopsided carcass began to display themselves with unspoken lechery.

Mindful of his distraction with Lady Horner Kate engaged me now in more forward and loving glances and we chatted nervously and circumspectly about the forthcoming event. I could see that she was full of tension. She had a long part to deliver.

"You have spilt wine upon your chin. Here."

She leant over and dropped a folded napkin beside my plate. I opened it gently. It held a scrap of paper.

"I will meet you in the old gatehouse by the moat at a little after twelve," she had written. She had added a postscript in an even tinier hand: "I will explain everything. I love you."

I could hardly believe it. I became excitement incarnate. I felt astonishingly strong, yet gentle and full of endless affection. Yet there was still a strange fight in my nature. I looked over at her sharply. I was mad ever to have entertained one shred of distrust towards her. The distrust and the sexual desire had been inextricably bound up together. At this moment I stopped lusting after her. I had begun to find a better, and more unclouded being in myself. If I had been duped, had it not been all my own fault?

I reaffirmed to myself my promise that from now on I would be chaste. However much victory might call for celebration later. No longer would I be running a race with that nemesis to which she was always about to reduce me.

18

Women are Angels Wooing

Still no de Houpeville. This is the chapel. We have begun the play. Here once the cross of Jesus hung. Wolsey's men despoiled it. They melted down the chalices to endow an Oxford college and school dedicated to the dissemination of hypocritical virtue. They smashed the delicate porcelain statue of Mary.

Now my twelve nymphs and goddesses celebrate a more profane sacrament. That of Jupiter's manhood. The head of the Church looks on. Una, the blazing light of the truth, a woman clothed in the sun. This is her church. She frets, like any stood-up lover waiting impatiently for her sweetheart to turn up. She keeps turning to her old Lord Cecil who, like a father with his small daughter, gathers her hand and pats it comfortingly.

We are into the third fable. There is yet another flaming marital row between Jupiter and Juno. At least I can relieve my feelings, although my verse is wooden and undramatic. I lack the insight and passion of better makers of plays. My rows become common slanging matches. But the scolding match is how drama began. John Donne, esoteric metaphysical poet, who tried to put his thoughts on love in as many distorted postures as he attempted to coerce his mistresses to adopt in bed, is trying to be popular.

Juno is asking Jupiter for a divorce. This gets a laugh, as the political implications are driven home. "A divorce, a divorce, my kingdom for a divorce!"

My lines ransack and plagiarise other plays. But Jupiter and Juno will never divorce, no more than did Adam and Eve. The laughter swells, as I fail to be able to remove my headpiece, that of my best disguise – the beautiful white bull which swam out after Europa.

So I have to deliver my lines tugging and tearing at my papier mâché horns, and shouting, roaring like a bull all the time. Juno has to lend me a hand, too, which adds to the hilarity, for she is tugging at the folds in my neck, while abusing me with the foulest and most critical epithets a woman can apply to a man or a faithless god.

Kate naturally appears like a divinity when she is angry, and Jupiter, who had just raped Europa among the spunk and froth of the waves, while her garments fluttered around her in serpentine loops, wants his Juno more than anything. He roars and bellows with marital lust. All this is highly decorous, I have to say. There may be flimsy dresses and suggestive glances, but shameful deeds are not shown, only described in the most fanciful words and images.

Twelve trumpeters, adorned in purple velvet and bearing gold chain, enter the back of the chapel and commence a resounding but ear-splitting fanfare. This announces the arrival of the Duc de Houpeville.

Thank heaven.

It will give me time to have my head cut off by the property people. Yet I did not mind the Duc's absence. His presence brings the approach nearer of that moment I dread, and that only I will see. Whatever happens I will be caught. I can only pray that Topcliffe's intelligence will turn out to be false.

A strange little figure, small, in balloon-like breeches, and with flaming orange stockings, flits into the view finder of my blurred and befogged animal mask.

"I must beg ze pardon aff everyone," he announces in a thick accent. "It is zo silly that we to miss-teak ze road."

He seizes the Queen's hand and hops on to a stool specially made to elevate his tiny trunk, to whisper some cajoling flattery in her ear. She positively vibrates at this attention, like the plumage of a male peacock. Her paragon prince has arrived at last.

Well, heaven or hell, the masque goes on. Enter Atlanta, to run her race with the apples, giving the stage assistants a chance to finish hacking me about the head.

"Oh," says the Duke, "I am zo sorry to miss dis charmante entertainment. But I beg you no to stop, please, on my behalf. What says Madame L'Isle, our most gracious sovereign on earth?"

Elizabeth positively writhes with satisfaction at his compliments. For a moment or two my heart leaps with joy as I believe she is going to call off the rest of the masque in favour of dancing.

"No," she says in her most sweet tone. "Mr Donne will be most sorely disappointed if we suspend his fancy."

Would I . . . ?

Women are Angels Wooing

II

I must now describe the climax of my entertainment in more detail, for it was meant to be outright flattery to Elizabeth and to the English nation.

Because I – Jupiter, that is – had entered the "embrace" – to put it nicely and discreetly – of Aegina, Juno punished the isle of Greece that bore this name with a terrible plague. I did not know why, but our Queen specially loved this fable. Like the plagues of the present age it first claimed the lives of those most devoted to curing it.

Decaying corpses lay everywhere, the most loathsome stench filled the air and even the vultures, the dogs and wolves, shrank hungrily away from touching the flesh of the dead.

This was the final climactic effect of Jupiter's unbridled desire and of Juno's need to punish his victims, who themselves only became victims through the ill-fate of his passion for them. In these stories there is always reassurance for the old and the ugly. In fact, in our age as in all others, I see much evidence that good looks are a curse. Even the puritans would agree with this diagnosis.

But Juno's revenge is reversed, for Aegina's son to Jupiter, who has neglected the religious rites due to his father, prays directly to Jupiter to acknowledge him as his father. Jupiter, in the end, only too happy to be virtuous and to atone for his venery, hears the prayer.

The thunder and lightning of the stage effects instils wonderment and scares de Houpeville, who clings to the hand of the Queen, who on most occasions is more than a man – but intent tonight on showing herself a woman.

To replace its plague-emptied land with citizens Jupiter turns a column of ants on his neglected oak-tree into upright and thrifty men, called Myrmidons. These are meant to be – in symbol – the hard-working and virtuous subjects of our Queen.

During this rousing paean I was the god off-stage. The *deus ex machina*. I watched the little frog. The saltpetre flashed in the stone baptismal font, and I could see the ranks of courtiers behind the Duc and the Queen being forced to open. I thought of the snapper or pocket dag Topcliffe carried with him and meant to use.

I cannot say what impelled me – beyond what might be called a normal death-wish – but using my divine and theatrical licence, and imposingly masked in gold as the godhead, I thrust myself into the audience behind the Duc. In the style of the Italian *commedia*, I improvised on my need to find a perfect example of the Elizabethan gentleman.

With such an alibi I propelled myself forward into a position where I should meet the man who was edging his way towards his rendezvous with the Duc.

Behind my mask I could not make out who it was, if indeed I knew him. But once I was by his side I seized the cuff of his shirt, and plucked him from the throng. I now had my own ambiguity: I had chosen: or so I could tell Topcliffe.

> "Here in mockery
> And in cuckoldry
> We make sacrifice
> Of our god's device"

Here was the man who was Juno's perfect embodiment of male virtue. The ideal and chivalric Englishman.

I was well beyond shock or fear. I could only experience recognition in a kind of strange state of acceptance. For the man was Jasper Underhill, looking most bemused, but completely unruffled.

The ideal and chivalric Englishman. But suddenly the horrific suspicion crossed my mind that this man was not real. I was conscious of a mortal coldness and felt as if I should never again be warm.

Underhill bowed, showed off a lively curve of the leg, and accepted the audience's enjoyment of his quite regal fashion with palpable satisfaction.

"I have saved your life," I whispered furiously to him from behind my mask, yet wondering at the incongruity of my words. And my mind, for once, then worked with the lightning speed of my assumed persona. "You must pay me back by saving my brother Henry who is in Newgate. Topcliffe is ordering his death tonight."

"*Touché*," answered Underhill loudly. By which I knew he would do what he could.

And as he answered this I confirmed the wildness of my supposition and the vow I made earlier in the chapel when I feared my own surrender to jealousy. Yet I was well beyond any public betrayal of my frenzy.

I stepped forward to achieve the grand reconciliation of Juno and Jupiter.

> "Fie on lustful fantasy!
> Fie on sin and luxury
> Lust is but a bloody fire
> Kindled with unchaste desire"

We play our scene, Kate and I, with electric force and with many feelings between us unresolved, which flashes the message that most actors, when tearing a passion to tatters, have no idea or understanding of themselves at all.

When Kate and I are tied together in silk, at the climax, I hail the Queen and her partner the Duc. From around her flesh-tinted but well-stockinged hips Kate removes the golden string with the silken sphere which is knit with Minerva's knot, and hands it to the radiant Queen.

I can see that this is totally unexpected. The Queen applauds and ties it to herself.

> "Love calls to war;
> Sighs his alarm.
> Lips his sword are,
> The nuptial couch his arms"

Some of those in the audience must be asking themselves, as I am, "Will the knot be freed tonight?"

III

When I left the hall some hours later the festivities and dancing were in full swing. In spite of my encounter with Underhill I had recovered my buoyancy: while the masque had been a triumph, the Queen was dancing ecstatically with de Houpeville, and they played all manner of games and diversions with the ladies-in-attendance.

The house was ransacked to gratify Elizabeth's wish to indulge in hide-and-seek with mirrors, and the dark smoky glass they found was dusted and washed. I was continually complimented. I believe the guardian angel that serves those in love was on my side.

I brought a servant, Thomas Grey, with me and we rode under the big trees in the park which swayed in the fresh, early summer night. My servant became scared at the shadows cast by the big bushes.

"What's the matter?" I asked him. "They are only trees."

"But trees are like the arches in the chapel," he answered. "Make me think in hushed tones."

"Are you frightened?"

"Yes, sir. Frightened we might be heard."

"But no one can object to what we are saying." I explained I wanted him to be on guard outside the summer lodge.

"What if Mr Topcliffe comes?" he asked me. "The torturer with the crafty eyebrows and that twisted sly mouth."

"What makes you think of him?"

"He's everywhere, isn't he, sir? Look over there. Isn't that a musket barrel flashing in the moonlight?"

I was starting to feel uneasy myself. I had arrived late. Fortunately we reached the path where you had to walk the rest of the way, so I left my horse with the man, with the instructions that he should wait there for me. It was a completely still night and – reassuringly – I could hear the unabated sounds of music and merriment holding sway in the house.

It was quiet where I strode down the walk, bordered by a thick hedge on both sides, to the little old gatehouse by what was now the lake. I could see the house, which was dark and shuttered, except for the first-floor window, where a light shone through, throwing its gleam out on to a spreading oak, which I took to be a portent of renewal, as in my masque.

I called gently. I waited for a time, watching the oak-mullioned window and its ceiling moulded with Tudor roses. I imagined treasures of old wainscoting and elaborate doors and clustered figures of chimney pieces. I eliminated all idea of a bed from my mind.

A sudden shiver went through me. A clock in the house struck one. Half an hour I must have waited already, which meant that Kate was an hour late. But I was sure that she would keep her word.

I waited a further half an hour, or so I thought, during which no one turned up. My imagination began to play games with me. What if Kate had been abducted by Topcliffe? What if she had fallen asleep and lay in the room? Suggestion became so powerful that I went up to the house and seizing the creeper that climbed the wall, began to hoist myself by its trunk up into a position where I could see into the room.

Then the unexpected happened. A sound of explosions and shouts and cries erupted from the palace and continued for some

Women are Angels Wooing

minutes. This in turn brought Grey charging down the path and struggling to restrain our two horses which he held by their bridles and which had worked themselves into a high state of excitement.

I held Pump. Grey was thrown twice as he tried to mount, but as I had managed with my first vault to climb on to Pump, I was geared off straight into a fast gallop in the direction of the uproar. I glanced behind but saw no Grey.

It seemed on my arrival as if a small skirmish had broken out in or around the palace, with smoke, noise, screaming women and the general and complete confusion and hysteria of the servants. Upon enquiring of the first person I met, a boy from the kitchen or the stables, I was told, "The quality has left."

"You mean the Queen?"

"The Queen?" he squinted at me strangely. "Long live the Queen," he went on. "But there weren't no Queen here."

"But I saw her with my own eyes." I felt like whipping the boy and raised my crop. I was beside myself with anger. He received the message.

"Well that's what I bin told to say, sir. By my Lord Burghley, no less."

I leapt from Pump and entered the hall where every light was still blazing. Here I found Egerton in control, although he, too, seemed unusually flustered.

"Ah Mr Donne," he greeted me. "I believe there is some strange commotion in the heavens tonight – an unusual conjunction of the moon and stars. Jupiter in Mars, or Venus in Saturn. Something very odd indeed is going on!"

I set no store by this, for I knew that the Queen had already consulted John Dee, her astrologer, on the outcome of the night's events.

"So, my Lord," I answered rudely, "where is the Queen?"

"Gone. Left. I think her astrologer is in trouble. He failed to warn her. I wouldn't like to be in his shoes."

"And where is the Duc de Houpeville?"

Egerton sighed. "Gone as well."

"They went together?" My heart bounded with revival. Hope the hellcat was all that was left to me.

Egerton: "In different directions."

"So." I hesitated. I felt lead on my chest. "It didn't go well for them?"

Egerton peered enquiringly at me, as if, for once, my knowledge of events was greater than his.

"I mean, later . . ." I went on. "Good heavens, Lord Keeper. In bed."

Egerton suddenly became a shrivelled-up old man.

"It did not go at all, Master Donne."

"But you knew of our sovereign's intentions?"

If Egerton did, he would not show it. His Queen was by no means the same as my Queen.

"Take a look in the ante-chamber to her bedroom, Master Donne."

I did as I was told, running up the stairs two at a time and narrowly failing to wound myself on the threatening outstretched pike of an attendant who tried to bar my way.

I was not alone in the presence chamber. The room was full of noisy gleeful laughter. My Lords Oxford and Essex were here – the latter on parole – and they could hardly contain themselves for joy. They were embracing each other, and dancing and singing and jumping up and down.

"It's off! It's off! It's off!" they chanted in chorus, like a pair of naughty will o' the wisps. My Lord of Oxford was so full of exuberance he pissed over a state chair. He had a jutting ugly little prick like a knob with spikes on.

On going nearer I saw why. Oxford had not for nothing staled over the most decorated chair of state. Velvet-upholstered, studded with fine brass, its dark wood gleaming with the glacial dimension of polish applied by a generation of Cecil retainers, it had its own macabre incumbent. A dead thing lay there. I shuddered and felt sick at the sight.

It was the body of an ape. It wore a powdered and decorated wig in imitation of the Duc. Around the animal's neck a rope had been attached. A notice was pinned to its belly. DEATH TO THE FRENCH.

I noticed new books piled on other chairs, and stacked over the fireplace. The title was enough to send any Frenchman scurrying back to his native shore for snails and garlic sauce.

DISCOVERY OF THE GAPING GULF WHERE ENGLAND IS TO BE SWALLOWED BY A FRENCH MARRIAGE

So. The puritans had been at work again. I saw the unknown coming towards me like a giant nightman about his grisly occupation. I wanted to upbraid those drunk flowers of English chivalry for their short-sighted gloating.

"It's Mr Overdone – I remember you," said Oxford. "Writes about his mistresses going to bed and how," he added with falsetto flourish, "I am naked first!"

"And falling stars," slurred Essex.

"I'll teach this mermaid to sing," said Oxford. "Come over here, you naughty mandrake you."

I do believe my Lord of Oxford had some gross intention with his uncovered pillock. I turned on my heel and vanished. Downstairs and outside I met Egerton again.

"So you see what happened?"

"Only too well," I answered regretfully. I made as if to leave.

"Where are you going?" asked Egerton.

"I have an appointment. An *affaire de coeur*."

Egerton sighed.

"Young man," he said, "compared with you, a man on a barrel of gunpowder with a fuse alight is safe. My advice to you is to fly. Catch up with de Houpeville. In that direction" – and he pointed to the east. "Use your dramatic credentials. Never be seen again in England."

I mounted Pump once more and headed back to the gate lodge. I counted Egerton's words at nothing . . . I would give Kate one last chance. And then, again, I owed loyalty to my man Grey. He might have broken his arm or leg.

When I reached the yew hedge walk near the house this time I did not bother to dismount. Seeing or hearing no sign of Grey or of his horse I galloped straight down the path between the two sides of the hedge with the light in the bedroom as my beacon, its glow wondrously swelling and enticing me as I came nearer.

But I rode straight into a party of armed men, some six or more who surrounded me and grabbed my sword and pistol from me. I noticed one or two of my helpers from the masque.

"Well-met by moonlight, Mr Donne," boomed the voice of Topcliffe, who went on to air his knowledge: "Didn't I hear that line in a play of a summer night's dream? Not like this nightmare, eh?"

"Ill-met," I corrected him. He laughed even more fiercely.

"The fairies have departed, Mr Donne."

"Where is Kate? In God's name where is Kate?"

"Kate? Kate who?"

"You know, Mr Topcliffe. The one who played Juno. You sat next to her." You dabbled in her palm, I thought to say. But as if reasonableness would work, I was pleading in a decent, fair-minded voice.

"But how do you think we knew to find you here, Mr Donne?"

"Then you must have arrested her too, even tortured her."

This time he guffawed. He really enjoyed his diabolical role. "Oh no Mr Donne, she told me of her own free will."

The injection of bile and jealousy threatened to tear my head from my shoulders.

"Where is she now?"

"I don't know, Mr Donne. All I know is that you are to be guest tonight. In Westminster. My house."

It was well known that Topcliffe had a unique privilege, granted him by the Queen, of a private rack built in his own home to examine prisoners at his convenience.

"On whose authority?"

"I don't need any authority but my own."

"I insist on seeing the Queen."

"The Queen, Mr Donne, is a woman. You ought to learn, Mr Donne, never trust a woman. The gender of 'nightmare' is female. O wicked sex, perjured and unjust."

"I insist on seeing the Queen."

"Come to think of it, I did spot that Kate of yours. She left after the play. With a tall foppish fellow called Underhill. Rather than pass the time of day I'd have such useless dandies drowned in the vapours of their wit. But they serve my cause, Mr Donne. They give the aristocracy a bad name. He'll know how to keep her occupied."

The last word was pronounced with a sly, dirty, double meaning.

A rider had roped my legs under Pump who murmured with consternation and while I felt faint and senseless I was jogged into life and pain, and they led me from that vain bubble of hope.

They seemed in a hurry and were joined by others that spurred the horses on. Behind us there was a great flash and a terrific explosion. The choice and picturesque gatehouse with its four walls of yellow brownstone buckled and split, faltered and fell in a cloud of smoke and dust. My mind was as blurred and blotted as our Surrey hills in an early morning drizzle. But I knew it had been meant for me.

PART THREE
A Falling Star

19

Riders

I am in a priest hole. The darkness is complete. No crack of light, not even a glimmer. My throat is dry with the dustiness of age-long timber. So perfectly has the carpenter done his job that I cannot tell if it is night or day. I question. Can this be my grave?

Not yet, for the hunters are on me, battering at my feet far away and below like the hounds of hell. Voices infiltrate the walls. More hammering and a sound like a shattered trumpet as the gate is unbarred. A woman's piercing scream. A roar as men flood the hall. A rush of shod feet from room to room.

The house is ripped apart. Floors and walls are battered through. My heart knocks away in my throat as loud as an armed intruder on the postern hammer. Cannot the whole world hear my heart?

More minutes pass, then the climax. With my eyes closed, I am resting my head against an itchy cobwebbed beam when it dances alive with the vibration of feet. A cloak brushes against the refitted boards which closet me in secrecy. Within a yard of my head a pike foot strikes with a sudden thump. Talking voices. Silence. Thudding and vibration of feet. Splintering wood. Whispers. More talking voices. More splintering wood. Silence again.

In my hand I hold a rosary, a superstitious wreath of prayer that I have always studiously avoided. I want to emerge of my own free will. Another numbing blow within three inches of my face. I crick my head back to avoid the pike thrust.

Suddenly: "Are you better, Mr Donne?" A slow and surly country voice.

I discovered with relief that I was awake. Such nightmares were all too frequent. But reality was only by a hair's breadth better.

"Er . . . Thank you, yes, Green, I am."

My guard had hair which was nearly red, and eyebrows darker than his hair. His eyes were lively hazel. Whitefaced, he had freckles and had once been my captor's groom.

"Dreaming again, sir? The other night you were walking up and down the room in a frenzy. I had to pour a pan of cold water over you."

"I'm afraid so, Green."

I was stricken with a sense of betrayal. How could she have left me without any word or sign? To rot, to be tortured, even to die. I preferred not to eat or drink what Green had now brought me. Any nourishment served only to add fire to my pain. My head would burst. How could she have done it? I could not believe it was deliberate on her part. Yet it must have been. There was no other answer.

"No, thank you, Green."

"You have become dangerously thin, sir."

I had. I was but a shadow of my former self. I did not mind much if I died. I had nothing to live for. Even worse than this, I had no way of talking to anyone, for they had kept me locked up since they had taken me away from Hatfield House.

This imprisonment had lasted six months – or so I counted them. No one had come to question me. No one threatened me. No one brought me a confession to sign. I was tolerably treated, and if I had wanted to eat, no doubt I would have been well fed. As it was, I took meat and beer only once a day. Green told me I was in Westminster, in Topcliffe's own tall house, here as his personal prisoner, and this was enough to keep me in a state of constant terror.

"Have you seen a woman with Mr Topcliffe?"

"You keep asking me that, sir. No woman. To tell you the truth, I don't think he likes women. But he took your horse, sir. He likes horses. No doubt when they let you out, you shall have it back."

"How did she go under him?"

"Proudly, sir. Like a prince's mare."

Even Pump betrayed me with Topcliffe.

"He has the woman somewhere, too." I swore. I bit my lip. I could see Kate at his direction playing the whore, and began once more a bitter and silent railing against her. Comparison with the most treacherous women in history was no exaggeration. She had conspired against me from the first moment I had picked her to play Juno. I had convinced myself, against reality, that it was otherwise. I had been blinded.

I now believed that she had contrived, in the first place, on that fatal day at Court, to place herself in my view so as to work my downfall. What was the reason? Had she always been in Topcliffe's pay? Perhaps she was a committed puritan, as Burghley had said, and wreaked my downfall because of the poems I wrote about corporeal fancy. She had always meant to chasten my flesh and strip my spirit of wantonness.

I did not want revenge. I wanted only to know why she had behaved as she had.

"Give me further instruction on riding," I said gruffly.

The one solace of my captivity had been Green, who had tutored me in becoming a better horseman, so that I could not wait to try out his instruction. If I was ever given the chance to ride again. I doubted this, the more so when I heard the wailing and screams of tortured men down below me in the house.

Green was thrusting his pale, moonlike countenance at me, and I was taking no notice.

"There's little time, Mr Donne. If I was you, I would take your chance."

"Take my chance? What do you suggest, Green?"

"Well, sir, in a little while the master will be back."

I had often thought of escape, but where could I go? I still felt so wounded by Kate that I was at heart an invalid, bent before all else on my own destruction. If she did not love me, who ever would? Most of all, if she did not love me I cared nothing for myself. I had no reason to go on living.

When Topcliffe had told me that Kate had left with Underhill, I had not believed him. To know the master of the rack would soon be back in his house – although it could have meant my death – filled me with joy, for if I could no longer be with Kate, I cared for nothing else. The last thing I cherished was my freedom.

I fell asleep, dreaming again. As they took me out it was the tiny things that caught my attention. Kate came into the open, with a surge of faces behind her. I tried to smile at her. I was sick and faint from the fight upstairs. She did not seem in the slightest distraught. Perhaps she was relieved.

I tried to pray. I noticed the unpolished saddle and tack of the horses, an old bucket, a pair of shears, the grooms pulling water at the well, bursts of their dialect, the yapping of a new litter of pups in the manger. I noticed one of my captors had hairs like a sow sticking out from his nose. I watched them brush down Pump and fasten a martingale to her noseband and tighten her cheek straps. I was led out and lifted upon her, my arms still bound fast with cord, my feet again tied under her belly by a thong.

As they urged Pump forward I gazed numbly at her cropped

mane. Why had they done that? Her trot bumped and jerked me up and down like a puppet. I did not want Kate to witness my humiliation. I wanted to tell her that racked carcasses are not easy to dissect. I mumbled my request to my captor, but received no answer.

This time I was awoken by an unusual commotion in the streets outside. There was uproar, the clash of metal on metal, cries of instruction and fear, the shriek of frightened or unattended children.

Then waves of lamentation, the misery and the music of grief and anger. All this was filtered, distant, but outside something enormous was happening. Had the Queen died, that there had broken out such universal and uncontrollable grief?

I asked Green what it was.

"It's the good Earl. He's dead, sir. And what high hopes we had in him!"

"You mean my Lord Essex?"

Green nodded. "He's lost his head, Mr Donne. Three times the headman whirled his axe."

I must have been asleep all night and well into the morning.

"So you went to the Tower?"

He assented again. Had I even been guarded?

"I wouldn't have missed it for the world. It was an execution in a million, Mr Donne. He confessed all his weaknesses, saying how he'd been puffed up in his youth with bawdy and the love of pleasure. His sins, says he, were more in number than the hairs on his head. He prayed for everyone, most of all for his Queen. He took off his doublet and stood before everyone in his scarlet waistcoat.

"What a fine figure he was, Mr Donne: tall, bareheaded, his long fair hair flowing about his shoulders. He knelt at the low block. 'Lord be merciful to thy prostrate servant,' he cries out in a clear rising voice. Then, with difficulty, his head come off. The headsman seized it by the hair, raised it and shouted, 'God save the Queen!'"

So. The Queen was not dead. The enthusiasm with which Green spoke brought me sick to despair or suicide. I suffered with Essex. Disordered in mind, petulant and pathetic as he was, the Queen had let him down. His betrayal was one of disappointed hope. No wonder he raved in fury and told her that her conditions were as crooked as her carcass. No wonder he stormed into her room late at night when she was dressed for bed. No wonder he pushed her to the point where she could never forgive him.

Riders

I heard footsteps on the stairs in the passage outside: of heavy shod feet. A large powerful man. The footsteps approached my door. Green stiffened with fear, as if he did not want to be caught talking with me.

The rounding up of Essex supporters was complete. The crooked state, mirror of the crooked carcass of the Queen, had yet again crushed its opponents. The chief ratcatcher was home.

Two guards entered. They dismissed Green. They were serious and professional: their clothes were covered with mud, their visible skin flecked and smeared with killing.

Sweat was running down my face. I bit my lips and tasted blood. I could only just stop myself from moaning aloud. This time, I believed, this time it really was the end.

"Follow me," one guard ordered. I did as I was told. But where was Topcliffe?

20

The Infiltration

I followed the two guards down through the tall maze of winding passages and stairways out of Topcliffe's house, across an inner courtyard to the main iron gates, where a coach was waiting with an escort of four mounted and armed guards. They forced me to climb into the coach, which was dark inside, with barred windows, so I could barely make out the other occupant.

The door was locked behind us, and the coach rumbled forward. I was now in a prison on wheels.

It was the end of a cold and foggy winter day. The greyish light behind us was turning into a dull reddish glow without any brilliance or incandescence in it – a weird tint that hung over open spaces to the west.

In the aftermath of Essex's execution London was ill at ease; although Essex had failed lamentably to raise public sympathy, the rabble was discontented and wanted change. The authorities were alert and vengeful.

Conspirators would be run to earth; those denounced at sixpence a head – with a pound if hanged – would include a wide range of the disaffected. In lonely streets that night the silence would suddenly be broken by voices of terror, by blows of iron, by streams of oaths, by prayers for mercy – then again succeeded by an even more harrowing silence. Cuckolds could dispose of their wives' lovers: lovers of their whores' bridegrooms.

My travelling companion, slumped in a corner, still slept. I felt little horror at my discovery of his identity.

This was Topcliffe, licensed madman with a homicidal mission to wipe every Catholic off the surface of the globe, dedicated religious zealot whose litanies were chains of flailing iron. Topcliffe, who used spikes to pierce the liver, wires to noose round the genitals and hoick them off, who sliced the eyeball with fine sharpened blades. How could the Queen make use of such a man?

We were face to face again. The years he had spent in the

The Infiltration

unrelenting practice of evil had changed his features since I first observed them. His evil had become an illness of the mind which had in the process of time grown into his face. In York he had looked like an Oxford master, blond and intellectual; now he carried a beak and a blotched, lustless face. Tangled grey and white straggly hair coated in grease. Fleshy lips. He had been slashed in a fight, or so it seemed, and the obscenity of his countenance was crowned with a dirty bandage that hid one of his eyes.

I made no effort to talk. I directed my eyes through the barred window at the desolate streets. The wheels of the crude carriage bumped violently and grated horrendously. Once we knocked down two or three youths who played idly with a ball, and two fell wounded to the ground and lay there. We did not stop. Their friends abused us and brandished their fists. Still the executioner did not move.

He was expecting me to plead for mercy. To throw myself on the floor. To renounce my evil past. To reveal my accomplices. Only the disturbed emotions of the innocent quietened such monsters.

But I could do no such thing. By now my fierce indignation would stop at nothing. I longed to be tried, to air my grievances publicly in front of the highest judges. I was sure I would have supporters. I knew I would find the Queen taking my part.

Above the clattering hooves of the horses, and the wayward tracking and grinding of the wheels as we continued east – I began to believe that our destination must be the Tower – I heard a voice emanating from the heap opposite me. It spoke softly – at once unmistakably.

> "Alas, says he, so oft have I been warned,
> Hell has no fury like a woman scorned – "

and then a familiar laugh.

I could not believe it. The man sitting opposite me in the coach, under escort of arms, was Underhill.

I had not spoken to him since the masque of Jupiter, where I had, as I believed, saved his life, and now here he was, disguised as the man who would have his blood: victim and murderer in one.

I was too struck with amazement to speak. But I had no doubt that he was real.

He went on softly, "But the real problem is, who is the scorned woman? Was it really the Queen, or was it Robert Devereux, the Earl of Essex? It's a bit like the problem of Judas, John.

"Did Judas betray Christ, or – perhaps crucially, and to turn the problem on its head – did Jesus let Judas down in the traitor's high expectations of what being a disciple would do for him? Ergo, did Jesus betray Judas? There's a lot of Judas in us all, John, me included."

"I would love to discover this," I replied testily, "in the security of knowing that I will be alive to finish the conversation."

I added, "What really worries me, Underhill, is where is Topcliffe?"

"Oh," said Underhill nonchalantly, while looking at roughened, painted hands whose elegance could not quite be masked, "polishing his soul and preparing for eternity."

"You mean he's dead?"

"If not actually, then well on the way to the everlasting bonfire. He was pursuing a suspect towards Dover when he so frightened his horse that it refused to gallop. He lashed it ever and ever more violently; it could take no more and it reared up, snorting and leaping from side to side of the road.

"He kept whipping and cursing the animal and then hot as fire it charged off. Two hundred yards down one of Her Majesty's rare pieces of cobbled road it planted its forefeet firmly in the ground, striking fire and smoke on the flint, then for many yards as if shot from the mouth of a cannon, Mr Topcliffe became a projectile. You must know the wicked man's epitaph:

> Betwixt the stirrup and the ground
> Mercy I asked, mercy I found."

"His horse?" I questioned nervously, suddenly overjoyed at this brave and boisterous jade, wondering if like Caligula's, it shouldn't be rewarded with a seat in parliament. The gruesome apparition of my friend sat up, scratching its eye under the bandage.

"What do you know of the horse?"

"It's probably Pump. More than probably. Certainly."

"Ah," said Underhill expiring with a sigh. "That would explain it. God guides everything, you see, John Donne. Your clumsy and maladroit horsemanship prepared the way for the death of the most evil man in England. Well, if you want your horse back, I know where she's tethered, for I myself passed the spot only two nights ago."

The Infiltration

"What's your purpose with me, Sir Jasper?"

This increasingly unreal situation was now hideous. We still rode under the escort of the Queen's pikemen. Nothing, not even our escape from our escort, could be counted on. I was far from safe.

"O quieten down, John. What cannot be eschewed must be embraced. I said I would come to save you. Here I am. Embrace me, my friend. Topcliffe is dying. Your horse is in Kent, awaiting collection –

> There was a young man from Kent,
> Whose prick was so long that it bent;
> To save himself trouble
> He put it in double
> And instead of coming he went.

We shall ride again, you and I, John, as we last rode from York. You shall retrieve your chestnut mare who has done England such wonderful service. In three days we shall be in France."

I then remembered.

"God help me, you bastard," I said to Underhill quietly. "What have you done with Kate?"

II

He had gone completely white. His mouth opened, as if to reply. His face was convulsed in supplication. As for myself I was ready to crack with impatience. She had been false to me. She had sucked my blood, then invented with his help a cheap death for me. If my heart was brittle, his was black. Would I not have just office on my murderer's accomplice? I boiled with revenge.

Between us no further talk was possible. Our own escort was quickly surrounded by a superior power of armed men.

"Who are you within?" called a voice. "Prisoners of the Queen? If so, tell us your names and rank."

I craned my head to look outside but our horses, under the control of a groom, had not halted, but trotted on quickly.

We were in the Strand near Essex House and unknown to both of us there must have been several score or more of armed men, armed citizens mostly, but with some nobles and their retainers, who at the execution had taken to the streets. Although they were mustered in harness, they would not be allowed to pose any threat for long. But for the moment they were ugly and menacing, so much so that some of our escort had melted away.

Underhill had delved like lightning into his travelling bag. In an instant most of his disguise as Topcliffe had gone. He had snatched out of the bag a hat that was banded and feathered and made of silk. He had advanced his rapier with its gilded hilt to catch the eye and now he flourished a heel-length silk cloak of elaborate design, which, both within and without, was fitted with crystal buttons and embroidered with gold.

"Who goes there?" demanded a second voice from outside as our horses skidded to a halt and the shafts buckled and threatened to break. My anger with Underhill was so extreme that I was of half a mind to denounce him to them as the murderer. The supporters of Essex would have shown little clemency had they believed they had captured Topcliffe.

"Sir Jasper Underhill – " I answered (Underhill was still desperately between identities) " – with a prisoner of Her Majesty's, the poet John Donne."

My name hardly produced a surge of sympathy, but some of the assembly knew Underhill.

"Strike his irons from him," commanded an elderly but powerful armed man. Two retainers took me courteously from the carriage and by the road they cut my fetters. I chafed my wrists and ankles, and surveyed the scene around me, wondering what action Underhill would pursue. He was out of the carriage in one bound, conversing earnestly and secretly with one of the leaders. I believed that he was convincing him to continue the journey with him and telling them that he would again assume, for their safety, the disguise of Topcliffe.

While I pondered what I should do next, aware that this was a momentous decision that would affect every future hour and day of my life, I could see that a new escort of Essex ringleaders was being formed. These men, dressed now more modestly as the Queen's guard, would escort Underhill and those who accompanied him in the coach to the Kent coast where they could embark for France and freedom. I bent down to rub my ankles more.

"Come along, Donne, we're ready to leave," called out Underhill.

I decided to make a bolt for it. My departure was so swift and so unexpected to the others that no one ran after me, or even gave me a second thought. I knew my way from Essex House at the east of

The Infiltration

the Strand, to the mansion house where I had decided to plead my cause. For some ten minutes or so before I reached my goal I exulted in the way that I, for once, had outwitted Underhill.

Standing on the steps of York House, the Lord Keeper's domicile, and just about to enter it, I became conscious of a letter that had been stuffed into my doublet pocket. Feverishly opening this – only too aware that I might be watched while reading some incriminating piece of evidence that might then be snatched from me – I found that Underhill had written inside:

"I am sorry, John, you have seen fit not to journey with us to sanity. Your mother will be desolated. Your friends hope only for your well-being. The frog Duc enjoyed your masque and offers you employment as his master of revels whenever you wish. He returns by me this token, which he believes you will know how to interpret, with the earnest hope that it will help you when you have need."

In the folded paper was the satin or samite moon that I had once fitted to the waist of Kate.

21

A Convert

"Ah, Donne," said Egerton with a warm clap of the hand to my shoulder, followed by a fatherly embrace. "You appear like a man who has forgotten how to smile."

"I request your audience in private, Lord Keeper."

Egerton was in his element, mopping up, saving bloodshed by convincing the insurgents to surrender: the artist mediator and conciliator, the flower of English genius. Even now mud-stained men in harness with defeated and drooping eyes were being led past me and consigned to the keep.

"Well, I hope you have important news, young man," Egerton said when we were alone. I was surprised that he kept no guard with him, for I could have been ready with a long blade.

He possessed an uncommon trait: he trusted what he knew. Even so I had to lie, invent a story about Her Majesty's safety, and how I had intelligence of a group and their intentions – at this late hour – of overthrowing the Queen's authority.

"My dear fellow," said Egerton with a disconcerting yawn, "tell me another!" He poured me a cup of wine. "But what of you? You look as if, like Aeneas, you have been down to hell and back. But the greatest surprise is my seeing you here at all. I had thought . . . um . . . how should I say it, that you had . . . mm . . . made flight. When did you return to London?" he added casually.

"Return?" I answered dully, feeling the charge of a heavy and full red wine on the pit of an empty stomach. "I've never been away!"

"But weren't you in France?"

Egerton glanced around anxiously, as if he feared attack and needed a guard near him. Likewise, for a moment, I shook in case I should be searched and the silk disc and letter found. What if they thought I had made halek with the Queen of England?

"I have never been in France, my lord."

Egerton stared at me incredulously. It was then I could see the strain in his face. "But you left that night with the Queen's suitor and with that scheming Catholic girlfriend of yours."

"Catholic!" I cried out involuntarily, but then choked back my frantic and sudden agony.

"Yes, Catholic," said Egerton, like the bass line in a plainsong chant, as if for emphasis.

I vowed silently that, until I had no more life in my spongy liver and veins, I would sound out the bottom of this mystery. I cared no longer to have Kate as my wife: she was much more than this to me now. An overwhelming enigma that, to have any sense or purpose in my own existence, I needed to understand.

The best way to proceed with Egerton was honesty. I sensed that at any moment his pressing business would tear him away. But I had to have an ally, here, in the Court, to make my life tenable.

"I have been in London all along. For the past six months, or so I ascertained, I have been a prisoner in Mr Topcliffe's house."

To mention that name was like lifting the thin crust off a volcano. Red-faced though Egerton was, it was a horseman or farmer's red face, the skin abrased, the veins eroded by the wind and rain, for Egerton's nature was phlegmatic. But now the blood rushed to those veins and his face pulsated like an invasion beacon.

"Topcliffe! Topcliffe!" he thundered. "What was that murdering Lucifer doing with you? More than this, what were you doing with him? If you were not in France, *I* needed you, John Donne. I needed propaganda . . . support," he spluttered and coughed.

"But he had me chained in his house," I complained angrily.

"The man has always behaved as if he was a law to himself. It's our good Queen's fault. And Walsingham's. She plays all her ministers off against each other. Grrhugh."

Growling wasn't enough for him, and he hit his fist down hard on the table to regain control of himself.

"If Topcliffe continues to act outside the law like this, he will answer for it."

I kept quiet, although I knew that he had already answered for it. But not to the law of England. A wise head, as my Lord Burghley used to say, keeps a close mouth. How I wished the old fox was here to protect me, but he had died.

At this moment the presence chamber door flies open. Egerton draws his sword. But it is a friend of his, Sir George More, a bald barrel of a man with a red cap of skin over his cranium and a full fleshy mouth.

"Why, what's the matter, George?" asked Egerton.

"Good my Lord, pardon this forced entry." Seeing me, the knight backed away as if he would exit stealthily and ignominiously.

"Now you're here, pointless to make an apology," said Egerton.

"Only my overpowering grief has impelled me to burst in on you like this."

"Who have you lost now?" asked Egerton tetchily. All the Court knew this knight as a noisy, sorrow-ridden widower who had lost his wife some two or three years before and had never stopped proclaiming her matchless virtue.

"My daughter. My daughter Anne," wailed the old man and abandoned himself to a rage of impotent sobbing and lowing despair like some great bovine lump bellowing of her dead calf in our Surrey meadows.

"Dead?" asked Egerton.

"Might as well be," he nodded in agreement. "But worse. Abused, stolen from me. Seduced. Corrupted by spells and medicines. No longer my daughter."

"She made off of her own free will?"

"She was beguiled by a magician. She is but sixteen."

"His name?"

"Captain Sphacto."

Egerton swore softly to himself. This was, as I was soon to hear, the new head of Sir Thomas Walsingham's private guard, a Protestant of Portuguese blood whose parents had sought asylum in London. "You shall have redress under law. But first you must fetch them both here."

"I don't know where they are," said the unhappy father. "How glad I am I have no other child."

I spoke up. "I know Captain Sphacto's watering place. I will go find him, and return your daughter."

I knew Sphacto of old. We were fellow hunters of the female sex. I needed action. I had the measure of the man who now had a perilously high place in Our Majesty's security system.

"Leave us, Sir George." When the wailing father had withdrawn Egerton said to me, "This affair demands the utmost haste, Mr Donne."

"I shall require money, Lord Keeper. And what shall I do with Anne More when I find her, and have freed her?"

"You said it, Donne. Keeper." I frowned.

He separated his title into two syllables. "Keep her. She needs a

A Convert

husband, and you a wife. I tell you, John Donne, she's a spectacular catch. Mind you, the old man has squandered all his money."

I blushed, for as a matter of honour I still burned to settle the question of Kate.

"How shall I support her, sir?"

"You are hired. As from this moment you are my secretary. You will live here at York House. This is what you were promised, and this is what you now receive. But can you really deal with that sorcerer Sphacto? He's a very dangerous fellow."

"I believe so. I think I know what Sphacto's sorcery consists of. I don't believe in magic."

"Nor do I, nor do I," answered Egerton heartily. "I'm the brains-in-the-belly Englishman, what? And you, John Donne, the airy and metaphysical, shall serve me!"

He went to the door and called out.

"Where's that member of the Commission that haunts York House? Fetch him here at once."

He came over close to me and seized me by the shoulders. "I thrived on insecurity once, John Donne, like you. I played in the dark labyrinths of Popery. Like your friend Sir Jasper. I helped Catholics. It's part of growing up. The end of one rebellion leads to the end of another, what? Let's have more wine."

I sipped my wine thoughtfully.

Egerton continued.

"There is only one way to quieten people. Compromise. This is why our Queen so wisely changed the wording of her title from that of her father. He was called, 'the only supreme head *on earth* of the Church of England'. She modified this to 'the only supreme governor *of this realm*, as well in all spiritual and ecclesiastical things or causes as temporal'. Bit of a mouthful!"

My God! The member of the "Commission" called in by Egerton turned out to be the Archbishop of Canterbury, a blunt practical man, but decked out in his full regalia.

"Here is our 'infallible and absolute' minister! Eh, Archbishop?" Egerton roared with laughter. The cleric maintained solemnity and silence.

Archbishop Whitgift administered to me the oath of supremacy which up to then I had avoided so successfully. The Archbishop was a strong advocate of the use of the rack in the torture of Catholic prisoners.

"This corporeal oath," he told me, "is also so that we might enquire into your private speeches and the conferences you have with your dearest friends. Yes, that we might know of the very secret thoughts and intents of your heart, so that you may furnish both matter of accusation and proof against yourself."

Egerton seemed pleased. I had – but at a price – money, occupation, and the promise of a wife.

"John Donne," pronounced Egerton, "you are a symbol, a turning point in the history of this country. Since I first met you, I have always believed that in your choice lay the future."

"Security," the Archbishop echoed him, "rests upon spiritual authority, my Lord. This, in turn, is based on the purity of the Church."

The purity of the Church? I felt like Madam Suppository birding in men's purses. Amen, I say, to all. I was the death of the English soul.

22

Quelque Chose from Court

I was enjoying the unusual optical laws that worked in the London sky on a walk over London Bridge and into Southwark. They were burning so much coal now in London, with so much new smoke in the sky, that the City and neighbouring Westminster were beginning to have their own systems of weather. The light and dark played upon each other, and in the struggle of sun and smoke, aerial graduations and confusions created whole new worlds of filtered and leaking lights, and cloud ceilings of unusual softness and richness. Like our religious soul, London concealed its vast embryo state in veils of haze.

Casually, or perhaps with the lightest of intentions, my steps led me to the brothel called the Bunch of Grapes. I had been here recently, for it had been the first place I thought of in connection with Captain Sphacto – knowing his predilection for a certain kind of select stew – and the nobleman's daughter. If Sphacto had been involved, he would have brought her here. But there was no sign of him, or of her.

It was now some six or more months after I took the oath given me by Whitgift, and my heretical zeal had somewhat abated. I had given up my intention to please Egerton in the matter of a wife. I had sought Anne More for a while but had not found her. Henry had not died, but clung on tenaciously in Newgate.

In the Bunch of Grapes a private room could be had for threepence, and choice made from a wide range of goods who, in a casual and relaxed way, would chat, laugh, sew or preen themselves in the lower chambers, so that men might choose at their ease.

Now one girl in this gathering, of an unusual sensibility, apparently highborn, undoubtedly different, caught my eye. She was tall, her hair was dark, her eyes wide and innocent, and she had the fairest, most unblemished skin I have ever seen; fairer and clearer and softer, or so it seemed, than even Kate's (I no longer had her near me for comparison). She had an incomparable childlike beauty.

Her eyes were downcast as if she was a stranger to the shame of her profession. When I enquired of her state I was told that she had been pledged by a bankrupt, drunken father against redemption of his debts.

She had a good face, and I asked if she might be brought to my upstairs room. The pander would not let her go.

"I want twenty pound for her virgin knot," he rasped at me.

He had a youngish face and clever dark eyes; his cheeks betrayed a love of wine, but he was fit and sportful-looking. Good for some jokes, I should say.

Where should I find twenty pound for a woman's untried crack that had hardly twenty all year for my own modest rent and living? And yet I have to say my urgency was extreme. I was caught in a delirium of desire such as would have kept me awake all night. I felt I should burst or explode with a rage of lust.

"How do I know she is what you claim?"

"Search the market, you'll never find such a fresh and bushy maidenhead," he went on. "I kept her these six months, secret in the country, to build her up."

"Before I assent shall I not have at least the chance to talk to her?"

There must have been something about the extremity of my condition, as well as my nobleman's attire and well-spoken manner that gave the bawd confidence, for he motioned me swiftly away. One of the dirty brats who served the ale led me upstairs to this bare room which had a bed of straw and water in a pitcher and a shallow broad basin.

"How long have you been at this game?" I asked the girl when we were alone.

She sat trembling in the chair opposite me while my eye burned and my heart drummed. One leap and I could have had her. Was I, after all, responsible for the overpowering lust of my own nature, or was it not foisted upon me at birth by my stars? I could have enjoyed her there and then, passed her back to the bawd for nothing, claiming I had done him a service by ravishing her, for certainly, as I could devise, no one had as yet forced her.

And given time I could have worked her in, paced her so that she suited a dozen men's manège.

She sighed – eloquently. Her eyes pleaded towards me with pity. Yet I could as easily pretend it had never happened. As the Roman author wrote, good was not good unless a thousand possessed it: no one ever rigged out a fair ship just to lie in harbour.

But something about her cleft my heart. Some extraordinary grace descended on me. It is hard to describe how or why.

I was ready with my cloak to blot out the light and act the rest – when – and I will never know why – an image of my first saint, Margaret Clitheroe, being pressed naked to death, exploded in my mind.

At first I was angry. I was outraged, my pride hurt at the interference. Defensive arguments rose to support my desire. We did not any longer need our self or person to be all of one piece. In my heart I could entertain a dozen hidden motives, acting out one, then another. I was happily double-hearted, bearing a second heart within the first: at the very back of myself lurked that shadowy enclave I now desired above all to release – the hurting guilt, the rebelliousness, the resentment of an all too patent and extended lust.

The girl before me was of a single image: her heart was whole and entire. It had not yet been destroyed.

II

What should I do? Rush downstairs and reject the pander's offer; or smuggle the girl out to St Albany, hide her in my kitchen and cellar while I found a home for her. Would she trust me? She had seen the lust, the rage in me.

She had started to whine quietly. Imagine my astonishment when I saw her close her eyes and open them, swivelling the lips – as if they were the more secret ones – in an unmistakable gesture of temptation. But as if this was not enough, her fresh healthy tongue came forth from her lips and started to move with a slightly lascivious, yet still tactfully feminine, sensual signal. Could I now resist what I had so firmly set aside?

She rose from where, wretchedly cowering, she had been seated away from me: O here was the recipe for a decidedly Protestant anguish. I was caught in something that I could neither accept, nor do anything to reject. I was helpless. I was entirely isolated. What spiritual resources which up to then I had been able to call upon, froze inside me. I was sucked under by despair. This was hell. I could not resist.

Licentiousness swelled around me: I was paralysed by desire. My emotions of holiness, of spiritual sanctity, were overwhelmed as the girl slipped her simple dress over her head, dropped down between my outstretched legs and applied herself to rubbing my member. I was ready to release myself from the darkness of separation from Kate and from her loss.

"What's your name?" I whispered.

"Anne," she replied.

"Anne?" My enquiry was murmured and half-hearted.

Even as she was then, holding and thrusting me inexpertly at herself, she gave me an expression of hard, still, gravity.

"Anne More."

I gaped at the coolness of her utterance, her pride in the depths of her shame. To dare to give me her name was an offer of trust, an appeal to the best side of me.

I stood up and fastened myself. I was floating into clearness. I was re-christened in that moment. For the first time I knew the renunciation of sex. It came upon me like the glitter of a drawn blade.

"Get dressed," I told the girl. "And take off that ridiculous hair."

I meant the murkin of nether hair, which brothel keepers forced on girls to make them seem older.

She looked at me directly and the expression still grave, but tempered with relief at her escape, struck me as the most sublime I have ever seen.

"You shall be my wife," I said.

But this would be easier said than done.

23

Prisms of the Flesh

My brother's face still pursued me. The large lips, the long aquiline nose, the huge and lovely dark eyes, and wide-arched brows, the long fine-boned fingers with which he would frame his face when he looked at you; all these I shared with him, but these now had become pronounced into haggard and exaggerated pointers of doom. The years in prison had devoured most of his substance. The rings about his eyes were quite black.

He took the eggs and meat I brought him and wolfed them down. Then, with the suddenness of people who suffer like him, his countenance changed to an expression of radiant happiness and enthusiasm. His face had a girlish beauty. He looked young again.

"I pray, John, I pray every day for you."

"There. I have come to see you."

I felt frightened even more when I touched his parchment skin when we kissed and I came close to his unnatural and glittery eyes. We were so close, so near that the looks we gave each other, the tones of voice, meant more than anything we could say. We were so like one another.

For most of my visit Henry was in an affectionate and happy mood, but I could only see one thing: his death. How can I help him?, I kept thinking. I could see that he had only a month or two to live. But we were on opposite sides of a great divide.

As I was leaving he leaned over close to me and whispered, "John, I love you. You can't change the blood in your veins. It will cry out in the darkness of night against your foolishness. Turn your back on what you know to be wrong. It is when we deny our instincts that we sin. We are all one family."

His prayers were useless, for I worked for Egerton keeping a record of Catholic publications against the English heretics, and answering blast for blast. Henry apart, who was my own flesh and blood, we had to make an example of Catholics. Much of my writing was directed against the German schismatics, the light empty brains of the French, and the faithlessness of the Italians.

Anne More was continually at odds with Sir George, who would not let her out of his sight. We were not allowed to meet. I wooed her with letters. I was a committed member of my Church, working in the household of the Lord Keeper, but this carried no weight with Sir George. His other daughters had married knights or baronets. I could not compete. But as a civil servant, one of the few members of the Court working for the state full-time, I grew self-confident, even overweening. I had power. Knowing the way favours were dispensed, sooner or later I would be able to divert some of them towards myself.

I had the appearance of the most odious of courtiers: glistering, painted in many colours. I wore a slashed doublet, or I went about with an ironbound chest, girt and thick-ribbed with broad gold laces. If I leant against a wall I might be mistaken for the picture hanging behind me.

I tried to satirise the Court, but I found I was passing death judgments. I called them satires. The more a poet knows, the more he has to become angry to digest everything. Some sentences I wrote needed years before they could release their venom. I also wrote paradoxes about virtue and virginity – nobody believed in these.

Anne wanted to escape from her father – and from Egerton's third wife, who was her guardian when she was in London. Egerton's wife, Alice, was the widow of Ferdinando Stanley, Earl of Derby; a complicated alliance, achieved in secret with Egerton's own private chaplain conducting the ceremony.

Anne was in law still a minor, but she wrote letter after letter trying to persuade me to elope with her. Secret marriages, she argued, were easy things to arrange. But in York House I noted the legal effects of clandestine marriages: the brides and grooms variously consigned to the Gatehouse, the Fleet or the Clink.

II

Years before, Philip, the picaresque ruffian of Spain, had sent his overweight galleons absurdly billowing full tilt up the English Channel. But the threat of England's annihilation went on: in spying, clandestine murder, piracy, and, not least of all, word battles.

One March night at the Hope Inn on Bankside I was arguing with a Spanish merchant, no doubt in the pay of the Escorial, who was accusing the English of having broken away from the true faith.

"We do not see God as you see God. Look at your Inquisition with its priests who torture victims to make them confess faith."

"Why don't you look at your Queen who tortures the priests to confess the true love of their souls?"

This made me angry. My hand was on my sword. "Don't talk to me about the soul. You Spaniards do not understand the meaning of soul."

"You English don't know how to suffer for the greater glory!"

"Exactly! And I thank heaven for it!"

I could feel my voice becoming slurred. In the room above the drinking parlour rented for a few pennies I had set myself up and kept some quill and paper for the dashing down of dark thoughts. Here were some patriotic sentiments my Queen would applaud me for, and maybe through Sir Thomas Walsingham reward me. "Should the world be a wearying and rewardless place?"

The Spaniard spat and rose unsteadily to his feet. He was pitched dazzlingly at the height of fashion and he tottered on his high-heeled boots to embrace me involuntarily.

"I am leaving you. You are backward. You can't even add up figures, for you jumble Roman and Arabic numerals in the same sum. Your city is full of embezzlers. Your sailors like Drake are ruffians and pirates. As for your much-vaunted literature . . ."

"Our literature is just beginning – "

"You mean it will be great for a while – then abruptly end."

I laughed with scorn: "What a ridiculous view: our poets will be the glory of the world."

"Oh, yes." The Spaniard coughed. "While you engage for the next few years in the heat of the struggle. But if the Protestants and puritans win . . . that will be the end of the wholeness of spirit in your lives . . ."

"Nonsense. Literature itself is no more than a livelihood."

I looked at my drink. Really, I ought to be upstairs and not debauching my energy in talk with this ridiculous fellow – in his preposterous clothes. He stank of cheap civet. No doubt he never washed. All the gold and might of Spain would not adequately support him.

This colloquy with my Iberian counterpart was cut short by the invasion of the inn parlour by a group of Walsingham's men, distinguished by their black and praetorian appearance and their tight military bearing and discipline. The Spaniard hastily took to his heels, vanishing like the devil.

They came through the large parlour slowly, staring at each person in turn. They had a bloodless, cold look. They had no fathers and mothers, for they were mostly foundlings, trained to have no other allegiance than that to the Tudor monarch. They picked out one or two men – and a pretty girl whose nubile bosom was bare.

I had some status in this place: it was known that I had contacts at Court and memory of my disgrace over Kate, more than a year ago, had enhanced rather than tarnished my reputation. I had spent much money here, too, in recent weeks. Emissaries had come to me from France, imploring me to join my family – and I had sent them packing.

Stephen, our host, walked over. He appealed to me.

"Mr Donne, sir, can you help our Pauline? Say she is your god-daughter: or that good Queen Bess needs her at Court. You know what those men will do to her."

I did indeed. There would be cold-blooded freedom taken with her in the inn-yard outside: she might, if she knew how to play her cards, win herself a pass to France.

I had no desire to cross the path of these ugly brutes. I was also concerned for Thomas Grey, who was again my man-servant, and who had begun to entertain the room with some of my songs set to his lute. But when these soldiers walked in he fell ominously silent. He rose to go.

"What is your name?" asked one of the vermin.

"Where do you live?"

"Are you a married man or a bachelor?"

The others laughed crudely. I am not sure what distorted instinct prompted Grey to leave. It was not very wise.

He turned on them, trying to be affable. "My name? Where I live . . . Truly, I mean to say, 'To relieve myself with a good piss!'"

He was trying to humour them and this was fatal. I rose, for I had caught sight of a familiar face, that of Captain Sphacto, the fast-talking rogue who, incongruously, had been given the captainship of this band.

"Captain Sphacto – John Donne's the name. In the old days we swapped many a yarn outside – and inside – my lady's chamber – "

He perused me up and down. Anne had confirmed that he had abducted her. I dared not raise this now. He had wavy jet hair, a rather sharp, quill-like nose. The well-formed mouth had a hint of ugliness at its edges, but this was well concealed. I felt the sweat rise to my temples as his blue but bloodstreaked eyes rested on my chin – not quite meeting my own.

"Donne, how's the old *stella in monte veneris*?" he hooted with joyful *bonhomie*, which did not for one moment reassure me. Nor did his hearty clap on the shoulders.

24

Captain of the Guard

"Please tell those friends of yours that the man they question is no conspirator. Just a harmless musician – "

Suddenly Sphacto pulled me by the shoulder over to a pillar. I feared some rash change of temper in the man.

"I'll find it very hard," he smiled, showing one or two teeth missing, giving his visage a more lowering and ominous aspect. "One of their company has just been murdered. He had two travel permits out of England into France and the word is that the murderers or murderer made for here, and were in the Catholic pay of my Lord Dorset who wanted them for novitiate Jesuits he wished to spirit over to France."

After this Sphacto, my friend, if such he was – it being a very provisional kind of friendship built on shifting sands of allegiance – gave me a whiff of fatality.

"Well, what do you know of this murder?" he asked.

"Nothing. Why do you question me?"

"We know he is here. It will only be a matter of time before we lay hands on him. There is a thirty pound reward."

I had to conceal a certain satisfaction in the disappearance of one of that odious bunch. I knew nothing of the circumstances. Fortunately Sphacto had lodged it firmly in the grey ventricles of his devious brain that he wanted to hear a song of mine, and so of his own accord he went over to Grey and commanded him to play it. Grey sang in that delightful careless voice of his:

> "Go, and catch a falling star,
> Get with a child a mandrake root,
> Tell me, where all past years are
> Or who cleft the Devil's foot."

Sphacto had a merry, music-loving soul, an innocence and goodness trapped inside him, in spite of his entanglement in the murky exercise of power. I could forgive him when he became so easily transported, enjoying and clapping to the song. Even the poor, brain-washed clotons, devils as they were, lapped it up. Sphacto ordered cheap Spanish wine for everyone.

> "Teach me to hear mermaids singing,
> Or to keep off envy's stinging,
> And find
> What wind
> Serves to advance an honest mind."

As Grey sang on I noticed a man rapping at the window: I recognised him as my brother's servant, Finch, whose appearance at once spelt trouble, because of the link with Henry.

The singing became wilder and more jolly.

> "If thou beest born to strange sights,
> Things invisible to see,
> Ride ten thousand days and nights . . ."

As the others were well occupied, and as my host was doing his best to lure his daughter away from the soldiers' poking sticks with every possible dainty and forcemeat – as well as the choicest Rhenish and Savoyard wines from his cellar – I slipped out of the parlour.

I asked Bernard Finch why he was here. We were in the Pannier alley yard behind the Hope. The smell of rotting tripe stank in my nostrils. It was growing cold; darkness was fast gathering pace.

"My Lord," he gasped. "I did it for Henry."

These wretched Catholics. They had so much greater reserves of energy than the rest of us.

I should have given him away then and there: I was being watched myself, I could easily be arrested. To call out Sphacto would have been best. But I now had before me the spectral memory of Henry's lovely face, with my mother's appealing eyes set in it.

"I suppose that I approve the deed," I remarked stuffily, "but I cannot condone the cause."

"Good. You have your brother's quickness," said Bernard. "But you must help me before I am taken, or can escape. I have two passes – and there are two supposed to be in the inn to whom I was to give them tonight.

"There is – or was – a third for Henry. But I fear that they will not come till later, that Walsingham's men already know who they are, and I fear especially that Poley is here somewhere, in disguise. What if they are captured – and the passes fall into Poley's hands?"

Poley? I scowled at the trillibub sellers. Here was the new rag-raker in the dunghill, the new scavenger in the veins and bowels, the new evil in England's intestine war. This original author of wickedness had cut his teeth as an accomplice in Christopher Marlowe's murder at the Bull Inn at Deptford.

"But who are this pair?"

Involuntarily I was seized by such a huge shudder that I had to steady myself against a wall. For Henry's sake I was being drawn into this alien business. I had only to call Sphacto to earn myself an informer's purse of £30; a schoolmaster's wage for eighteen months. With it I could devote myself to my epic on the Fall of Man, something that, with an insider's knowledge, I knew a great deal about by now.

I could hear Grey in the Hope's parlour starting a new song:

> "Oh do not die, for I shall hate
>   All women so, when thou art gone,
> That thee I shall not celebrate,
>   When I remember, thou wast one."

They had lit the lamps which burned brightly on the tables and in the vine-branch brackets. Grey had accompanied me at Hatfield. Now he was sustained by that which sustained me: love of words and their sounds.

> "But yet thou canst not die, I know,
>   To leave this world behind, is death,
> But when thou from this world wilt go,
>   The whole world vapours with thy breath."

"Well, sir, I don't know how to say this," Bernard was telling me, although I hardly paid attention. "Henry died last night." I turned to him, only dumbly connected to his meaning.

"Henry died," he repeated. "I stole the permits for him. I couldn't bear to see him suffer any more. Here is your brother's ring. To give it to me was the last thing he did on this earth – it was the last thing he could do – as a token."

Captain of the Guard

Henry was dead. I kept saying this over to myself. I could not truly register it. I could not connect anything. I did not know whether I felt grief or profound relief. But I was free of certain obligations; free from blackmail, and from my own need to save him.

I was in a daze.

> "Or if, when thou, the world's soul, goest,
>   It stay, 'tis but thy carcass then,
>   The fairest woman but thy ghost."

I could hear Grey's voice as Bernard repeated: "I pass it to his brother."

At last some instinct of survival hit me, like a douche of cold water between the eyes. "All right, give me the permits. For whom, originally, were they made out?"

"Secret envoys who were parties to a treaty to be signed between the Queen and France."

Bernard then described a man who could only be the exquisite figure of Sir Jasper Underhill: but he said he would be travelling with his wife: a young woman of exceptional beauty. That Underhill was married was a new twist, although I had heard that he had contracted a bride who was, they said, the wonder of Europe. I felt too stunned and weary to reflect on this further.

Bernard refused to name Underhill, but it was clear to me that it could be no other. Both would be, hinted Bernard, an enormous catch for Elizabeth's ministers behind her back and their capture would deal such a blow to rising Catholic morale that the counter-revolution of the papists and the low breed of Jesuits would never recover from it.

Had no one told Bernard of my new inclination, and what I had been doing of late?

From inside his cloak Bernard found a crucifix and held it in front of me.

"Swear by this and by the soul of your dead brother that you will do the best you can."

I wore Henry's ring. I had the permits. I had no hesitation, as God is my witness. The desire to act so must have been the well of the deepest power within me – however much propaganda and self-interest propelled me to do otherwise. As I swore to do as he said I felt free.

"Now give me some money and leave. I'll try to make my escape . . ."

161

Bernard accepted whatever available coins I slipped into his hand and was gone as quickly as he had come. I hid the permits in my breeches while still wondering numbly on the identity of the female traveller to whom I could now afford such surety of travel; for these were warrants from the Queen herself, and could not be countermanded.

> "Come live with me, and be my love,
> And we will some new pleasures prove
> Of golden sands, and crystal brooks,
> With silken lines, and silver hooks."

Grey was still performing steadily on my behalf while the host had successfully detached Pauline from the toils of her would-be rapists. But I had no sooner joined Sphacto, who turned to me with a beaming and approving smile as if I had not at any time left him, when from outside came shouts and whistles. The men that Sphacto had posted there had seen Bernard. The hue and cry was up. Sphacto spoke to me in a low voice.

"As I said, I knew he would be coming here!"

Sphacto surveyed me with those puckfist, frontless eyes in which were hidden hooks and baits. "You know about it, John."

I paused. My heart beat very fast. Was he about to accuse me? I bit an inward lip but tried to show nothing in my face.

"I know you do," Sphacto continued. "It's no good pretending that you don't, but I am wise and clever enough to see that you have been sworn to secrecy by someone in authority higher than I."

Thank God. He assumed that I, as Egerton's secretary, was working nearer to the Queen than he was. My masque had elevated me into a better position than I bargained for. Sphacto could not have known that, since that night in Hatfield, the Queen herself had completely ignored me; since his father's recent death Burghley's hunchback son now guarded her interests, and he was no friend of mine.

I believed that wisdom lay in adopting a cautious and circumspect attitude to those extraordinary privileges I had once enjoyed. Tied on a leather string I carried the satin disc around my neck.

But to Sphacto perhaps to be out of Elizabeth's favour was as great a mark of distinction as to be in it, because it meant that you had penetrated to an inner core of people to whom she reacted as if they were her family: we were all primitively bonded to her.

This is why, in spite of my suspicious behaviour, he had deferred to me. This is why he had freed Thomas Grey and had clung so close to me.

The deviousness of our political system supplied me – at that moment at any rate – both alibi and the possibility of future bluff. I could help the Catholic pair that, on Henry's dead body, I had sworn to protect. It could even be the safer course of action, as my mind could envisage – as I placed myself in Sphacto's shoes – the agent murdered deliberately as a matter of policy to give Underhill and his woman in disguise a safe passage out of the country.

Elizabeth was trying to make a secret deal with the Pope behind the backs of her ministers – in nature like her father all over again, but the reverse side of the same coin.

Suddenly – as I saw it – God had not only given me Henry's ring to watch over me, but had supplied along with it the safest course of action. And if this were not so, I always had for myself the third pass in reserve.

Sphacto then said, "I shall have to round up and search everyone here." His bloodshot but closed-up eyes were watching the landlord who was extending a protective arm around Pauline.

"Her, too," said Sphacto, curling his lips. "Women know where to hide, but we know where to look – " Sphacto then laughed as I, half convulsed with fear, concealed my reaction.

Sphacto winked. "Not you, John," he said conspiratorially.

Just then, at the dicing table, I noticed Bernard's face. He had – I shall never know how – managed to wheedle his way into the tavern and even now was occupied in a game as if he had been here all evening. But another player stood behind him and spoke to him softly. One of Sphacto's men.

Bernard drew a long-blade Italian dagger and I could see him thrust it almost into the guard's ribs. Bernard then seized him by the hand and motioned him to leave together with him.

I started to move over to where the two of them were walking away but at this moment the agent grappled with Bernard and my brother's man had no choice but to stab him which he did in the arm. Blood gushed everywhere. Bernard ran out of the room towards the lobby. Another of Sphacto's men who carried a musket fired a shot after him. Pauline and her customers screamed and crouched behind the tables.

I turned my back on the incident for fear that Bernard, losing his head, might seek safety with me. When I sensed that I could not in any way be of any help to Bernard, I joined in to assist his capture and pinioned his arm, winking at him at the same time to show him that I was on his side.

His grey eyes, bloodshot with terror, shifted quickly down towards my brother's ring. But I was determined. I would not forfeit myself. I would deny him.

I survived.

As he was dragged out of the parlour to a barge waiting at the wharf near by, Stephen, our host, relit those lamps which had fallen to the floor and spoke to calm everyone down.

Grey took up his lute, joined now by a recorder and a viol:

> "Sweetest love, I do not go,
> For weariness of thee,
> Nor in hope the world can show
> A fitter love for me;
> But since that I
> Must die at last, 'tis best,
> To use myself in jest
> Thus by fain'd deaths to die."

But far from reassuring everyone and emptying the guard from the parlour, as I hoped, there now seemed to be some new faces which crowded the tapster as he drew ale. I felt suffocated by the hot, tallowy atmosphere but I dared not leave.

Then I spied Robert Poley, glorified murderer and horsethief who, now he had publicly reformed and embraced the creed of a Calvinist, had become a second Topcliffe. Spotting me Poley came over.

"Well, we are honoured tonight!" he observed cynically. "It's not often that a humble city tavern is so graced with company." I turned to Grey, who had broken off to consult me about the song.

"Captain Poley," I said, "is one of the reasons that this present age of Queen Elizabeth is so rich and illustrious."

"You say 'present', as if you expected it soon to pass," Robert Poley sparred.

"I am a citizen of all epochs. For me all time is *eternally* present."

The boy appeared with glasses and a bottle of usquebaugh, Poley's drink. I told Grey to play something more roisterous.

"May I ask you a question? Purely for my own enlightenment. As you see, I have no secretary," he needled me on my position.

I searched his face a moment or two before answering. His was a handsome blond aspect, but there was something icy and controlled beneath the surface, some dark sacrament that held this man together. They say that he had once, like Hercules, been subject to fits of madness, but that these had passed, leaving him ashamed but so proud that he would always crush the feelings of guilt and his fear that the fits might return.

He was, therefore, always on edge, his eyes darting about to hunt for signs of suspicion, or a stare perhaps, that might be an excuse for him to act. He would stand, hover rather, over his prey ready to catch the slightest movement in a man's mind of anxiety or fear which would tell him that man hid something else. Like attracts like and Poley the persecutor sought out the fear he wanted to put down in himself. The enemies of Elizabeth bore the same personal stamp or profile as her police.

"What *is* your religion?"

I knew when to meet a probing look, and was an adept at fencing with unspoken energy, storing up love to meet hate and dissolve it in well-being. I could see the question that was not being put, the emotion that was masked in remote or roundabout expression. But just then, as people are, I was flippant.

"The ecstasy of flesh and wine."

I had made a terribly false move. I do not know why, but it slipped out, perhaps some pocket of tension in me I could not account for – what was the name, or even just the presence of the mysterious woman? . . . more probably a reaction to the death of Henry. One only ever masters others when one has mastered oneself. Example is all that one can give.

I bit my tongue and swore silently. Above all this puritan had no sense of humour. First law. You do not send up God's elect. I am not sure which number of the elect Poley had given himself, perhaps it was the 251st thousand and fourteen (he told me once himself in confidence) but he had his place and number intaglioed on his chest. His behaviour was impeccable.

Poley's fingernails tapped the edge of his glass.

"So you do believe in the wine becoming the blood of Jesus? Ecstatics believe in miracles."

I thought of the glory of the miraculous, of all the superstitious glory of our Elizabethan age. Like O'Hearne's golden bubble, one day it would burst, leaving only a film of glittering slime.

"No, I'm a rebel and an atheist. I don't believe too much in priests."

The lines in the side of Poley's face relaxed.

By now my mind was racing. And how could I conceal from this arch-plotter the rapid and sudden energy flowing into my own scheming liver?

"Drop this fooling, Mr Donne," Poley sternly rebuked me. I felt an easing. Somewhere I had managed to check my dislike and hostility towards him. "A deadly enemy of England is expected here shortly, and we cannot take him and his companions into custody – on the Queen's express orders – "

"Why is that?"

"The moods of our Queen are like the moods of God. We do not question them."

I knew this man was lying. He would do what he could to organise providence and acts of God. I had heard of this strange inward armistice of our withered virgin pear. But she could turn like a cyclone.

"Then what will you do?"

"We will stop them leaving England until such time when our sovereign's mood changes again, and we again need to make an example of such people. We will not have to wait long."

Suddenly I saw my own significance as owner of those three permits which gave the right to their bearers to leave the country.

The slight flush of blood that rose to my cheeks could only have been observed by someone who was truly free inside and able to register what happens to others with a clear mind. This was beyond the ability of Poley.

"I expect you know who he is."

I had no idea. But I knew it did not do to be ignorant. So I gave Poley the nod.

"Do not reveal it – on Walsingham's express command. For he will be disguised and it suits us as much as him to keep unknown his person, for if it is known that one such as him is tolerated, word of our weakness will spread, and papist spies will say we are weak –"

I thought I now knew who the stranger was. But I did not believe a word that Poley spoke.

"Do not forget how courageous he is. He is the bravest of them all."

Coming from Poley these were, as I noted with irony, commendatory words indeed. Then the host came over to me and asked me if I would take a turn with him outside, for he wanted to usher his daughter out and smoke a pipe laced with hemp.

Captain of the Guard

II

In the meantime and unknown to me – Grey told me later – a couple had entered the tavern and their servants had carried their luggage upstairs where they had taken a room and an ante-room. Their names had been given to the host as De Frampul. They had requested that Grey should play for them and he had felt awkward, unsure what to do because he feared any withdrawal from his secure role as musician downstairs might again land him in danger.

He informed them that he would join them in a minute or two; downstairs, finding a substitute, he again slipped off. Who should he find on his return – to my amazement and disbelief when he told me – but Captain Sphacto in attendance on this couple.

Grey said that he was struck by the woman's rarity of beauty. She wore the latest chopines and a stunning dress of white beneath her travel cloak and hood. Grey wondered if she had a child. But he was sure that the woman was not as self-possessed as she tried to appear. When she turned to look at him Grey knew her at once even though she had greatly changed. She was deeply taken aback.

"Upon my soul," said Grey. "You've changed, my lady" – and adding in his cheeky fashion – "you carry a rondel dagger. You must be ready for danger."

"Every lady needs some protection."

"Spanish is it, my lady?"

"I would not know," she answered.

Captain Sphacto was talking to the man – "a notable hot fornicator!" All this was reported to me, although it hardly put me in a good light. Many directly imputed to me feelings and actions which were not mine. My master Ovid had stolen his own wife and made her the mistress in his verses – while I had turned many of his verses into my own, so that you would believe me their subject.

"Oh, I have met him too," said the man.

Sphacto said, "But even so an honest instrument of procreation, who genuinely seeks to marry and inherit according to his inches. Men are jealous of him."

Sphacto had got wind of the Anne More episode.

25

Likeness Glues Love

No more. Not if they see me now. Not if they recognise how I am aged and have become blurred and blind – and my sexual instinct alone undimmed, unblunted by time. But then I was kicked in the stomach, I was doubled over. Stretched, beaten to bursting point. I had just entered. Suddenly I wasn't breathing any more. I was living dead with shock. My eyes were riveted on her. That brighter-than-being face had turned from where she characteristically was looking into the air – a head always better in profile than seen full-face, for she was too thin, but a face to be laughed beside in bed, soft, utterly feminine, yet also primitive and instinctive and animal. A face of change, that moved with the season. A face that stirred with its passionate nakedness and vulnerability the animal curled in the breeches.

I had not seen her for ages. It was not much more than a year, yet it seemed a lifetime.

I have learnt the uselessness of apportioning blame, regret and resentment over past events, for the past, far from belonging to any of us, is a pattern of shifting sand that takes on the print only of the present mood like a hand or face pressed into it.

At that moment I felt clear as I have ever felt clear: she had left me in order to educate herself, in order to be free, in order not to become a wife and mother but an independent being like a man, leaving to me the burden of starting a family on my own. And yet here she was, exactly at the point where she had been before – an unfinished epic still, a collection of motifs and themes for the great requiem mass of all time. Still incomplete. As woman is and forever will be. She was still just a girl, with beautiful shining eyes. And just then they were full of tears.

Likeness Glues Love

II

Over in the corner of the room stands this other shadowy soul. Then John Donne, who despised memory, had the recollection of seeing the same man before, many years ago. In York. When they crushed Margaret Clitheroe. Then, as now, the man was a stranger.

But when he came forward this time he could see he had changed. He never looked at Donne. But he seemed to be looking at Donne somewhere else in a mirror.

"Hello, Kate."

Kate laughed.

"This is Sir Golding de Frampul." This time it did not matter what name he went under. I knew who he was and would not give him away. As always.

"John Donne: a great visitor of ladies; a great frequenter of plays; a great writer of conceited verses!"

Such was his mock introduction that I pretended to be flattered. The voice had an even more nonchalant, more suave ring than when I last heard it; I suspected that had we been on our own there would have been even more lewd jokes than before, more impertinences about the private parts of women. But ever since that wallop or shock of seeing Kate had overtaken me I was in a new rage of possessiveness such as I had never felt towards her before.

Now I blushed and panted for that which I had not.

Sphacto was here, too, playing a double-game. He probably had a shrewd idea that I had the visitors' permits, but did not know exactly for whom I worked – how high up my connections went, whether I could be commanded or should be deferred to.

I looked again at Underhill: should I help him gratify his deepest wish in life, his most profound ambition, and if I did this, was I not helping the enemies of England?

I could help delay the inevitable, the martyrdom of more priests by granting him the passes, but could I really postpone his sought-after agony by helping him to escape the country? For I knew that even if he left the country it would be only to take Kate out of danger. He would return.

But what did Kate want? Did she want martyrdom? Were they travelling companions in their faith or did their love and closeness go deeper? Should I collude in their design?

I was a muddle of contrary thoughts and feelings. I wanted Kate: again wanted her smell, her soft and caressing voice, wanted her fully, but especially wanted her naked. Yet I was now chaste, and promised to another. I was trying to earn self-respect by my abstinence and was succeeding. For Anne valued me in my waiting.

Could Kate have taken a vow of chastity? Could it be that she had renounced intercourse? What if, like Vibia Perpetua, she now put her womanhood at the disposal of her faith? Or like Paul's companion, Thecla, when paraded naked before the most powerful ruler of the time, Alexander of Antioch, she could resist his advances.

"Mr – Sir er, G – has," I explained, "been trying to set up merchants for the sale of sweet wines from Amboise."

I knew that I was fighting with myself to do the most difficult thing of all. To be good. Not to be selfish. Not to be jealous. To escape from those times with their powerful memories when I alone, and with distorted desire, had wanted Kate: to see that she should be shared with all.

It seemed like a good but sour joke, that was all: the sale of sweet wines – the blood of Christ, I mean. What a devilish euphemism. This was the way I told the truth.

"Are you the same as before?" I asked her so that only she could hear. "Was I awake? Or was it I who was asleep?"

She answered: "I wouldn't have come if I had known you were here."

"You ran away from me – and left me to face the rest."

"There were reasons."

"There were no possible reasons to do as you did. To take me to that point in order, then, to betray me. You might have stopped earlier."

"I hated you – because of what you did – even now I still do – "

Captain Sphacto strides over to us which stops us talking any more.

"Lady de Frampul, have you and your husband decided to spend the night here or – if not here – will you please tell me where you intend to stay?"

At the word husband I feel myself colouring. I know it is untrue, I know Kate and Underhill are not married, yet suspicion is not rational. I also know the force of Underhill, and I wonder if he might not have wavered. In spite of his tall and comely figure nothing pleasant emanates from him, nothing which seeks to be approved, which wants flattery, or even recognition. Yet I like certain qualities in the man so much that I wonder if I am not grossly unfair. After all, it is I who want to be liked, to get on with

Likeness Glues Love

everyone although, as far as certain people are concerned, I have not shown much aptitude. And now the passes are in my hands, I have something to barter with.

Married? It would have been all too easy. Underhill may have been a Jesuit, as I suspected. And even if he was, he may well have thwarted the Pope's rule. Some priests do.

Protestants had the privilege of having wives restored to them. Henry VIII gave the Church many heirs and, judging by the general reprobate nature of clergymen's sons, also bequeathed an endless line of criminals and rebels upon the nation.

I can speak of this for I had seven children myself. Of those four sons that live, one is of a sound and perfect nature, but another a complete rogue.

I know a celibate will serve God best, using in the saving of souls the energy that his family takes from him.

Yet when I think that Underhill might have possessed Kate – even in a non-sexual way – it upsets my judgement. Above all else, I had to know if it was true.

Sphacto looks over at me.

"If you want my guess, it is that Bernard Finch left those permits with Mr Donne here. He is a difficult man, is Mr Donne. One never knows what he intends or why."

26

In my Albany Lodging

Kate appears: at first I think that it is more giddy work of an astrologer. But then the frail jig of light on Kate grows into a pool and then into a beam. A gust of wind blows, and it becomes impossible to tell that she is still here. But I can feel my eyes balk at the vision.

"Can you find me a drink?" she says with those steady blue eyes at their most provocative and ethereal; her face is supplicating and tender. I rise to my feet. I can feel my legs giving way.

She brings a candle to us and puts it on the table. I also need to drink. Somehow I have to clear my head.

I pour aqua vitae into a cup.

"You're looking so well . . ." she says to me as she takes the drink. "Does the Queen still send for you?"

"They say I have much displeased her."

"Are you not drinking?" she asks me.

I seize a cup and drain it. But I do not know that it is already empty. I hold up the cup. As she cannot see into it the gesture means nothing; I am full of such empty flourishes; my whole personality is composed of such tricks and egotistical ape imitations.

Deception is in the air. I am someone else, and that someone else is still in the state of being formed. Kate says softly, as if she can read my mind, "It is not too late, John: it is never too late."

She is now in the chair. My eye rests on my empty cup. But the gentle expansive gaze of her lovely sapphire eyes on my face is an invitation to strike out from the coast-line into a sea of oblivion. I long to say that my need, my love for her, is as all-consuming as it ever was.

"I have promised someone else . . . to marry," I say flatly.

My face is a blank, as if I have drawn a curtain across it behind which all kinds of plots and machinations are being formulated; agents of schemes run backwards and forwards, like men loading a cannon from the breech, their match ready to ignite the powder in the hole.

In my Albany Lodging

"And do you love her?"

The wick dipped in melted sulphur . . .

"She trusts me. She does not watch me . . ."

Kate stops me. Can I withstand her compelling beauty? Since she has gone away it has redoubled, as if something new has possessed her and made her even more the essence of what she was before. She is herself and yet someone else. She has none of that raw unfinished need for me on which I tortured myself.

"I hope you do not blame me." She motions for me to pour her more spirit.

"Why did you not write?"

"If I had written I would have given you pain."

"You have changed much."

"I have travelled."

"With Underhill?"

I bite my lip. I wish I had not spoken.

"I have met your mother."

"She is not very likeable. I take after her."

"I am humbled . . ."

"You knew all along the difficulties and uncertainty under which I laboured. You were watching over me, judging me – giving me marks for my performance – in more senses than one – ready all the time to draw the net tight about me and see me – well see me . . ."

"No," she answers; "I forgot who you were. I didn't reckon the days."

"Well I did. Had I not been rescued by Sir Thomas Egerton I would be in Newgate. Like my brother Henry, who died there."

Kate recoils as if I have wounded her on her most sensitive point. She then asks: "May I tell you something I have been meaning to tell you for a long time?"

"With a happy ending or not? A sad tale." I cannot rid my mind of its habit of sexual innuendo. "Well, perhaps the right ending will spring up to end the tale."

"It is about a simple and naïve girl who came down from Scotland where she has a very fierce and independent father and no mother. Her father's life has been shortened by the death of his only son, and the cause to which he devoted his whole working life – a death he met in York."

I blanch. I remember. The last time I had been in York. Many years ago. That hot but perfect day in May. Egerton had hinted at it, but I had been too stupid to understand. So he had known all along. The death of that beautiful young woman crushed beneath stones placed on a door. That day I had become beside myself. I had been drawn into a duel. I had needlessly slaughtered another young man . . . The young man. The ridiculous young man . . .

"Do you want to know what really happened – and why . . . why I first got to know you?

"They brought my brother's body by wagon back home to Edinburgh. He arrived in the night. My father was upwards of seventy years – he had only married first when he was in his mid-fifties and then my mother played him false as only a headstrong, coquettish beauty tied to an old man can. She was intent on having some fun, that's all – but she paid dearly for it, for she caught the boils and fistulas off some golden-haired apprentice."

I still hate to think it is other than it was. That there was some predisposition in our fates, even, is bad enough, but that it should be a conscious will, a special seeking out, on her part. I could not simply believe that it was revenge.

"All my father's love was centred in the life of his only son. In him he saw the chance to have re-created the glory of the family – *his* family, not my mother's – as well as the continuation of his seed into the future.

"I recall the scene so well. Torches leapt and stabbed like spear-heads as they brought the body of Edward through the apartments of the mansion and carried him to his room. Here his dead body was placed on the bed. Then my father, with white hair and stiff straight back, proud in his noble lineage, although now a cripple, was placed on his litter and carried by two captains to his bedside. I myself followed my father, and then as I stood beside the bed, between dead brother and grief-stricken father, I became completely terrified. For I realised that this death of his only son had entirely robbed my father of something even more precious, if that was possible."

"Oh, no," I answer, for I see where this is leading.

"Yes. The first thing he asks me is, 'Who killed my son?'

"I name your name, for after that fight it is well known all over York.

"'That name', says my father, 'you'll never forget it.' 'But it was in fair fight,' I protest, 'the young man John Donne might equally have been killed, and there was but a year or so between them.'

"'My son was killed by an older man,' he went on, but there was no reasoning with him. I was only thirteen myself, and how could I

In my Albany Lodging

then see that what my father next made me do was a morbid figment of his own mind, which had been turned with grief over Edward's death?"

"What did he make you do?" I ache to take Kate's hand, but I know that if I do it will upset her.

"He made me swear. He bound me to his feeble mind and his diseased will, and made me swear. The words he used were in a curse that even now has a power to turn me back into that awful state I was in when I first met you . . . He made me swear 'to root out John Donne and before the face of Almighty God who is my witness, to bring about his death, ruin or dishonour in revenge for Edward's death.'"

Kate has gone very white, the effort of confessing this has taxed her to the very core.

I could hardly breathe. My eyes in some look I can only call unique caught hers. For I knew that in that moment my identity, my whole being would live or die.

"So, is the person you name still his murderer in your eyes?"

This seems suddenly to check her, as if the whole notion has become too much, or as if there has been this conflict which has never fully been resolved.

"While we were first together, and when I was still set on revenge, but the revenge of a fully grown woman who was prepared to use everything – "

A sigh escapes me as I realise the full implication of this. The inconstancy of hers that I set down, those tantalising qualities, as well as my own answer, all this was an essentially false response based on something concealed in her which I did not know about. I can no longer in any way claim that my poetry ever represented a truth; my songs and sonnets which appertain to the fickleness of my mistress, my licence granted to her to live out her wayward nature, it all came from the fact that Kate, through the burden of grief laid on her by the death of her brother – and by her father's curse – could not, however much she wanted, love me.

"But then I found someone who somehow was able to bring me to peace. Someone who was able to bring me to the point where I could forgive John Donne."

At this point there wells up in me so much regret and bitterness that I cannot help blurting out, "But not before you sought a revenge of your own making – and carried it out even to the destruction of that man who killed your brother!"

She is about to say something, but she stops.

"Did you always know?" I pursue her.

What I mean is, did she always know when, stage by stage, like the most cunning of courtesans or petticoat punks she embraced me even in the Queen's own chamber in Richmond, leading me as unsuspecting as Agamemnon led by Clytemnestra to the point where I could be blown up in the gatehouse at Hatfield.

"I was confused. Until I met the man who released me from the oath my father made me swear. He overcame and bound me with a spirit stronger than my own. And then, John, at the very last moment, having plotted your death, I saved your life!"

I was stretched on something worse than Topcliffe's rack.

"And who was the man?"

She looks for a moment as if she wants to tell me, and in her there is something which I can only describe as penitence, but it is swiftly taken over by defiance, or – at least – restlessness. Her eyes fill suddenly with tears as she rises, leaves the table, turns back to look at me and walks from my room.

27

The Boar Hunt

Diana, goddess of virgin and intellectual women, is on the side of the hunted animal, the bloody, perjured rage of hate such as women will harness one day. The furious animal has been unleashed, in revenge for a farmer king who has offered honours to Bacchus, but has neglected her altars. The beast ravages his land, trampling crops and savaging vine clusters, murdering flocks and slaughtering cows, until a band of heroes vows to bring it down.

They track it through dense forests, through sedge and marsh grass and through supple willow groves where – still acting with the will of Diana – it tramples and crashes its way through tree trunks and swamp. Seeing its foes ranged against it and as they hurl their spears, it turns to meet them.

Diana leaps to its aid and steals from their spears and arrows the tips of iron. It charges down on its bold adversaries, tumbles them over and plunges its tusks into the Arcadian Ancaeus, ripping open his groin, from which his guts slide and slither in a mass of gore, and soak the earth in a crimson river.

"Ancaeus' rash bravery has done this to him," shouts Theseus, who cautions that they fling their weapons from a safe distance.

They bring down the mighty animal.

28

Infinity's Sunrise

First thing the next morning a man brought a letter from Anne, who was still with her father, Sir George, at Loseley Park: it exhorted me more than ever to elope with her.

Anne wanted me to arrange our marriage along the lines of Egerton's secret contract. Anne said that we could have a similar ceremony at the Savoy Chapel in the Strand. Once upon a time a hospital, the Savoy was now carved into many small tenancies which gentlemen of fashion who owned no London house lived in as town residences. These precincts were a "liberty", free from the power of Church and civil courts. The Chapel was often host to clandestine marriages.

I wrote back to Anne a letter saying that I would arrange our secret marriage at once. Anne had a strong mind of her own. I knew that I would lose her if I did not fall in with her wishes. I intended to put Kate out of my thoughts for ever. She may have been acting a better and more justifiable role, but she was still acting. I had wanted her to belong to me, but I was sure she never would.

There was a sudden and peremptory knocking downstairs on my front door: I feared the authorities. I went to answer the door and found Kate. The feelings of yesterday returned to pierce my aching heart with fresh pain.

"Come in," I said coldly. She followed me without a word to the upstairs parlour, where we sat down. She did not look so well or radiant as yesterday, but like the face of the countryside which can change so suddenly when the balance of the air is upset, she had a menacing and purposeful air, as if bent on destruction.

Without waiting I began at once:
"There is something I must tell you, which I failed to put before you yesterday."

I could tell she had come for a purpose, but could not work out that purpose. She looked indifferent to my words.

She removed her gloves and placed them carefully on the table so that the fingers dangled over the edge, like the udder of a cow.

"So. You have decided to marry."

"Yes."

"To whom?"

"I cannot say."

For a while she said nothing. She betrayed no feeling at all.

"The Devil has this country by the throat," she observed in a neutral tone of voice. "Would you want your children to grow up in such a land?"

"I have no choice. Anyway, it is all changing. The Protestants are winning, and do you know why? They appeal to the basic instincts, not only of Englishmen, but of all men universally."

"And of women?"

I ignored this. But it was true. English women were still mainly Catholic in feeling. But my natural belligerence soared to the surface with nervous relief. I was in the mood of one of the articulate and self-congratulatory masters.

"England is small. To order society we have to give a place to everyone. We know the value of scarcity. People are scarce and last but a short while. Thus it is we base our safety – the very foundation of the state – on taking a man's life from time to time. A valuable life: of one of the best, most educated – the flower of chivalry and wit. (Had not I heard this before?)

"There is always the chance that the condemned man can at the ninth hour spring that dramatic conversion, even then he may be spared . . ."

"Like you, John Donne," she said gently with a smile.

I went on. I could not stop. I must have wanted to obliterate her presence, her influence from my life. Yet I could see that she, by starting the argument, had manoeuvred me into showing myself in my worst light, therefore confirming her most critical feelings about me to herself.

"The crowd is cheated of its offering. The pikemen called in to protect the victim. A condemned priest's apostasy can be worth a thousand new adherents to the Church. We are subtle technicians in the capture of souls. The City of London knows that Protestantism serves it best."

This was all lies. In my heart I did not believe a word I was saying.

"In France it does not," she said quietly. "In Italy it does not. Look at the new hospitals in Italy, the advances in medical cure and practice. They are leagues ahead of you."

"Well, no one here minds too much about that. For an Englishman the most important thing is to keep out of the hands of a doctor."

"Look at all the learning that has disappeared; how the monasteries supported music – and especially charity."

"If you want to tell me that the English are a bloody-minded lot, I couldn't agree with you more. Arrogant, unstable, vindictive."

"Is that what it means to be God's chosen people?"

"Most people think this way," I say with a certain trace of bitterness. "But I can't say I do myself. I long for their certainty. I have the feeling that God has rejected *me*. Anyway, if God has rejected me, why did you come to see me again? Who told you where to find me last night?"

"Let's just say I had informants."

"In high places. Government servants, no doubt. Soon you'll be like Eve once again, preparing to lead me into . . ."

"Please," says Kate, urging me to forbear.

I go to help myself to a glass of wine and pour Kate one. Even though it is before noon.

"Well, what has brought you over the river a second time? Not a desire to give work to the boatmen, I'm sure."

She says nothing. I flash my brilliant eyes into which I feel some irritation from Niobe, our cat, fly . . . "And what miraculous power over love do I have, that I can banish mourning a neglected husband *and* the revenge of a father . . . ?"

Kate looks at me steadily. "You must let me have those permits. They were ours by right before they were stolen . . ."

"To what price will you go . . . ?"

She says nothing but her eyes tell me, "Any save one."

"So you did come for a reason after all. I suppose I must now listen while you trot out what a great man Underhill is. How he is on the same mission as Edmund Campion."

"Shouldn't it be your mission, too, John? You choose to deny it, to grow cynical about it, even to play at being on the opposing side. But you are fighting too, aren't you? Stop pretending to yourself that you are not."

I turn my back on her. I have made up my mind. Even though the ceremony has yet to be performed, I am a married man. Kate's new faith, like that of Margaret Clitheroe, is for ever lost. England has no need of a soul, for it has a good mind.

"If your brother were here, he would not believe his ears."

I raise my glass and swallow its contents. The wine tastes odd. Kate turns ashen-white. She has risen from her chair. What next I wonder?

"I shall never understand how you fell in love with me when I so carefully held you off . . ."

I break in harshly: "I didn't ask to be put in the position where, even against my own will, your brother's temper provoked me beyond any kind of endurance!"

"As children," Kate went on, "we were taught right and wrong, but no one corrected our tempers. I know my disposition. I have been unhappily married once already. When could I ever have looked up to you?" Her fury is all too plain. "When were you going to grow up and *dare* to be yourself?"

She has pushed herself to the limit of the hurt that she can give me.

I recognise now that all of us, myself as well, will attack what we love until we cannot bear it any more and then we stop. We dislodge pain and resentment in ourselves by hitting out only to feel, in the end, that we do not want the pain we have been so keen on giving to hurt what we love.

I am about to answer her but I stop, look at her and gasp.

She is holding in her hand a small, deadly-looking knife.

"Don't drink again!" she screams. I have the glass in my hand, raised to my lips.

"I have drugged you. A moment ago when your back was turned, I put hebenon juice in your glass."

She shows me the phial.

"I am determined you shall come with me. If not then I stay here and we die together."

My force of mind begins to ebb.

"How did you know how much to give me?"

"I want those permits."

"No."

Kate moves from where she is standing.

"Soon you will be asleep. Underhill and I have arranged your departure."

"I still refuse."

I want to say to her that it is my love which threatens her and this is why she wants to get rid of me, but the room is closing in. Everything is slipping from me. My heart beats very fast as I summon every force to battle with the drug.

"I understand why you've become a Catholic," I say to her. "Because with your father as he was, and with your brother dead, you never could bear the responsibility of loving someone. You always just wanted to be loved, a one-way flow of energy, a traffic you can continually raise your hand to, and call out 'stop'!"

"Give me those permits."

Kate lifts the knife above her head and takes a step towards me, yet while she does so I can see the Devil behind her imposing himself on me, a proud figure, that of her father but with the features of Kate creased and heavy with age.

The Devil gives way to an even more grotesque and painted double of himself behind the beckoning harlot of a young woman, luring me as Kate had lured me. I knew at once who it was.

It was not her father that I had failed to overcome, but her deceiving mother, the hidden whore in Kate who had tempted the hidden whore of my mother in myself, and now held me over the battlements with a blade at my throat.

"You think we don't want to go the whole way," had said her brother. "I'm not setting out to sea just to make me sick."

I break into a further sweat. I can feel the poison hammering in my blood, building up like a great wave of the sea to batter and break my heart.

Suddenly Kate is at my side, ministering to me something else which I can swallow with ease. She speaks quickly.

"I must have been drawn to where I knew I might find you – as if by fate. I was sure that I would never see you again. But now, or so I feel in this last minute or so, I am just as sure we can avoid the danger of an unequal marriage, and that I shall, if I marry you, escape discredit and misery. I could never go through the grief of not being able to respect my partner in life . . ."

Her words career out of joint as I take her in my arms and kiss her on the mouth. The boy I killed was the other side of me. I had killed part of myself. Kate's revenge had stopped her growing. She had remained an unopened person; her thirst for revenge had destroyed her identity, until she met the other half, her brother's killer, who would give her life.

We were made for one another. We both had something to forgive.

She closes her eyes. So do I. For the first time I can make love with closed eyes.

Infinity's Sunrise

II

But now began my true tragedy; the beginning of my end. The end of my beginning.

Was it that I preferred to remain close to my dark and evil past, to keep it by me as a dictionary or reference book to define past faults, and hold myself from failing again? Was it love of my country that decided me to stay? The green grass on the other side tempted me, but I knew every blade in my brown and balding lawn.

I was deciding for the future: for the plague of love, as it was in the most chilling signs promised, would once more depart. The bodies would be conveyed away in the night, the houses shut up for a month. Then they would burn rose-vinegar, treacle and tar, to sweeten the rooms. I was praying to Jupiter. Acknowledging power.

After the plague there would be a return to human and wanton sensuality. Women would be adored; marriages thrive, twins and triplets born to most women. Not only in the birth of children, but ecstasy would show itself in dress – coats become unbuttoned, women's bosoms unlaced, tightness and closeness to the human form, above all a clinging to those private parts which excite desire, would become the be-all and end-all of fashion.

Even when the plague had gone, there would still be plague blindness in men's hearts as we interiorised our past – that of history as well as that of our own lives – into images that would live with us always.

For in such manner does everyone respond to the threat of annihilation passing: not only did the fairer sex wear artificial hair, low blouses and spill their beauty for every eye to see, wearing short skirts that men may see their bottoms and other forms indicative of sex. But – and this more than anything enrages the puritans – they also wear pointed chopines!

And what about the dances of death that would be performed? And what the harlots and orange-wenches would do to bring back to life those who mock and act death!

I may have started a family of my own already. But I had a sense of irretrievable loss; something had struck me down. I was laid low with jealousy of my former self. A part of me was amputated.

And now I was married.

After the ceremony was performed at the Savoy Chapel we had but a few hours in which to consummate our union. Anne returned to her father's house in Loseley Park. I resolved at the first possible chance to let Sir George know. I quaked at the consequences. I was moving into even more danger. I was sure the Lord Keeper would support me. But what would the Queen think?

PART IV

The Torch of Flesh

29

Underhill's Secret

I was seized by the throat by Bacon. Since the trial of Essex, at which he prosecuted with such fiendish and clever intelligence, Sir Francis Bacon had risen to rival Egerton in power.

"You will fetch us those two friends of yours. You are a traitor to your Queen, Mr Donne, unless we have both of them safely under lock and key by tomorrow morning. And we know you have committed fornication with the woman."

I had given Kate the permits. We had said goodbye.

As I walked through crowded Charing Cross and past the Bermudas I reflected that my life really had come to its limit. All I hoped for at the end of it: a measure of wealth, comfort, esteem from my friends – would for ever be forfeit. Whether they found an agent and gave him a few pounds to make an end of me, or whether they arraigned me on a charge and brought accusations against me in the courts, my life would no longer be worth living.

I thought of the virtues of Anne my wife. The word wife meant everything to me. She had stood by me. She waited for me. By dithering and not writing to her father I had behaved selfishly towards her. I should have taken up a position in the Church long before. I could have been a bishop with a dozen or more house-servants, not just the useless Marion I had, who was fit for cleaning fish and plucking fowl but little else.

As for the state of my soul, I might as well forget this. My body would die in some unsuitable, painful and humiliating fashion, and it would decay. My soul would wander painfully for ever, just as it had in life, in a purgatorial search both for improvement and forgiveness.

It hardly helped much to reflect on these things during my walk back to my lodging. Kate and Underhill would now be on the road to Kent (if they had not already caught the ferry at Gravesend).

Should I not seek out some of my remaining family friends in Yorkshire? Lie low until the authorities had other outrages to fill their minds. With such a government as we had which consisted of a few men who did not trust each other and tried to keep everything tightly within their power, not everything could be controlled at once.

Their memory was short. Like middle-aged women every new crisis made them forget the last. Records were scanty. Identification rested almost entirely on a shaky recall. A year could put a great distance between a hunted man and his pursuers.

Yet a heaviness had settled in my heart. A kind of fatality, as if I did not want to run any more. The sheriff, the magistrate, whoever was at home to meet one – I would greet him with a blithe heart. I was not prepared in any way for the person I did find there.

II

The light-hearted, careless laugh was still intact. "Hear for your love, and buy for your money," he sang,

> "A delicate ballad of the ferret and the coney,
> A preservative against the punk's evil."

"Why are you here!" I asked Underhill. "Has Kate been arrested?" Then I felt too exhausted to speak. I collapsed in a chair. "I was expecting . . . " I stuttered.

"I know," said Underhill with reassuring warmth.

"You better leave at once. Poley and his hell-hounds are after you and Kate. I don't know why, but I would prefer just now that you should both be safe."

"Or dead?" he added in a gentle mocking undertone.

Underhill stood quietly and immovably by my window, a tower of strength, impassive and serene. He seemed to have energy left over from himself to give me all I needed. He behaved towards me as if he were the soul of kindness.

I felt ashamed of myself and of my weakness. With an enormous effort I raised my spirits, but how could I be kind towards Underhill, when I still felt he had robbed me of Kate?

"But if I stay, you will be safe," insisted Underhill. "Is that what they are saying? Then I must stay, and you must go. And when they come, as they will, they will find me."

"I have a wife now." I looked away from him, frightened he might probe my confidence on this issue.

Underhill's Secret

"You can send for her. Kate will help you both to escape. Take your wife with you."

"I never want to see Kate again."

"You still love her."

"I am married. Our lives have taken different paths." I thought how it would frighten me to see her again, so beautiful and young and animated as she still was. "Seeing her again has upset me."

"Women are created just for that."

"I wish I had never met her. She claims that she belongs to God."

"Yes," Underhill sighed, "she has plans to withdraw from mankind into a convent, yet I doubt that it will last."

"If man had forgiven what God has forgiven then I would have married Kate." Underhill regarded me with an encouraging glow in his eyes. I had an ungovernable impulse to blurt it out: "When I killed that young Scotsman in York I had little idea that he would turn out to be the brother of the girl I wanted to marry. It seems unbelievably unjust. I confessed the killing to a priest, to – Underhill, are you listening to me, for you arranged it? – a Catholic priest. I might have been hanged for my confession. Yet I believed in it." I spoke faster and faster. "The fervour of my soul on that night was such that I was under the spell of God. I belonged to him. Never has this happened to me since."

This was the first time I had ever put into words my feelings about God and this whole terrible circumstance and these words seemed to gather stature and importance as I said them. I could not look Underhill in the face, and, to be truthful, part of me still blamed him with unforgiving bitterness for taking Kate away from Hatfield House.

"I knew all that," said Underhill quietly.

"You knew it?" I looked at him aghast.

"Kate told me of . . . her plans for revenge."

I was pale but suddenly I felt the blood pounding to my temples and saw a mist of blood over the darkness of my own brain. My old murderous, jealous Adam surged to the surface. Kate had told Underhill in confidence, Kate perhaps had whispered intimacies of our liaison to him.

"Kate was the ultimate betrayer, wasn't she?"

"Oh, no, John," he interposed calmly. "She was in love with you."

I laughed. "In love? What a preposterous notion. Unless you could mean the love that a wild beast has for its victim as it hunts him down. Kate was no more in love with me than a tiger with its prey."

"Kate would have killed you in Hatfield. But I met her, and we talked. I dissuaded her."

"You?" I interrupted. I simply did not believe him.

"Yes, me. Listen. You both had the keys to one another's souls. But she was ahead of you, John. If she had destroyed you, she would have destroyed herself. But she saved herself – and, it may be hard for you to believe this – you too have been saved."

"This has become far too metaphysical for me," I countered, distrusting his assurance. I was trying as best I could to seem unconcerned, yet I feared that any moment Walsingham's men would interrupt us. I gave Underhill a dark, anxious frown.

"John Donne," Underhill declared. "What is a soul? Have you ever thought? Is it just a pleasing motion of mind that we sense? Or is it the very essence, the centre of being?"

I rose from my chair and went to look out of the window. I was more sure than ever that soon they would be here. Yet what was said mattered.

"I regard the soul," I answered honestly, "as something that is an equivalent of the sexual part, or more precisely woman's centric – "

I stopped. I looked into those bright dusky eyes of what now seemed like blue and which always appeared to me so naughty and lecherous, so that I never could believe the man was a virgin, for he had the face of a satyr. I saw that it was I who had created Kate in the imaginings of my heart. I said, "I feel continually pursued – by the Furies. By the shadows of my father and my mother."

He thought. After a while he answered me.

"Your testing is not over," he said.

"Will it ever be over?"

"If you provide the right answers to the questions."

"But am I responsible for all that is happening to me? Look, what *has* gone on? Did I not invent Kate in answer to my needs? Did I not drive her to become revenged on me in the way that she did?"

"Yet nothing you did in this whole business seemed to be your fault."

"But of course it was my fault."

"So who did it?"

"You mean, did God do it to me? Was it that evil old God the Father wanting his revenge on me for flouting his will? And what

Underhill's Secret

did I do wrong according to the habits and fashions of the age in which I live?"

"It could have been the accident of your birth. I mean the stellar influences." He did not mean it. He was provoking me.

"Oh, yes, it could. It could have been that my liver was not functioning properly. It could have been that I did not say my prayers in the right way. Yet the world shows me hundreds – no, thousands – who behave towards themselves and others in a far more evil and disgusting way and yet nothing bad ever happens to them."

"You have been singled out."

I turned on him. "You'll be saying next I'm a Calvinist."

"No," said Underhill. "It wasn't God who picked you out, John Donne. You singled out yourself. You became a 'self'. You were curious about everything. You would not admit of limit. You would not stop searching, stop trying to find out. You wanted this freedom, of a kind that only begets a desire for more. This is your reward. The world."

"You think I should now stop?"

"I'm afraid you never will. You have been corrupted by a desire for the truth. Did you not write in one of your unprinted poems that religious truth was like a castle or a woman to which one lays siege:

> He that will
> Reach her, about must, and about must go;
> And what the hill's suddenness resists, win so."

I remained silent.

"Did you not also speak directly to your God, 'For better or worse take me, or leave me: To take, and leave me, is adultery'?"

"I have written worse than that!" I cried out sharply.

"But John," Jasper Underhill went on sadly. "You have a problem. You are still trying to make Kate responsible for your predicament."

Had I really committed the ultimate blasphemy with Kate? Made her God and worshipped her? I cannot ever tell the truth of this.

Underhill continued patiently, "You must give up trying to solve everything. As if you could do it all by yourself! In the final reckoning do you want God to neglect man and so leave him to his own devices that he will destroy himself? This is the way to go about it, you know."

"You mean I should take pity on the Almighty. Is that what I should do?"

"Respect the fact that mystery is above reason and sense. Be content to leave it so. The mind of God is like the mind of woman – ultimately unfathomable."

"If only I had not wanted to possess Kate."

Underhill gazed deeply into my eyes. His own flickered with a thousand lights and suddenly they were the very opposite of lazy.

"Kate confessed the murderous intentions of her heart to me. She had planned your execution, to the last detail."

I could see the dust of the collapsing gatehouse by the lake, as it folded in on itself. "And why, may I ask, did you want me to live?"

"Because I knew you were free from guilt over the death of her brother."

I was well aware that, in O'Hearne's schoolroom, Underhill had witnessed the provocation I had been given. He could not have seen into my soul; yet his words implied something more.

I raised my face towards his, full of anxiety and questioning, but also of danger. I knew Underhill was a more powerful person than I, and probably highly skilled at self-defence. Was he armed?

"*I* confessed you, John."

He paused, to give the words time to sink in.

"And you have always been . . . " I could hardly get the word out.

"Yes. I have always been a priest." He looked at me with lowered eyes. "I'm sorry, John."

So. I had known it all along. From the first moment I saw him. When he and Margaret Clitheroe had exchanged that calm indefinable look between themselves. The man's vocation had shone out. Yet why had I refused to believe it? Because it had something to do with my mother and I wanted to squash in me any allegiance to her deeper feelings. I rebelled against the greater love she had shown for priests than for her own sons, the greater confidence she had shown them in telling them her secrets, the greater intimacy given to them of her true self. She had not trusted me with herself.

I went and seized him by the loose folds of his doublet. I screamed at him, "For God's sake, for God's sake and for mine, get yourself out of here before it's too late!"

But even then the knocking on the door began. Underhill was caught.

Underhill's Secret

Before I went to answer, however, I pleaded with him to go. Even though I had an exit contrived through a back and secret stair, into the matured and leafy bower where a concealed door gave freedom to the street, he would take no action to avoid capture.

"John Donne, gentleman. Is one of such name at home?"

They did not push me aside. They were nothing to do with Cecil or the Council. Just amiable and slovenly part-time constables dressed in their ancient perpetuance. Armed after a fashion, one with an arquebus, more for show than effect, one with a backsword.

"We have a warrant, sir, for the arrest of John Donne."

"But on what charge?"

I could hardly believe that it was me they wanted to arrest.

"Bit of a queer one, this is, sir." The constable leant his arquebus against the wall. "Let's have a look . . . "

They squinted at the warrant. "Unlawful matrimony, it says here," said another of the men.

"I don't believe it. Are you sure?"

"Aren't you, sir? Marriage is so quick these days. I knew a maid married in an afternoon when she went for parsley to stuff a rabbit."

"No . . . no. I thought it was fornication written down here . . . " I had dropped my voice, so they could hardly hear.

"On the 25th day of June at the Savoy Chapel . . . "

They proposed to take me to the Fleet. I told them to wait. I packed a bag, and ordered necessaries to be brought later by Grey to the prison. I said goodbye to Underhill, scribbling down an address for him where he might remain in safety, for he would neither use his pass nor take benefit of mine.

We were now in the final throes of our life and death struggle. Which of us would win? Which of us, that is to say, would prove to have the greater moral authority? Had I known in Hatfield that Underhill was a priest I would have made him marry me and Kate. But now I was paying for my marriage to Anne.

"Too bad about the Fleet. But a nice bowling green they say. Better than the Marshalsea where they sent Mr Brook, the witness to your wedding. Wouldn't like to be among them pirates and rowers, and other water melons."

"Felons," I corrected him furiously. "You mean felons!"

30

Royal Divorce

My breath stops short; I seem to feel my life stand still while I listen to the Latin spoken by the captain of the gentlemen pensioners. The emissary has arrived at the rendezvous which I have arranged. An agreement has been drawn up between myself and the Council, to which Underhill, whom I contacted at the address to which I had sent him, has also been made a party.

The time is four in the morning. The meeting is to last an hour. After this Underhill is to be given some hours' grace to make good his escape. He will be free – for these first hours at least – to leave the house and London. I do not trust anything about it.

I have made the agreement which has also secured my release from the Fleet, where I wrote again and again to Anne's father (who had discovered our secret elopement and become so enraged that he had demanded my arrest), and to Egerton. In those weeks when I languished in jail the slanders against me had multiplied. In my sense of poverty and common rank I grew weak, became ill and took to my sick bed. My debts, my Catholic connections, my affairs with ladies at Court, my reputation wriggled in Thames' ooze at its lowest tide.

In my final desperation I had penned a most grovelling letter to my Lord Keeper suggesting that I knew where to find Underhill and promising the whole of my future life to Egerton's service and that of my wife. "If your displeasure sever us," I ended my missive, "Anne's peace of conscience and quiet would be for ever wounded and violenced."

Now the encounter has been ineluctably set into motion I feel myself draw back. I want to tell the priest to fly – to save his life before it becomes too late. Yet even now, with the imminent arrival of the Council's officer, it is too late; any attempt to alert Underhill might be a pretext for my own sudden, and second, arrest. This time my release would not be so easy.

I hear the knocking. I hold my breath, imagining what could be happening next. From where I have hidden myself I cannot see the front door. I have mounted the rickety wooden stairs to the attic above the boathouse, which is by the water to the south of the Devil's Tavern, off Essex Street. Here I have sat down on the straw, pulling a tattered curtain across the front of me. Here I will be able to watch the encounter, and listen to what passes between the pair. Through a gap in the roof a slit of star-studded sky is visible. Below me four great torches of resinous wood flame up. At the far end roars a great fire of logs and coals.

But as soon as I see Underhill I sense a darkness overwhelm me. His defiance. His incredible stupidity.

The gentleman pensioner cannot refrain from challenging him.

"So you're dressed like the Devil himself!"

The other guards laugh.

The mocking and vain wit has dressed for the occasion in the most flagrant way possible: he has donned an extreme Jesuit garb, a gown and a cloak, advertising his connection with the darkest power. They say Lucifer, the black angel, has a more perfect knowledge of God the Father, because he was the most trusted before he fell.

"Would you prefer I was a hypocrite and came dressed as I was before?"

"Why didn't you ever go out before in these clothes?"

The answer, as I knew, was that he would have been caught at once. "Instead you had a disguise and assumed a false name. No decent person behaves like that."

"Ah, you wanted to catch me quickly and put an end to our work for the salvation of souls. Saint Raphael did just like me. He assumed a false name, and his incognito helped him to do work God entrusted to him."

"So why have you changed now? And why are you here?"

My heart seems at once almost to stop beating. If they have set a trap for him, Underhill has set an even bigger one for them, of which I now have an intuition for the first time.

I hear the gentle swish of water and the steady creaking of oars. Then silence. A few quiet words of command. Then the officer Underhill is due to meet draws into view, a tall dark figure well-muffled against the damp and cold river air. It is the identity of this person which freezes the blood in my veins. I cannot see the face, which is turned away from me, but I know who it is at once.

Dressed to kill, a carrot-wigged Jezebel, it is the Queen, whose sight provokes in me positive loathing. Is she now set to devour another man in a gesture both of blood sacrifice and of guilt? I look down at those long and cruel Italian hands.

"I wish to be alone with the priest," she tells her gentlemen pensioners. They consult among themselves. One goes to remonstrate with her, but she refuses to listen.

She takes off her cloak. She motions the priest to sit down at the table on which have been set lamps, a bottle and two glasses. As Elizabeth lolls somewhere inside the serried complexities of her raiment, a superb self-decorated image of regality, the horror of this utterly unexpected situation strikes me with an almost physical blow. For a moment she is just like a doll. I can hear the faint quacking of mallards on the water outside.

"Is that wise?" asks Sphacto, whose voice I recognise with a further chill. "What if he puts you under a spell?"

I am equally frightened of Underhill's power. The fear of what might happen to England if "Father Edmund" has his way makes my senses reel.

"My dear Captain pensioner," replies the Queen, "if you think an old woman such as I will be susceptible to the papist charms of Underhill, then you do not know your Queen. God is a remarkable man, as the Dowager Duchess of Suffolk used to say in Mary's time, and we are his chosen people."

That farthing catchphrase again! I want to vomit. Sphacto bows and withdraws. But I know the Queen too well to believe that she has come here with so hostile an intention towards Underhill. But Sphacto, and especially his master, the comical little hunchback monster Robert le Diable, want blood sacrifices. They know that however much sympathy a priest's death will awaken, in the long run, like a hammer pounding on a stone, it wears away adherents to the faith.

There is a long silence which attends the departure of the guards. I wonder who will speak first. I look down on the Queen, hooding my candle-strained eyes, and once again she has changed. Where I have felt violent hatred towards her, for those huge unatoned crimes of hers which were often merely the by-products of her vacillating and contradictory moods, I now feel that under Underhill's influence the essential beauty and truth of her personality may be about to emerge.

For she is transforming herself, before my very eyes, as if she was a creation of my master Ovid, for all her advanced years, pale and beautiful, so that my heart begins to ache for her, and I begin to

Royal Divorce

superimpose on her the many younger faces she once had, as if in a vision.

At last she breaks the silence.

"I wish to make confession to a priest," she says.

II

I am stunned. Such a bombshell from the head of the Church. I rage in my heart: should I not stand up and denounce my sovereign Queen, call in the gentleman pensioners, tell them of this terrible lapse, and stop it going any further? But if I have to open my mouth, or in any other way reveal that I am listening I will be dead in an instant. Worse, they will hang me like a starling in Tyburn and cut off my privy parts. This is a secret like that of Actaeon surprising the naked Diana at her bath. Reveal it and I am turned to a stag. Moreover her word against mine, she will deny it. And she would win, because she would then believe intensely that she could never have said what she had said. And so, would God believe her confession? I ask myself. All we Protestants are products of a split mind.

While Underhill begins to say in Latin the words that prepare the way for the Queen to make her confession I drift into fantasy. The Queen is seizing hold of the priest's virgin member and stroking it till it hardens and she is saying, "But if I made you take me, if I swooped down on you like Venus on Adonis, and possessed your virgin manhood all for myself?" An eye for an eye, I dream, a virgin for a virgin.

"I could not stop you," Underhill is saying. "I could only pray for you."

"But don't you think," the Queen continues, "that I deserve just one selfish gratification in my life of self-denial?"

"That is not for me to say," answers the priest.

"I have prayed – I pray every night – to your saints. To your Jesus. I have a crucifix in my own very private chapel. My puritan ministers are in despair."

"My Queen, take your hand away," answers Underhill sternly. "I cannot vouch for what might happen."

The Queen hesitates: like an eagle poised to swoop, she instinctively begins to position herself to shed herself of her robes.

Like an open flesh shambles, she quivers: the secret places of her body are there to be taken.

But it is with words only that the sovereign undresses herself.

III

"That is your prerogative," Underhill was saying. Both were seated. Elizabeth toyed with food, and offered some to Underhill.

"I have no brothers," she said. "I have no father and mother. Many times I have been called a bastard. My mother was officially judged a whore. My mother's marriage was called utterly void . . ."

"But you are here," said Underhill firmly, "to confess your sins."

"I confess my father and mother's sins."

"Of course – in so far as you believe them to be your own."

"They are. And as we become older they become more so. All my life the sins of my mother and father have stalked me: they were there brooding over me, first thing in the morning when I awoke. Last thing at night they harrow me into bed."

"Tell me what you can."

"No one has ever, or will ever depict the tyranny my father was able to exercise in his bedchamber over his wife, and over his children. He dandled me on his knee, and sometimes I could feel his mighty pole of manhood stiffen under the royal hose. Think what having a father who murdered my mother did to me. And for what? Jealousy, purely imaginary jealousy – itself no more than retrospective frustration for not having a son. Shall I explain further?

"My mother was beautiful beyond belief: thin, delectable, and saucy; she had wonderful dark and abundant hair, fine eyes – the eyes of the Irish, a firm strong and full mouth, a head set on a long neck. She had all – and I mean all – the fair parts of woman.

"But she also knew which side of her bread was buttered, and how to play along my wicked father's bellowing lust for all she was worth. She could stretch her fair cheveril conscience to receive my father in bed, before they married, while he could never distinguish between what he wanted and what was right. He saw himself as Jove, forcing himself into alien animal shapes (and self-flattering emotional distortions) to have whom he willed.

"My mother understood him, with her ferocious, middle-class narrow-minded virtue, she made those fat red cheeks, and that ever-swelling royal belly, puff out with even more explosive lust – and perhaps more, that desire to make sure her belly was barricadoed with his child. He had divorced his first wife, Catherine, for the same reason of illicit fornication that he was committing when he married my mother.

Royal Divorce

"But there was nowhere his jealousy could hide. Once awoken it could not be called back. As my mother had skilfully fanned it with an enchanting skittish laugh, a sweet, white, pappy bosom, a sight of ungartered inner thigh, or sometimes – for his royal eye alone – a glimpse of the mystery his mind fed on since the disastrous, sexless match with Catherine of Aragon like an obsession – how could she bite it off and contain it once she gave in?

"At first they had a roaring time, yet who could say it was a true marriage? All that nonsense from Leviticus – 'thou cannot uncover thy brother's wife's shame' – over Catherine of Aragon, having married his brother Arthur before she married Henry! Arthur had died and left her a widow – to claim the marriage was not lawful was nonsense. All that money torn from the choirs, and stones and living flesh of the medieval Church – had been spent on justifying my father's divorce, and legalising his need for adultery. Emissaries, advisers, holy men by the hundred were beheaded. Coffers emptied, bribes well placed for legitimising this crooked Zeus's passion for infidelity. Could marriage ever be the same again in England?"

Underhill remained silent. What was he thinking? I could see he was free from speculation. He made no judgement.

"Let us not even say my father loved lechery, or cultivated subtlety, or even gave of himself with disinterested desire to satisfy his partner. Yet who can ever peer at such royal cavortings and divine them correctly?"

True, I thought in my secret listening post.

I continued to feel terrified at such royal revelation, bound for ever to remain silent. Only now, with my own death the mere brush of a lark's wing away, can I reveal the truth.

As for what the divinity said – and as one who has passed his life measuring the correspondences between a man's behaviour between the four posts of his bed and the state of his soul – I can, with authority, state that her father was no great shakes in bed. Bang – in it went, the flint lit the cannon, and it was over with a ruptured breach, a cry of pain, a brief wash of tears – a soaring female pride, perhaps, at receiving the sovereign package and – let's hope – even the issue. The King's divine right. But once the kill had been made, the blade wiped on the bedcovers, it was back to war, meat, and claret. Sex was a mental attribute called possessing.

"Can you wonder then, at how tortured this ginger-haired, wispy little angel of his daughter – or so they told me I was – could become. My very claim to the throne rested on a dubious legality, and an utterly spurious moral claim. How cold, how deeply ruthless and self-contained I would have to be, even at the earliest age, to evade any pitfall – and what a supreme survivor I would have to be.

"Alas, my mother was no survivor at all: her own image swallowed her up. She believed in herself completely, she had blind faith in her prettiness, her seductive eyes and playful belly. She enjoyed herself as a dream, enchanted by the glory and richness of the trappings, but not in any way aware how the Court tugged on the strength of my father and would tear or whittle away anyone who was not as strong or clever as its collective intelligence.

"My father's huge possessiveness was no protection to her: she was but meat which fed him; and who believes all that talk of Henry needing a male heir – pure piffle and nonsense. He was like me, his daughter, his proof of not wanting to commit himself to a member of the opposite sex lay in changing wives five times. But I was cleverer than he was, for I learned the only true lesson he gave me – which lay in not entering into marriage in the first place. I married my kingdom and learned six languages.

"Imagine my poor mother, finally, slain for a purely fictitious notion of sexual infidelity under the King's nose when she herself had just miscarried his son and true heir, triggered by the shock of one of his careless, manly accidents. Had he loved or honoured his wife in any decent way – defended *her* faith in the way he later bragged under the twisted papal title Defender of the Faith – he would have refrained from love and secured her lying-in against mishap.

"But his manliness, so called, crushed her in this second blow, a second aggression to cancel out the first because he could not curb his headstrong tyranny.

"I would not trust my wants to any man. My mother was caught merely whispering, smiling on someone else – flirting quite harmlessly – poor girl; a month or two before, she had shed all that blood losing her son and had herself miraculously survived the loss. She needed to boost her self-confidence, needed reassurance that others besides that brutal old ox could find her attractive. Did England's Sun King ever understand?"

She was in tears, but she still spoke firmly.

"All my life, Father, through my purity and uprightness I have tried to atone for the sin of my father. I believe that since the day I was born I have been ill on account of my father's great crime against the soul of his nation."

IV

A sudden chill descended on me, an icy claw of Gloriana seized my backbone, and I wished more than ever I was not here. I had seen into her heart of darkness. I had been a witness to the infamy of her family. To her need to confess. I could see how, in its extreme reverse, her virginity had prolonged her father's tyranny and adultery. This witnessing of mine would become my wound while I was called upon to assume chameleon shapes of monster conformity and compliance which would be snapped over me, clipped over my senses and mind, with strings and assent.

There now breathed out, expanded, spread, exhaled, such a glorious spirit of love and confidence from Underhill, whose sudden and remarkable energy reached even me. The pale forehead of the Queen was still rucked with pain, creased with torture. She bowed her head. Underhill dragged a chair to the fire, and ushered the Queen to take a seat nearer to the warmth, which she did with docility, almost humility. They now sat some eight yards from where I crouched over them and I could see fully into both their faces.

They spoke quietly. But I awaited the explosion, the reaction in the Queen. She had given too much away – and she would want to seize it back.

"My Church," the Queen was now saying, "is an institution which is supposed to mediate to the world the eternal and universal wisdom of God. But it is rife with its own petty issues and ambitions. Do you know what drives my bishops? The desire for money."

I could not agree with the Queen more. This in the future, with the demands of my children and my wife, would fan my support for the rewards to be won in the new Church. The Church had to move with the times and adapt to the new aspirations and desire of the people.

"You speak good sense, my liege. But all institutions have an evil side."

"Peace!" the Queen interrupted. "No more of this. I hate theological debate. I'd sooner listen to cats howling at the moon. What's true today in man is never true tomorrow. The hypotheses of yesterday collapse tomorrow."

"You wish to be reconciled with Rome?"

She was not listening. She went on regardless.

"The Church that is married to the spirit of the age will be a widow in the next."

My heart went black. My senses began to scatter. Our Grace's madness was indeed becoming serious. Burghley once said to me how when the fit was on her she would accuse him of those things she most feared in herself. She had once called him a collapsed old pair of bellows.

Underhill sighed. For a moment I caught the look of a hunted creature in his eye.

"What would your people do?" he asked quietly.

"They would follow me. They are tired of insecurity."

"But how could we negotiate? If only the Pope was an Englishman, as he once was when Nicholas Brakespear was Pope. But he is not aware of the conditions in England."

"I thought the Pope was infallible," said the Queen quickly.

"No. His inspiration is not by any means infallible. It is only his pronouncements, made with the full weight and agreement of the Church behind him, which are deemed infallible."

The Queen was not listening.

"I tried," she said bleakly. "I gave myself to de Houpeville. He had the token of my love. A disc of samite. Is failure a sin? It was too late for me to have an heir. It is too late for reconciliation with Rome."

I swallowed with relief. Could she be believed?

"Your Grace," said Underhill quietly, "it is never too late for anything."

She laughed. "You are a man and a priest, and there are some things you do not know. Would your Pope make me a bishop?"

I began to feel a little easier. No one could dismantle Elizabeth's final identity.

"I cannot commit the Vatican," answered Underhill uncertainly.

"I am head of the Church here, you know. God damn it, I can make myself a bishop if I want to."

I cannot even to this day understand why, but Underhill became angry. He clenched up. He began to shake. He pursued the way out by silence. But she could read his mind.

"Why do you scowl? Stop looking at me like that. Why should I not be the first woman bishop of the Anglican Church? If I so decide, none shall oppose my consecration."

By an almost superhuman effort of will Underhill managed to stay seated and maintain his silence.

"You want to stifle me, Mr Underhill. You want to destroy my soul, to stop me being myself!" She screamed out these words, then put her hand to that wide gaping mouth. She breathed heavily. It was too much for Underhill, whose mortality had caught up with him.

"Then why don't you become a bishop?" he challenged her.

"Nothing," she was still staring hard at him. "Stop looking at me like that, Mr Underhill." My heart was beating fast. I had wondered why but I could now see why Underhill had not absolved her from what she felt were her sins. I could so clearly understand the connection between her father and herself. She *was* her father. He played the Devil as a boyish, bluff but evil tyrant. He was a Tudor. While we ordinary mortals had nightmares in our sleep, Henry and his daughter lived them. They made the world take part in their private phantasmagoria. The mad put constructions and dark intentions where they are not. They elevate whispers into shouts. Telling them something once becomes a thousand times. All through this century the Tudors had planted their illness in their people and nurtured it.

"I am not looking like anything, Your Majesty. I am your good subject," he added.

But he had challenged the Queen. I can vouch for the fact that he gave the Queen no evil eye, and used no magic, but to contradict her wrongful charge was the greatest insult he could offer her deranged personality. It was, at any rate, taken by her as a sign of weakness. Weakness in man opened only one course of action to her.

"Yet if I free you, Mr Underhill, and make an accord with Rome, and let everyone worship according to their conscience, the country will be much greater and more powerful."

Underhill clearly resisted the impulse to take her hand.

"Otherwise I will die lonely and without faith, with no guarantee that my kingdom itself will last."

Underhill began very gently to smile. As a child recomposes itself after a quarrel when it feels the pelican blood of its mother's kindness asserting itself above the pain, so Underhill caught a true spirit of love kindling in his subject who was at the same time his mistress.

"Let us take bread and wine and celebrate the sacrament."

I wondered because she had no hesitation. She agreed. She had been starved spiritually and she needed food and drink.

But as Underhill rose and prepared the table, as Jesus had at his last supper, taking out his secret Mass-kit and arranging bread and wine to fulfil the holy mumble-jumble, something gradually alerted the Queen, and she awoke from her trance.

I believe now, that ultimately it was the humility that she could not find in herself. She feared forgiveness, for she feared the self-forgiveness which would mean that she would have to become someone else. She could kneel in body, but not in spirit, for there was a whole structure of powered authority behind her which spread through the Middle Ages and found its culmination in the Wars of the Roses, won by her grandfather, Henry Tudor, Earl of Richmond.

In her was as a forest, an avalanche, a myriad, many-sided power of command, a million brain cells attuned to every nuance of control, every impulse of the power and its opposite poles of superiority and inferiority. She would not part from this. For in this race she was always ten moves ahead of others. She had more sense of danger than anyone. She was more virtuous. More chaste, more abstemious, more learned. Better read, better succoured with singing and dancing.

But all these were competitive things, reflecting the men that she had surrounded herself with, and whom she devoured in order to please the husband whose moods she studied, while she inspired him, set him to work for the best in himself.

"Do you put yourself forward to die, Mr Underhill?"

Underhill stopped his reverential preparation.

"You are so gifted you should live, Mr Underhill."

If he found this – even he – a little threatening, he did not reveal it, for he went back to his work, still saying nothing.

"None of us can presume to take on the mantle of Jesus," Our Grace went on. "By presuming to follow in his footsteps, won't you be making an outlandish claim for yourself, Mr Underhill?"

Underhill answered: "I have already followed in his footsteps. I am a priest, bound to celibate vows and married to my Church."

"My Church is essentially the same as your Church," Our Grace countered. "I am proposing to unite them. I will issue a proclamation. You shall become an English bishop, the legate of Rome. I order this on the spot. The unity of our Churches shall be proclaimed at once."

Underhill's large and docile eyes smiled their disarming beam on the Queen. They held no reproach but he knew what was coming.

"The idea is a commendable one, Your Grace – "

"Then it shall be implemented."

"But impossible at present."

"You shall make it possible."

"I cannot defy my own Church."

"Then leave it. Leave it, Mr Underhill."

Then there was silence. And that was all.

Royal Divorce

V

After some moments, "Shall I go on?" asked Underhill with the utmost gentleness.

"Yes."

She said the word with an extraordinary impulse of warmth and generosity.

Both were approaching the moment which could never be turned back. Underhill was preparing the Mass. In a few moments he would be Father Edmund. Then the great miracle would happen. The godhead would be here.

He would be alive. Not flaunting or declaring his primitive power like Jupiter. But in human flesh and blood. Jesus would be here, while the Queen and Father Edmund, they would possess him in as sure a sense, if not surer, than ever woman had been taken by a man, or man by a woman. Jesus would be eaten, he would be swallowed, he would be devoured, he would be flapdragoned, it would be lawful eating. The word made flesh would be eaten. My brother Henry's words were about to come true for ever.

I slipped. To regain balance, I, John Donne, voyeur and poet, placed my foot on a weak and cracked piece of the ceiling, pressed my weight on it, lost my balance, and came crashing down on to the bed of fresh rushes below.

Suddenly the Queen's guards were everywhere.

"Seize him, seize him!" she commanded, pointing to me.

Numb and shaken I was lifted unceremoniously by both arms to my feet. I struggled free, shaking wattle and plaster dust from my clothes. I opened my doublet, ripped my shirt apart and found the disc of silk around my neck. Tearing it loose and solemnly raising it up before me like the Host from the chalice, I held it for the Queen.

"Your Grace. I was told to return this to you by the Duc de Houpeville."

I half expected her to laugh. To pass it off well. But her sense of humour had gone for ever. It was as if she had been hit by a bolt of Jupiter's lightning. She was a primal being once more. She put both hands to cover her eyes, to hide herself from the glare of reality.

"Let him go."

She parted her hands from her face. She stared at me. Her eyes were swimming in blood. Her long Italian hands began in silent convulsions to tear her dress and her front became all unbuttoned. I could smell the anger, an acrid, bitter mid-life smell discharged on me like a broadside. The anger of conflicting emotions and squashed feelings.

"You may keep your wedding knot, Mr Donne. May it choke you! You shall never see me again."

She turned her back on me. Her men escorted Underhill out to her barge. She followed slowly. I could hear the beginnings of hysterical rage. For once the mental power and energy were not equal to the volcano of personal conflict that bubbled to molten lead inside her. Her Majesty was fissured with a brain storm. Her fainting and faltering will was paralysed. She had lapsed for ever into danger.

Her departure was followed by the arrival of dawn. The sun rose over the Thames. The oarsmen had left the big boathouse doors open. The buildings along the waterfront became bright and kind, the thin pall of smoke over the City melted into a careless and revealing haze. The timber walls and rush-covered floor of the dark cavern in which I stood were flooded with a golden light which blinded me like a vision.

31

The Incubus of Terror and Examination

I watched Underhill's torture. I became convinced that he would not die. I knew where he was. I knew what was happening to him. His torment was my torment. His humour and abundant love of life diminished almost to extinction. But he felt no desire for revenge or retribution against his captors; he withheld from maiming himself by descending into a rage of anger.

I doubted if I could have withstood what he withstood. I, who otherwise lived inside his head, could not have done so. I had little of his miraculous power of disengagement. He had won control over himself.

He lived in a very very dirty, filthy cell. Love had raised its palace in the place of excrement. The Tower minted the Queen's money, radiated her love of power, but also contained her most secret shame. The cell in which Underhill was lodged was damp, ill-lit and hidden away from the more illustrious footsteps of relatives who visited the aristocratic captives. These waited cheerfully for change, for a new liberal spirit. Everyone believed that it would not be very long before the Queen was dead.

"Today, Your Grace, we jerked a roller on him some fifteen to twenty times. Once we tore a scream from him by the sharpness of the agony. His body lifted from the floor without a will of its own. He hung in the air ten or fifteen seconds in total pain, sweat pouring from his whole body!

"Then we let him sink to the floor. He started talking to Mr Donne and his family and in particular Mr Donne's mother. He was in a delirium . . . "

For while she was still alive, each evening Robert Poley would catch a boat from the Tower's flotilla, have it rowed upstream to Westminster, or, more frequently now, to Richmond, to inform her of the day's torture and the prisoner's reactions.

"Did you question him about the escapes?"

"All the time, Your Grace. We wanted to know dates, the names of the people whom he had helped to train, how he recruited new priests and spies."

"What did he say? Did he answer you?"

"Some he answered and some he would not. Once he asked only why there were so many friends in the room with him. I believe he was losing his wits. He asked at another time if he might not have time to collect himself. Captain Sphacto threw a bucket of cold water over him."

"Did this have the desired effect?"

"No. We went too far. So we had to give him the illusion and hope that the business was over for the day. We lifted him from the wooden trough. His eyes were closed, Your Grace. Only his body still appeared to live. After a while quite ordinary things seem just the same as torture. I've known of some that scream when we press the aqua vitae to their lips. I doubt he was aware by now that he wore no shirt or hose."

"He was naked?"

It seemed to matter to Her Grace.

"He complained he had a bracelet snapped tight round each of his wrists; my hands, he said, are unusually big. Rings of swollen flesh, we told him. He laughed like a child. Well, it is my birthday, he said; I suppose you're spoiling me with presents. Oh, he was strong, Your Grace, no doubt about it."

The Queen perked up. This is what she wanted to hear. The very resistance of Underhill gave her strength.

"And now he has had a taste of it? . . . " How she felt better. She might even rule a year or two longer.

"Well, we put the questions to him all over again. He became voluble, saying he dared not move his head because the sinews of his throat burned like cords of red-hot steel."

"Yet he still talked?"

"He named names. He listed places. He described circumstances; he gave us great lists. He said he would draw us maps."

I sighed with relief. I knew that none of this was true.

II

Robert Cecil: Has Donne confessed to you?
Underhill: I have no power to answer that.

The Incubus of Terror and Examination

Cecil: Have you confessed anyone in this land in the past few months?

What should he answer? Yes, the Queen of England?

Underhill: Through the Holy vows I have taken I am not at liberty to answer that.

Cecil: I command you to answer.

Underhill: In all humility, my Lord, there is one above of greater authority than you, who countermands your command.

Cecil: If you do not accept my command you are a traitor.

Underhill: To be a traitor, I would have to plot to overthrow the Queen's rule. I swear by God I have never done, and would never do, such a thing. I am the Queen's true and valiant subject.

Cecil: Then tell me whom you have confessed.

And here Cecil smiled: "I won't hurt them, I promise. What about Francis here? I would not be at all surprised if he had not crept along on the quiet to see you. And after rewarded you well for it!"

Those enemies of Bacon on the Council tittered with glee. Bacon blushed but said nothing. I noticed I had read Our Grace and her ablest courtier aright. Neither to deny or affirm a charge.

"Someone higher?"

The bloat-eyed Cecil himself, perhaps, weaving a thousand threads of stratagem, laying more plots a minute than the toad shoots spawn, might well need to disburden himself of his guilt and plotting in order to sleep with a quiet conscience.

"Everyone has need to confess some time or other, my Lord," said Underhill mildly and with commendable composure.

Cecil sprang on this: "Need? Who should ever have need to confess their sins before such uninformed monkeys as the Pope chooses for our lively entertainment to send to these shores. I suppose you need to confess yourself."

"Everyone should confess. Our sovereign's father, His Grace King Henry, would confess sometimes three times a day and would as many times hear Mass."

Cecil turned to the bishops. "Well, what do you say to that, my Lords of the Church? Has any of you an answer to make?"

"Everyone must needs make their private petition for their sins," answered Canterbury.

"But it needs not a papal lackey to overhear and spy into a man's talk with his own God," answered York.

Campion's Ghost

Cecil turned back to his prisoner.

"Well, what say you to these, Mr Underhill?"

"Some of us may be strong enough to send our pleas direct to the Almighty. But most of us need the support of an intermediary to put forward their case."

"Your case, Mr Underhill, is a hard one. But still I must return to my quarry. Who, on this Council, has confessed to you? My captain of the guard gave notice that five and twenty nights ago, before you were removed for safety's sake into the Queen's custody, a figure was seen to visit you – "

At this there was a certain flurry of consternation among the bishops; surely one of their number had been along for Underhill's comfort – possibly more than one.

"I am silent."

"Come, Mr Underhill. That will get you nowhere. You think to dominate me, do you, with your silence? To send your spirit into my head, to crush my soul and for your own to take it over. But I am not fooled by you, Mr Underhill. I am stronger than you. I will not be mastered."

"I will pray for your soul, my Lord. For your sins as well as my own."

He would not blink to say what he truly thought. He would not utter an ambiguous statement, then half withdraw it or leave its inoffensive face upright upon the table. You always knew where you were with him.

But even he was wilting under the strain: whether from words or the further expectation of torture, everything which for so long had made him clench with resistance suddenly weakened him on his feet. Perhaps it was the sense of slight relief that made him feel worse, for sometimes an improvement renders one more vulnerable.

Cecil noted this. He spoke kindly.

"Come over here, Mr Underhill. I wish to have a talk with you in private. Draw up a chair for him. Fetch him food and drink. The rest of you leave him."

Sniffing and baying, the whole parade of big-bellied councillors with their scarlet ostentatious hose and their trappings culled from the Queen's treasure box and other more dubious and hidden troves, suddenly breathed out and gave up the chase. With unified disgust and with an air of being cheated they turned heel and went out of the chamber leaving a dirty yellow wake of malodorous coughs, farts, cluckings and other yelps and whinnies and discontents. How their power-sated spirits longed for the ultimate sacrifice of Underhill to their ambition! They wanted to nail him to the flagmast as a supreme trophy.

Food and wine was brought to Underhill who must have been as ravenous as a wild animal. But he ate as someone past appetite: sparsely, fastidiously, making sure the meat and dainties did not cover him with grease.

"Our Majesty is sick of the blood-letting of good and holy men. You must renounce your faith."

"I cannot."

"You are but forty or so. You may live thirty more years. The times will change. Another will take my place. The Queen will die. Why do you put yourself forward to die?"

"It is not I who put myself forward. I seek only to do what is right."

III

Elizabeth was in Richmond on her own. Daily she was brought accounts of all that happened with Underhill. She commanded it.

She was stripped bare, to the naked soul. All of her layers had been removed, and this was the last layer of all. She must have blood. Blood will have blood. She had kept her kingdom together through the urgency of sex and murder. No wonder her poets talked so much of the rack, and of their "little death" in orgasm.

Here was her last victim, her last sacrifice, her last banquet of blood. The kingdom was rotten and propped up by hate. No wonder that just after she died it fell into the worst plague of my lifetime while a quarter of its people perished.

She sacrificed priests in the way that wayfaring captains told us the Incas in America made their blood offerings to primitive gods. Underhill was her last sacrifice. The last scapegoat of the virgin queen.

Now, preparing for the final injection of life into her soul, one last attempt at resuscitation, she was having spasms and convulsions as the poison began to flow through her system. She twisted, she contorted herself, she cried out in remorse, for she, like me, was killing the thing she loved most in order to feel pain and therefore to love and respect herself again.

What should I do? Cry out. Seek help. Deliver her up? Try to reason with her?

No.

Not even if she would see me, would I go to her. She needed the company of her ghosts. Sometimes they would appear to her without their heads, sometimes with them on. For now they could not answer back. She had them under her thumb.

She sobbed. She pulled her hair. She flayed her skin with her nails until the blood flowed. She threw herself on the ground and banged her head on the wooden floor. She tore her dress. She screamed, she shouted. She kicked her legs in the air. She uttered a stream of obscenities. She came to climax. Then she stopped, whimpering and quietly sobbing.

She reminded me of Kate. Who once opened her legs before my eyes, making sure I watched while she carefully parted the lips of her sex.

But Kate had survived all this. Kate lived. Kate would live.

And Elizabeth would die. Shortly. There was no need to go to her. No one would be able to approach her. No one to console her. She would refuse the comforts of the Anglican faith. Every final motion of the soul would be blocked and seized upon. Her forces were waning, her heart was growing cold; her unconscious soul, murky, confused and suppressed, increasingly dominated her actions and above all her mind. She would long to confess again. Yet what was the point of confession if, next moment, you put yourself once again in a state of mortal sin?

32

The Race Is On

I was supervising the new layout of Francis's garden. The son of Thomas Egerton, Sir Francis Wooley had, because of his marital problems, much neglected his estate. His wife, Mary, had taken over Anne and given her the protection her own home could not afford her. Breaking off my measuring I joined Anne and Mary where they sat on some bases of piers and broken walls of a once magnificent church.

Broad sloping pastures of velvet turf stretched out before us, overbrowsed by sheep of fantastic shagginess and huge, pliant-uddered cows. Everything in the countryside savoured of larder and manger.

Both began to instruct me with amusing barbs on the folly of my former days and how I had abused women so. Our friend's wife had just been reading a poem of mine.

"How could you?" said Mary Wooley, "compare women to fleas? Sucking the very blood of men, leaving not their most retired places free from their familiarity? Don't you think this is absurd as well as disgusting?"

Anne was blushing. She had to bear constantly the embarrassment of my former gall.

"I'm afraid," I answered, "the itch of the little beast was often similar to that of my own unrequited need for a wife." I forbore from mentioning that it was a woman that sucked the blood of her husband, Francis, and made him an often absent and ineffective provider to Mary and her children.

We rose and took a gentle stroll down lovers' lane, a hazel and willow tunnel which led to the frothing mill-race. But our idyll was soon interrupted, for from down the road came a clattering of hooves. Keen to know who it was I left the ladies and went to look. I saw a man on a big bay gelding, who dismounted at the end of the walk and pushed aside the leafy concealing entrance to hail me.

He was well dressed, in the latest Italian fashion, cap-à-pie the spirit of form. Tied to his saddle was that murrey red hat Underhill gave him on his escape from York. I could hardly believe it, for it was O'Hearne, my old shabby schoolmaster who now was decked out as I should have been, while I had fallen into slipshod and genteel poverty, a parasite on my noble friends and supporters; my shoes' leather was worn through, my hose and jerkin faded in colour and torn. Many of my friends from the Inns had advanced themselves to knighthoods, for there was a boom in litigation, and lawyers' fees were fat. I had stayed where I was.

"O'Hearne," I called out. "What brings you to Pyrford?"

Such was the general name for the locality, although it was to warn him against the politics and religion of my wife and our friend that I put on such a firm and haughty tone at once. It did not deter O'Hearne one bit. He came brutally to the point.

"I hear that on Sunday next at Tyburn is to be executed – " and here he paused as a trained rhetorician who reorders the natural drift of his sentences for effect – "Underhill!"

As if this was not enough he went straight on. "I hear that the Queen is soon to die. That London is to be punished with the plague for the excesses of her reign. That sooner than have sodomite King James on the throne of England, the Queen's puritan ministers plot to make England a republic like Venice."

The ladies, who had now joined us, were aghast and put their hands to their ears. Anne looked questioningly at me, as if to say, who is this madman.

"This is my former pedagogue," I introduced O'Hearne. "He has been in Venice and Naples and Sicily. He has developed a fashion for extravagant talk. I think it would be best if we withdrew in private."

Indeed it was, for such a poison of insurrection and wild talk burst out of O'Hearne, it would have infected not only me, which it did, but throttled and turned black my whole new hope of life. Let me make it clear. I had done with the past. To open up an old wound, to probe the leavings of injuries and insults, even of joys and ecstasies, to mourn a grief that had passed, this was an infallible way to inflame the brain and bring on new confusion.

"I'll tell you of the first day of his trial. Oh, it surprises me, Donne, that you were not there. I thought nothing would have kept you from such a spectacle. Where has the old John Donne gone?"

I would not succumb.

"For to be sure, Underhill made a spectacle of them. He made mincemeat of them. He exposed all their lies and preposterous theology as bumble-broth. He had laughter rippling even among the Queen's bench."

I did not want to hear this. I was painfully trying to make my way, to redeem myself, to crawl and climb – for both are performed in the same bent and fawning posture – to build a secure living for myself and family. I would have done anything to escape this torment.

"Egerton was the worst. Underhill exposed publicly all his papist past, and had his enemies, those increasing in numbers – "

"You mean the puritans and their creatures of darkness like Sphacto and Robert Poley."

"None other. He had them smirking with joy."

"So who questioned Underhill?"

"He had to give way to Bacon, who was cold and icy, and not to be caught. Bacon kept asking, 'If your God wants you to serve his will, why has he not let you go free? Why has he given you to us?'"

I could see what Underhill would have answered. But I did not point this out. Bacon, a wise lawyer and a genius at survival, could only see the virtues of selfishness. He had not the vision to see that Underhill might be worth more to his Church dead than alive. Soon there would be few people left in England who were not merely out for themselves. To those with distorted minds, virtue itself is vile. Nothing appears more ugly and threatening than the good.

Most of all I wanted to be left alone. Yet part of me, that secret part, that inward womb of spirit that my brain harboured, breeding an army of rebellious notions, wanted the overthrow of Bacon and his kind. I had to squash that part. I had renounced the Court. I wanted cheerfulness, peace and leisure to expand my thoughts. I needed to laugh and to unwind, but here was O'Hearne come to tempt me back from the false self to the true.

"I don't want to hear any more," I said. "I'll give you money. I'll give you all I have. Ten pounds."

For I could see in his eyes during his account of Underhill's trial that it was but a foregone conclusion, however cunningly Bacon and his cronies imagined they had tricked Underhill in the end. They could have condemned him and he been hanged without it. What was so sick and obscene was that they had to justify themselves in their evil – the old illness of Henry VIII. They had to feel that in what they did, however criminal it was, rightness was on their side.

"Underhill still lies in the Tower. We have a week before the sentence."

"Won't they wait?"

"Knollys and Norton and the majority of the Council want him dead now. If the Queen dies and he lives, he will be pardoned."

"There is no way of delaying execution?"

"Who could ask the Queen," suggested O'Hearne, "but yourself?"

I felt my gall rise. "That is out of the question!" I almost shouted my answer. I looked at O'Hearne. There is no doubt he had become a different person. Out of the atmosphere of poverty and religious persecution, he had grown. He had once been a man who minded his business, who had private little feuds and victories, who followed an interior and private course of pleasure and grief, perhaps with a few hobbies.

But now he had escaped the noxious vapours of his native land, he had positively expanded. His face had spread laterally; that tortured, hard and dual furrow on his brow had vanished. So had its fellows beneath his eyes while the crows' feet in his cheeks had blurred into forgiveness.

I saw myself in that same moment in a projection of my own future, battling endlessly against the ills of the flesh as they progressively mounted with time. I was never without a complaint these days. Once my lodestar had been my mistress's private parts, her low countries, her netherlands, her comfit box or naked seeing self. For a year or two after our marriage I did manage to hoist all this inspiration on to Anne and she had withstood its perilous onslaught. She had been but sixteen to my thirty years and the intensity had washed over her easily. But this became swamped with the blood and broken waters of childbirth; with John Donne, once the swaggering Italianate courtier, giving the midwife a hand and emptying the slop bucket and tangled arteries of the afterbirth down the privy.

I cultivated a different star: but was it the star of the east which shone over Bethlehem, or was it the star that shone over the Star Chamber?

"John, we are a good number, some thirty or forty, sworn by all that is sacred on our loyalty to Rome but also to England, to free Underhill. We want you to join us."

He seized me by the shoulders. I was strongly and emotionally moved by his appeal, for I have always loved O'Hearne, and look on him even now as my oldest and dearest friend. I was thoroughly disillusioned, too, with the Queen, and I knew there had soon to be a different order. The persecution would stop and if the Catholics kept

The Race Is On

the peace and abstained from plots, they would be allowed greater freedom of worship.

"What have you in mind?"

"What I have in mind is extremely simple, but extremely hazardous." O'Hearne frowned. "But can you be trusted with the plan? Won't you give us away?"

"I can be trusted," I said.

"And will you swear by the most holy of oaths?"

"I will swear."

"Swear on your brother Henry's head." I gulped. O'Hearne knew I would never break such an oath.

And so I was sworn to secrecy. To be in the knowledge of a secret is already to be part of a conspiracy. It was the last thing in the world I wanted. But how could I avoid it? I still loved Underhill and would do anything I could to help him live. Anything? Anything while he was there, that is. But if he was dead? I loved the man more than what he stood for.

Giving my excuses to Anne I sought lodgings in London, falsely claiming that I had been granted some money to provide an entertainment for my Lord Robert in the Strand.

And here we plotted.

33

Caesar Shall Go Forth

In that declining winter of the Queen's reign London was full of confused predictions and signs. They say that when beggars die no portents are seen, but that when princes die the heavens themselves blaze forth. Elizabeth's leavetaking of this world was hardly a blazing triumph. The astrologers had a field day peddling doom.

Among the wretched Catholics who clung on, the idea of the Golden Day was bandied about often: the Mass would live again, and everywhere among the poor and recusants it was said that England would become once more a fortunate and decent place in which to live and prosper. With the restoration of Popery would come Utopia. Merlin had foretold this, some held, along with the liberation of Wales.

But here it all became so misleading. The Great Una, the light of Thule, now dying in Richmond, had so often listened to star-gazers. Not only when the monasteries were reborn would the good times return to England, but a new king would come to the throne descended from the British hero King Arthur, whose heir, it had long been promised by the hawkers of deliverance from bondage, would free the oppressed and rule as a popular prince.

But wait a minute. Did not Henry VIII draw upon Arthur too, to help him throw off the authority of the Pope? Merlin was a prophetic shuttlecock, hit from both ends of the court.

Anyway, someone had to think up a good reason for the end of the Tudors, now that the cupboard was bare, except for their Scottish cousins. So they thought of Arthur and the eventual return of his line. All that was needed was to make sure that the new King of England was a blood relation of Arthur.

Powerful Merlin was again enlisted. Early Protestants called him the Devil's incubus, but now, when they backtracked and realised they could not do without him, he became the *learnèd* Merlin whom God "gave the spirit to know", who thundered out subversion to the Pope in Rome. If France and England were not to be reunified under the copulating spectre of Elizabeth and de Houpeville, then Scotland and England were, so reconstituting Arthur's ancient, if only short-lived, kingdom. Merlin lives on. The first Stuart was a long-lost Briton.

The crowd was not much bothered with this. The crowd, the English mob, was a thoroughly Protestant invention. Oh, I know there are some that will say, well what about the massacre in Paris, where the hammer of the Catholics, Walsingham, suffered his education in Catholic intolerance. Yet this butchery of the Huguenots, as Marlowe knew only too well, was masterminded by the Duke of Guise who paid the assassins in gold.

God bless our English mob. Its mindlessness, its zeal, its laziness, its greed, above all its lust for blood. Having been both Catholic and Protestant, I may speak with authority. As the Dean of St Paul's I speak without bias. Catholicism is opposed to the mob. It makes a virtue of deliberation, of calm, of space. The whole notion it embraces is that there is room for everyone within its structure.

Whoever heard of a popular Catholic uprising? The authority of the Church is against the crowd. The Church is frightened of rebelliousness.

Everyone who goes to Mass, everyone who receives the body and blood of Christ, does so as an individual. The sacred word belongs to him or her alone.

This is what terrifies the brain-sick puritans. They seek relief in the herd; they find reassurance in the volatility of the crowd just because it confirms their belief in the chaos and evil of this world. The squashed sexuality of the puritan who despises most what he would like to be and to have, finds its expression in the crowd's violent loathing.

The black puritan boar gores the loins of Adonis, so that Venus should be tortured with grief. Puritanism annihilates the feminine spirit.

As the Queen's wits grew airy and unhinged and she neither sought nor believed any spiritual comfort that could be found in her priests, so did normally staid people, the citizens of London, suffer a final upsurge of the poison she had been feeding them during the years of her reign.

In return for popularity she had been hiding her darkness in them, and now as she was dying, freed from the restraint of her terror and detached from the careful regulation of her ministers, so did that poison swell the body politic to bursting point and begin to crack it.

To the last her ministers were subtle and shrewd. Cecil knew how much that body politic needed a blood-letting so that its inner hidden imposthume should not blow it apart. And what, as his most puritan councillors understood, could be more of a sop to the anger of the crowd than the sacrifice of its very opposite in every aspect?

The priest.

He was the incarnation of everything that was opposite to the spontaneous, anti-authoritarian spirit of the crowd. A good man. A man of piety. A man of obedience. A man who believed in authority. In hierarchy. To them he was the perfect victim to be offered.

He satisfied everyone. The authorities. The middle-class people who upheld order, but remained safely locked in their houses with their retainers guarding them. His death would tame and awe the mob. The Protestant Church, because its liverish bishops could argue with the victim and convince themselves – having suppressed all opposition – that they were right. The Catholic Church, which would yet again prove its serene order, its dignity, and its restraint.

Would the victim be satisfied? Would he be prepared, like Christ, to shed his blood for many people? Would I, who felt so close to him, be prepared to allow him to do so?

No. I would do all in my power to stop him. I could not have him, in his death, overtaking me yet again and proving the superiority of Rome. I had to win something.

I had become a social nothing, a parasite on my rich friends, an impoverished husband and father who inflicted nothing but misery and privation on my family.

God had punished me enough. He may have broken my bones to set them straighter. He may have bruised me in a mortar like we do with flowers for their scent, so that I might satisfy him in my mortification with some fragrance.

I was tired of all this, tired of convincing myself that I had rather God frowned on me than not look on me at all, tired of believing that God's pursuit of me was a virtue while his total neglect would have been better. I wanted to be forgiven by God. But only on my own terms.

I wanted to believe in God again, rather than in that projection of myself that worshipped God for my own self-improvement through the Protestant form of religion. I sought, through pain, to flatter myself that I was good and deserving. Often I was a tortured puritan, bound and tortured by my selfishness. I wanted to believe, rather than to curse God for deserting me.

This was my final illusion. I would make one more attempt. I would join O'Hearne and we would free Underhill.

The race was on. We had a very good chance of success. The puritans wanted him dead, to increase their authority with the new king. We wanted him alive, because we wanted freedom of conscience. I wanted him alive. I did not want him to win.

But what did the Queen want? Nothing. Would she die first? Or would she first go mad? Would God – just about – protect her in her final moments? Would the Protestant Englishman be proved superior to the Catholic? Would England's splendid isolation be maintained? Would its independence be guaranteed?

II

Underhill had not given way by the end of the trial, nor did he comply with the wishes of the Council in the matter of supplying names of those who harboured priests, their places of worship or who attended. When so questioned Underhill would reply, *"tout le monde"* and simply give the names of everyone he knew. As he had the memory of an elephant he soon implicated the whole kingdom. They then accused him of dissembling his identity, of seducing young men, and sending them abroad to be schooled in the diabolical disciplines of Popery.

They were past masters in the orchestration of corrupt justice. Just before his trial rumours were spread about that he had turned Protestant, that he acknowledged all his faults in confession, that he was about to accept to become a bishop and burn Campion's "Brag" at St Paul's Cross. No one was allowed to see him. All over the country they arrested Catholics and taunted them with his treachery before letting them free again.

Before he left, O'Hearne told me of the rest of the trial. They had put up the stage at the south end of Westminster Hall and hung it with tapestries. They had sworn in twelve corrupt jurymen, most of them known informers, some of them fanatical Calvinists. The Queen's Counsel, Anderson, the Attorney-General, Popham, whose families had already been enriched with monastic lands, had conducted the case against him. The Lord Chief Justice presided over the trial. O'Hearne described how Underhill skilfully turned the charge of treason around on his accusers to show that they had only his religion to hold against him.

"In condemning Catholics," Underhill told them, "you condemn all your ancestors – all the priests of former time, the bishops . . . kings – all that was once the glory of England, the island of saints, and the most devoted child of the See of Peter. Why do you want England isolated? Why do you reject for the future its community with the rest of mankind . . . ?" This caused a mighty uproar because they all thought Underhill meant we should become part of Spain or, worse, France.

"So what was the day you were constantly threatening?" the accusing lawyer jumped in, seizing his chance to turn the tables. "What was the day that was shortly to come, if not that day when the Queen should be murdered, the Pope, the King of Spain, and all the other Queen's enemies were appointed to invade this realm?"

"Heaven and hell," answered Underhill, "you're like a jealous cuckold that imagines his wife is being unfaithful with every man she talks to or smiles on!" This provoked a bellow of great mirth in the hall, for everyone, and especially the members of the Council, knew that Anderson was a ferocious confiner of his wife, and hot in revenge, she was conducting a secret affair with a captain in the Beefeaters.

"You were known as a wit and a libertine," responded Anderson swiftly and suavely.

"In my youth, yes," answered Underhill. "Here's a crime I should answer for" – and here he looked around the lords. "I see you are all smiling," he said to them with complete and unaffected charm, and everyone laughed again. "The only problem today is that men persist in choosing mistresses as they do stuffs, for being fancied and worn by others. In my day," and the uproar started, for truly Underhill's wit had them by the short hairs, "we preferred the richer style which now lie untumbled and unasked for. Yet who would not prefer to be the only guest at a good table . . . " By now a tumultuous uproar had broken out, the faces of his accusers were bursting with rage and frustration, for no one would believe anything against a rogue who could make them laugh. "The trouble with the Protestant Church is that it needs a good hot sauce of Jesuits to keep its appetite alive. If the Church is the bride of Christ, as Jesus said, why can't you fall on your wife without the threat of a rival . . . " To save their dignity the judges brought the trial to its swift and foregone conclusion. Underhill was not allowed to speak again.

On the pretext that I was a confidant of Her Majesty and that I had married well and had the trust of some of the Council, I was persuaded by O'Hearne that I should bear to Underhill the details of the plan to effect his release.

"But what if he should not want to escape?" I asked.

"You mean, do you, that even he might be tempted by the martyrdom that will be his."

"Which would be the greater victory?" I asked.

"We will have to leave that to him to decide," O'Hearne answered. "I am convinced he will choose freedom. He is not the stuff of martyrs, is he? You and I, John, know that only too well!"

III

I felt no terror at going into the Tower to see Underhill. By this time my life had again become loathsome to me. My happiness had fled. I felt overwhelming shame at myself, and I could assemble little sorrow at the thought of the pain I might be causing Anne. If I died in attempting to rescue Underhill she would be unhappy because she truly loved me, but she loved me blindly and did not see how little I deserved her love. When she found out she would be bitter, but not for long, of this I was sure.

I did not mind if I was caught. Yet I have to admit that I believed O'Hearne's plan had a good chance of succeeding. The Jesuit John Gerard had escaped on a rope over the Tower Walk one dark night some years before, but our plan involved nothing so hazardous as attempting to slide down a rope and then to be caught in a boat on the Thames.

We had considerably more money and men at our disposal than ever Gerard had. Our plan was bold and simple, and would be performed in broad daylight. The political climate was very different. The opposition to Her Majesty grew daily. Londoners were indifferent to the fate of one more Jesuit priest, while many at Court, and even some members of the Council, believed the killing had gone far enough.

34

The Iron Man

They had him near the end, now, or so "Thrush" Poley and Captain Sphacto thought. They were determined to exact a confession from him: worse, they themselves believed, as madmen do, that he was guilty. They wanted him to confess their guilt, and free themselves from the hidden and buried remorse of their own crimes. It might be thought that years of coarsening the heart with cruelty, murder and secretive or devious machination might have numbed for ever its need for atonement. But no. The measure of the zeal of these torturers was their hunger for keeping Underhill on the rack, to torture him into a betrayal of his ideals. They desperately strove to make him their accomplice in crime.

They had an infernal consistency. They were convinced they would win.

"It can't be long," Sphacto said to Poley in the interrogation room of the North Tower.

"He must yield."

They gave sign for the man to increase the stretching. As for the prisoner, he had reached the absolute limit of hardship: no fresh air, no nourishment from food, stripped of rest, of light, there could not be found in his cheeks or lips a tint of any colour. The skin was dry as parchment, his eye sockets were pitted although a surly fever still pulsed in both of them. Lines of flesh overlapped each other in his cheeks and over his neck.

Sphacto and Poley crowed in triumph: they had transformed their sense of inferiority into fulfilment. Revenge over a fallen enemy. They drank in the spectacle. They gazed on his tortured form, to which had now been restored its foppish but torn elegance, the leather jerkin and velvet venetians of the former Sir Jasper. Poley, who they say had once been a King's chorister and loved to sing carols, suffered a paroxysm of the neck which he tried to hide; he whistled through his teeth and clicked his nails in triumph.

"So this time you intend to kill me?"

The Iron Man

"If necessary."

"But then you will be deprived of my giving in?" His voice quavered into the question, concealing the irony of his thought.

Sphacto gave sign to the attendant. But even then Underhill would not afford them the satisfaction of a cry of pain. He now flashed the insolent smile of a schoolboy.

I witnessed the torture from a corner. This was meant to be a training session, for the state did not charge the prisoner for torture on the understanding that apprentices could be present. Two or three other visitors were also here. Underhill was still not tamed. Even in the pose of that grim shadow that was now his body I saw a defiance, a spirit of resistance, a mocking, almost supernatural power.

I recalled that touch of fingers which many years before I felt in his friend's home where we stopped the night on our way south from York: "There are more things in heaven and earth, Horatio, than are dreamt of in your philosophy." I once again began to entertain doubts of Underhill's mortality.

"For the sake of heaven, confess," called Sphacto, who had in him some remnant of normal human feeling.

Thrush was annoyed and turned on Sphacto. "He will not confess," he snapped, "till that devil in him has been destroyed."

"Offer it food and drink. Offer it a different temptation. Try to draw it out." Thrush looked puzzled. Sphacto seized his chance.

"Free the prisoner," he told the attendant.

"What are you doing?" With a surly growl, Thrush now faced Sphacto. "Curse you, man."

"He'll die before he can speak."

At this point, as Underhill tottered forward, in his chill-lipped face there seemed a definite recognition that he had reached the privative limit. The skin adhered to his face like the wax of a death mask.

"I'm afraid . . ." he made a gesture as if it was all too much and collapsed to the floor. Sphacto sprang forward and seized him by the wrist, where he felt the pulse.

"Gone," he hissed at Poley, "his last breath's rivelled. Now look what you've done to him. It wasn't me. He was in his last stage of exhaustion. And you gave him the death blow."

"Shit in the Devil's arse!" exploded Thrush. "He's pretending!"

"Feel for yourself." Sphacto stepped aside, offering Poley the wrist.

The lips were parted, the eyes closed. Dull and brutal although Thrush was, the truth was dawning fast. He seized Underhill's wrist, felt the pulse and blenched.

"I don't believe it," he swore under his breath. "He can't be dead." Poley was breathing deeply with fear. "I'll make that cursed Papist confess . . ."

He drew a long knife.

Unseen by Thrush, who had his back to him, Sphacto had uncovered his naked rapier from its scabbard. His other clenched hand began to quiver as he raised the weapon. One eye went in one direction, the other towards me. He thrust the rapier deep into Poley's back. Poley doubled forward on Underhill, choked and coughed blood over his face. Sphacto leapt on to Poley and pulled him away from Underhill, who lay there gaunt and grave-eyed, his flesh bloodless, his lips like candle.

I was beside Sphacto by now. I laid my hand on his arm. Sphacto regarded me with keen curiosity. He had recovered and was filled with pride. With his braggart eyes he was questioning me; he still kept his weapon pointed towards Thrush, as if he feared he might return to life.

He seemed like a man carried on a log recklessly by the current, who sees another piece of wood bearing down on him in the entirely opposite direction. Should he jump to save his life? Sphacto thought quickly and jumped. I could see from his eyes that he would cause no trouble.

"Easy, easy my friend," I said. To show my own calm I turned and deposited my hat and cloak on a rickety, rush-bottomed chair. The visitors cowered almost hidden in a corner gloom which no wall torch reached.

He folded his arms. "I acted too late. Underhill is dead. The hangman is cheated. None of us will receive our bounties."

"Are you sure?" I asked.

"Sure of what?" he asked, apparently overcome with a quick wave of unreasoning tremor.

Through the barred windows of the torture chamber the cold early spring rays of the moon fought with the dim yellow of the corona.

"I did my best," said Sphacto. He turned to the torturer, who stood petrified in his white, blood-stained apron, throwing a great jellying shadow on the wall.

"They're not going to be too happy with you either, Burgess. I think the time has come for both of us to fly. Sir Francis and other members of the Council will be furious."

"What I meant was, are you sure that Underhill is dead?"

Sphacto jumped at my words, as if he felt a grip upon his shoulder.

I was amused. A kind of gentle clucking noise started to emanate from the sullen and inert form of Underhill. He was not dead. They say that certain mystics, through an inner power of concentration, can draw the blood away from the outer pulses such as those in the wrists. This could be one explanation. But let us just say that it was Underhill.

Underhill sat up carefully, wiping Poley's drying gore away from his face with his sleeve. Beside him the body of his torturer composed itself.

"I am not dead yet. But I am in a tight corner," he said, casting his eyes over towards Poley, whose flabby full red lips lay open and gaping, whose cold and ferocious eyes were now vacant. "I do believe Mr Robert Poley would have stabbed me. I owe my deliverance to Captain Sphacto. Allow me to shake your hand, my dear sir."

"What devilry is this?" demanded Sphacto, and turned his back. "I felt him dead myself. How can I be sure that it is not Satan from hell come to tempt me in the body of a Jesuit?"

"Captain Sphacto, when the good Queen dies as she must, on whose side will you find yourself: on Secretary Cecil's, or on that of Knollys and his crew?"

"Why, what do you recommend, Mr Donne?" He moved close to me. "Do you want to take Mr Underhill away?" he whispered. "For a thousand crowns we can deck out Thrush here like the body of Underhill, while you may disguise the priest as the vermin."

"Too damned easy," interrupted Underhill. "And what would we tell the assistants? Our good apprentices?"

"We can send them home."

Sphacto duly dismissed Burgess and the spectators.

"How do I know you can be trusted?" I asked Sphacto when we were alone.

"I was told to produce this letter, with the seal of Lord Mountjoy . . . " He reached inside his doublet and brought out a letter which I opened and read. It gave the nobleman's word of honour that Sphacto was committed to the cause of Underhill's escape, and had accepted a reward for life if it succeeded. O'Hearne and his confederates had been working hard. I believe that there would soon be hardly anyone of note in London who was not involved in the plot. I handed the note to Underhill.

Since he had risen to his feet he had remained standing. It was remarkable how the energy, force and determination had begun to flow back into his massive and tall frame.

"Really," he commented, "I don't believe I am worth rescuing. Truly the time has arrived for me to make peace with my deliverer."

"Wait till you hear of the circumstances of the plan," I said with relish. "They will tickle your fancy. It is so neat, so well contrived, so fault-proof. Like a play-plotting – except that it is real."

I explained to Underhill how he would be freed.

I left out one detail which entirely concerned myself, which was my own refinement and *coup de grâce* to this brilliant idea.

I was determined to turn the tables on everyone.

35

Death's Second Self

It is the day fixed for Underhill's execution on Tyburn Hill. I am waiting in a large house over an open courtyard just off Holborn, to the south, that the plotters have rented. I have been here all night preparing. In front of me I have a full-length mirror. I have had a cobbler fit platforms to my shoes. Otherwise I am in the long black robe of a Jesuit.

I have tousled and greyed my hair. I have put putty on my nose, like an actor. I have made my eyebrows grey and bushy, with extra hair and some glue. I have painted furrows on my forehead and lines either side of my mouth. I have fixed on a beard and trimmed it to an exact counterfeit of Underhill's.

Even now I can hear O'Hearne, some eight gentlemen and their servants at work in Holborn, digging up the roadstones, piling them to one side, so that Underhill and his escort will be forced into a diversion down a lane, past a garden under this house and into its yard. The escort, never more than a dozen men-at-arms who trot by the condemned man where he is tied to a hurdle and dragged by a horse, will be overwhelmed swiftly and locked downstairs in the cellar.

A new set of guards and a new prisoner tied to the hurdle will then proceed out of the diversion and by a different route to the one they entered by, back into Holborn. Nobody will be any the wiser. John Donne, alias Edmund Underhill, will proceed to his execution as planned. The crowd will not be cheated.

Yet as I approach Tyburn itself a further gentleman will step from the rabble and pull off my beard and demand to have a debate with the prisoner on the subject of the immaculate conception of Mary. Pretending to be alarmed the guard will pull the horse to a halt. The guards will surround me, hiding me from the crowd while they break my chains, in which space of time I will shed the priestly cloak, re-don the clothes of a humble artisan and melt away in the crowd. The soldiers of the guard, hirelings of O'Hearne, would then start a

229

hue and cry for the escaped prisoner, wreaking complete chaos in the crowd. The guard itself would disappear.

Underhill would by this time have reached a safe house in the north suburbs where he would remain hidden for a day or two, until the search had spent itself. He would afterwards, by easy stages, make his escape to France.

The tower clock of St Paul's strikes. It is seven o'clock. It is a Monday morning: soon Underhill will be fetched from the Tower and will meet the huge crowd which has collected at the West Gate, which will accompany him from the City to Tyburn.

Through the muddy streets of the City it will wend towards us here, following the prisoner and his escort, west along Cheap, past the old hospital of St Martin-le-Grand which has been rebuilt as commercial tenements and a large tavern.

Here thieves and prostitutes thrive, free from arrest among the French, Flemish and German Protestant exiles who work as tailors, felt hat makers, pommel and button moulders, silk weavers and stationers. Bladder Street will give way to Newgate Street with its flesh shambles, slaughterhouses, drinking shops.

The children are at school. The sucklings have been put out to nurse. The chicken farmers have gone to the north to collect their eggs for sale in the Meal market.

I await the arrival of Underhill. I feel like an actor about to make a grand entrance. I am not afraid. I have little doubt that the plan will succeed. Soon I will be lowering myself on to the hurdle, which as I understand is a business to be undertaken with care. I suspect that Underhill, given his size and the pain they have inflicted on him, will not be able to straighten his legs. There will be many rough places as the hurdle lifts and drops over uneven surfaces. It will be painful, but as I have suffered none of the usual tortures I will have none of the snapped sinews and wrenched joints of the true martyr who has survived one vast physical misery in order to make his final journey.

What I have told nobody, is that I do not intend to free myself along the route. I have money to bribe the hired guards to stay as my escort to the end. I have money to tip the executioners. If they no longer want to go along with me, I will make the journey alone.

I hope that I will be cut down from the rope before I have time to die so that I will witness and be conscious of the butchery done on me. Above all Kate will be proud of me, that I have had the courage to die as Saint Paul or Saint Alban.

Death's Second Self

I want to thank Underhill because I know he will be giving up to me the most valuable thing he has in life: his own martyrdom. Alive, he will undoubtedly do more good than me.

The appointed hour is almost come. A minute or two ahead of time there is a sound of great equine confusion and scuffling, the crack of a whip and a cry of command, as an unwilling dray is made to enter the confines of the yard, together with a dozen trotting, sweaty pikemen.

Things then happen so quickly I am dazed and blinded, but also curiously elated with a kind of unusual lightness. O'Hearne and his gentlemen and their servants, all with swords and pistols drawn quickly overwhelm the guard, who offer little resistance. They are bound and O'Hearne's men begin to lead or carry them out. Underhill is unshackled from the hurdle by O'Hearne. I am called down and I descend quickly.

Underhill seizes me by the shoulders. We embrace with love.

"We will see each other soon," he says.

I answer nothing. Does he foretell my deeper intention? He seems busy and happy too. At least he is not mournful, so he cannot be unhappy with the plot, as I believed he would be, to free him from dying the death of a martyr.

"I like your spade," he says, "it's better than mine." He tugged at my pepper-and-salt imitation. The glue held firm. I had been many things in my time. I am at last the Jesuit which God had intended me to be in the first place. This will be my master coup. Will God mind that I was stealing Underhill's death from him? Of course not. How could he refuse me his redeeming grace?

Hearing of my martyrdom Kate would understand how much my love for her really meant. At last I would be ahead of her, showing her the way. She would be in my debt. She would love me. I had written all my best poems; my fame, as lyric and as libertine poet, was secure. I would live on for ever in legend and I would have proved what I wanted to prove. I would have out-Kated Kate.

A musket shot rings out and all at once the air is thick with smoke, shouting, screams of pain, flying arrows and bolts. The authorities have heard of the plot and are reversing it. The guard that was to be my guard runs away. I shout in vain where I am trussed to my hurdle. In swashbuckling black leather, Sphacto appears, grinning from ear to ear with joy. He orders the first guard to be freed from the cellars and to resume their task.

This happens so fast that I am totally overwhelmed and mentally confused. I have given up my body to be torn, the proof of my manhood cut off, and I had felt secure. But now I am feverishly unhitched from the hurdle and thrown on the floor.

Where are O'Hearne and his men? They have all fled or been overpowered. So much for Catholic talk!

As if from nowhere Underhill appears. Scrambling to my feet I come face to face with him. I scarcely know any more how to put this story into words, so that it will be a credible picture of my state of mind. But the knowledge I now have of Underhill is different from that I have ever experienced before. He has always been great in bulk. He is even huger now as he strides and towers over me like a mountain. He is secure against evil. I have tussled with him over who shall possess heaven in heaven, and heaven on earth, or hell in heaven, or hell on earth. I have lost. I hate with a powerlessness which is the rage of humility.

He reads all this in my face as clearly as if it was written in a book. He moves gently round to confront his captors.

"Are you a ghost?" I ask his solid back.

After a little while he turns round again.

"Whose ghost would I be?" he asks finally.

"So you are not in my imagination, Underhill. You are not a ghost, an evil spirit or a fairy that's haunting me."

Underhill sighed. "These days magic is the national mania. It is collective folly of the worst kind – "

"Do I seem bewitched?"

"Not to me, John Donne." He frowns, "What are you doing?"

"Making the sign of the cross."

I am. I am abandoning the rational spirit of my faith.

"Then you agree that the order of the universe must be inexorably moral? . . . "

"I suppose so." I can't rid myself of my doubt. I am convinced once again that Underhill is a spirit.

"The Bible is full of magic. Moses' rod. Elijah's ring . . . Just tell me who you are . . . "

"It is too late for that, John Donne."

Underhill sings lightly:

> "The windmill blown down by the witch's fart.
> Or Saint George that O! did break the dragon's heart."

"Put Mr Underhill back on the hurdle!" shouts Sphacto. "Mr Donne, you are a free man."

Death's Second Self

"*Et tu, Brute!*" I say to Sphacto as they push me with their pikes over into a corner.

Sphacto laughs long and loud. "Not exactly, John, old rogue. I am not arresting you. I am on your side. It's you and me, the selfish ones, who go on living."

I then understand who is the true betrayer of the plot.

36

The Great Collector

"He is here

He is here as he was in the beginning

He is here among us as he was on the day of his death.

You are killing him over again. Just to go along with it is the same as performing the hangman's work yourself. He who lets it be done – "

"Silence the papist priest," shouted the Lord Keeper Egerton.

"Let him speak," shouted the people who became threatening to the officers who felt it would be wiser to let the priest have his say.

I had taken off my disguise. I had been cheated. My choice had been made for me. My other self had won. Now I had put on old clothes so I should not be recognised. I hid my face and I bided my time.

"Beat the drums! Beat the drums," cried out a voice. But the drums did not beat.

"He who lets it be done is the same as he who does it! It's the same thing. One goes with the other."

I heard, terrifyingly, my mother's voice.

"It's even worse than being the one who sticks in the knife. At least the commissioners have had the *courage* to do what they believed in. But when you let something be done, that's just the same thing. To be that feeble is worse than anything."

A growl of assent greeted Underhill's words. He was gaining support and was about to go on, but he stopped, shaken from his intense point of concentration by a sudden devastating sound that met his ears.

The clumsy and brutal ogress that devours human flesh had to keep herself alive: she roared when she feared that her prey might be snatched from her jaws. Usually she could make a joke of it and was easily diverted. She was always ready to gobble up anyone who fell on their face. But that day she had a dark, implacable wantonness.

The whole world was screaming and swaying. The priest heard

The Great Collector

below him, the trample of horses, voices complaining and clamouring.

He opened his eyes . . . the clamour died down. For a moment his eyes wandered over the heads of the people and up to the sky.

"Nearly sixteen centuries of Christendom have gone by since he bought back our souls for us. Today nothing flows around the earth only rage and ingratitude, a wave that sweeps souls away. This country needs cleaning up, but gently, like a mother cleans up her baby . . ."

"Enough treasonable words!" shouted Egerton. The crowd had grown impatient at this wooing before the act of darkness. I stood, as I stand now, on the threshold of eternity. I stood on the threshold of Underhill's eternity, not my own. He could not see my face. Beside me stood a girl who shunned me with her eyes and raised them on him.

I was depressed beyond belief. I had dipped in Underhill's dish and betrayed him. Once we had been together side by side and watched Margaret Clitheroe die.

Underhill smiled towards me and leaned down as if he were on the cross. The touch of the rope passed across his face. He closed his eyes for an instant, but then he opened them and smiled again. "I absolve the Queen in the name of the Father, the Son and the Holy Spirit . . ." I know that he said that for me, for only I could know what it meant. Then he offered his tip to the hangman. He was ready.

I drew a steady breath and pushing the rabble aside moved from where I stood to take up a position under the scaffold. Although I had sorted out some linen in order to soak up Underhill's blood I did not bargain for the great shower of blood which, some minutes later as the hangman and his assistant went about their grisly duty, I received as it streamed down through the chinks of the boards upon my hat and humble cloak.

I ducked out quickly from under the scaffold just in time to see the hangman chuck the butchered quarters into a great basket, together with the head of Underhill, which was destined to be set upon a pole on London Bridge, among the other parboiled and tanned heads. Children rushed to the basket to collect his blood to sell.

As the mangled limbs landed in the basket straw, an ear of wheat flew off in an arc to land on my chest. I clapped my hand to it to keep it there, but as I hurried from the place, now fearing pursuit, and eager to shed my soaking garments, I had no time to see that the ear was also sprinkled with blood.

I became fearful to keep the straw any time longer than an hour or two. The people had run off and left his remains. I had shivered under the cascade of his blood. I stripped off the garments where his blood had teemed down on me.

Afterwards I heard it told that the Lord Keeper Egerton had not denied Underhill his final identity. The old and fat nobleman, as forked as a mandrake root, within months of his own death, had thrown himself on the ground with a shriek of pain and clung to his mother earth as if she was a wheel which would not stop spinning.

I knew, in that moment, that Egerton knew: that since the very first day I had met him, Egerton had known all along. Why had he known? For he and Underhill had a close blood tie. They were half-brothers. This perhaps had always been, without my being aware of it, the affinity Egerton and I shared and which had made us friends.

I gave the blood-stained ear of wheat away that same evening secretly to a Catholic woman of my acquaintance who was the wife of my tailor. I had become scared in case it might contaminate me. Scared a poursuivant might hear of it and denounce me. I denied Edmund Underhill. At that moment I became a collaborator in the evil of the world.

My tailor's wife discovered a night or two later that within the blood-stained ear of wheat there was the face of a man, exactly proportioned in beard, mouth, eyes and forehead. It was that of Edmund Campion.

He wore a crown upon his head, while there was a star upon his chin. News of this wonder soon spread over the town, carried by gossip-mongers, malcontents, and by the penny press. The tailor's wife was persuaded to carry her straw to the house of the Spanish ambassador, where the nobility and the gentry flocked to see it. Even some members of the Council called by, putting on their most suspicious manner.

The authorities said that it was witchcraft.

My Play's Last Scene – February 1631

Charles I of England sits on his wide Scots bum – "Heroic Virtue" – married to the French papist spawn Henrietta – "Beauty" – such a spineless platonic pair as would float in from heaven in some insipid masque. Under his reddish golden hair, he has his usual simpering half-smile.

I plough on with my sermon.

"Our meditation of Christ's death should be more visceral and affect us more because it is of a thing already done. Can the mention of our own death be irksome and bitter?"

Many an evening I would sit looking at Anne as she sewed or knitted or attended to the children's needs. To protect myself against the authorities I had engaged more and more in the fight against Catholics. We were still resident in the house of Francis Wooley. By day I cultivated my life. I made an effort to care for Anne. I changed myself. I wanted only more children. I discarded my old personality and aspirations. If anyone asked me if I still wrote verses I repudiated them. By night I dreamed nightmares. Edmund Campion would appear in chains. Underhill in the manacles. Their metal would clank and resound in the empty chambers of my heart.

I had incurred the wrath of Egerton and his wife, which did not go, but my friendship with his son, Francis, strengthened. Francis's mistress, Joan, lived in London and bore him a daughter. Mary was compelled to acknowledge the mistress by bestowing her own name upon the child.

I was faithful to Anne and we had much perfect coupling together, but I felt my mother had put a curse on my marriage. In it I would find absence, darkness, death, things which were not. After Constance we had a stillborn boy. This time Anne's pregnancy had been especially difficult, with sores and lumps appearing on her legs, and a fatigue and darkness around her eyes which had boded ill. Visiting Paris soon after I had a vision of Anne pass twice through my bedroom with her shawl hanging about her shoulders, and with a dead child in her arms. We continued to have a child a year.

I had thought that the accession of James to the throne of England would change my fortune, but it did not. To the end of my days I wished that our plot to have Elizabeth married had met with success, for then I would have participated in the miracle of giving my country a Tudor heir and saved it from the Stuarts. In the good air and comfort of the Surrey countryside I grew into that purely English concoction: an eclectic ecclesiastic – and so I remained. I wrote against the Jesuits. I poured scorn on the conventicle of gloomy sullen saints. I still tried, for all my disgrace, to cultivate patrons, and in particular patronesses. I devoted laborious hours to my opiate and relief from all distress – study.

Although I felt God had deserted me I researched the problems of divinity and canon law. I addressed poems to great ladies and theological pamphlets to King James, who later rewarded me for my pious mischief. I also cultivated the airs of a gypsy, and moved in all ranks of society. I saw my home as my hospital, my dungeon, and the noise of my gamesome children often drove me mad, as I laboured always, too, to improve their, and Anne's lot. I had transplanted my wife into such wretched fortune, and I tried to make it up to her by giving her my company and what cheerfulness of spirit I could command.

I suffered the temptations of old, but I now had the proper means by which to deal with them: I would not banish a threat from my mind, but I gave it full place there, but would not act upon it, or even speak upon it. I would allow its emotions full play, however, and then I would subject my moods to a thorough and scholarly investigation.

So I withered and grew by turns. I conspired with my sickness. When a wound heals without being properly cleaned out it turns septic. The wound of my apostasy did not heal. Everything in my life when sounded rang out as though it had a crack in it.

Formerly I had annihilated women by flaunting my brain and my bawdy instrument, I had hounded them with my superiority so that they had no will of their own but were mere playthings of the flesh. It was myself that I would now cancel in images of nothing.

The swollen and caged husband I had had pleasure in cuckolding became myself – the coffined, imprisoned husband and father. As I had once teased and taxed women for their inconstancy so I now taxed and teased God for his.

My Play's Last Scene – February 1631

Anne built on and represented all that was good in me and worth keeping. In time she assumed, as if by a magical action of absorption or osmosis, many of the qualities of Underhill. Like the ear of wheat – but inwardly – she grew a personality of goodness. Perhaps, secretly and without acknowledgement on her part, it was this which I gave to her.

Well, I will talk to her in heaven, where all these problems will have their solution. For I, too, am shortly to die.

As for Kate I hear on good authority that she spends her days as High Abbess in a white and snowy monastery. Was it not I who grafted on to women my own capacity for betrayal, because of that greater betrayal I made of myself?

II

"There now hangs that sacred body upon the cross, rebaptised in his own sweat and tears, and embalmed in his own blood alive . . ." How I preferred coarse James, who slobbered over his meals, emptied his bowels in the saddle and stuck his finger in his favourite's codpiece. He had no illusions, like his son Charles. He knew faith and politics rode together like the whore and her client.

As long as you follow the form of worship outwardly, you can do what you like behind the curtains of your own bed. James could even take a joke against himself and his creatures who abused him for his pleasure – "Please you enter him and search him to the centre," wagged his court jester, Ben Jonson.

Blood alive? I see Charles stifle a yawn. The Queen would rather be whispering to her charms in secret, consulting her astrologer, praying to the papist cross she keeps in her own private chapel.

I would much prefer, still, to be worshipping at another altar, that of woman's centric part, playing the privileged spy upon my mistress's delightful spasms, worshipping the intricate purses, the aversely placed mouths that nature gave the fairer sex, offering myself as sport for every girl to practise on.

Then I could write with joy! Epithalamium after epithalamium took flight effortlessly as I panted impersonally after beauty. Amazingly, I spun images, deflowering the bride's virginity with the disembowelling knife of the groom's penis, giving licence to my loving pen as well as hands, ruling the dearest bodily parts with a

Campion's Ghost

wanton muse, opening the secret and forfended place to all searchers, to share its hot bestial sides with men.

But also refining love into a rare and perfect conundrum so that lovers will for ever, in their most close and intimate moments, dress themselves in my words and share them with each other.

I must stop this second sermon's raging. My outward self wavers and falters before His Imperial Majesty. I must take a grip on myself.

"There those glorious eyes grew faint in their light: so as the sun ashamed to survive them departed with his light too . . . "

As I hover on the rim of the eternal pit, wriggle in the lips of the whirlpool of twenty years of self-murder, I have left myself so little time. Like a high lute string I have been stretched to squeak tunes – and my strumpet faith has been richly rewarded. Doctor Donne, Dean of St Paul's. My estate is worth near £4000.

Moist with one last drop of my blood my dry soul still seeks you, Father Edmund, to burn off my rusts and punish me in my deformity! Often at night in my study I was visited by a dead face at the window. To dispel it I commissioned a dummy board painted in the likeness of Campion and had it set beside me for company.

How could I ever have belched and spewed out such hatred and blasphemy towards these men I loved, had it not been that, deep down and deep within, I was one myself. You, that I have so whipped, scorned and chastised, if your blood is on my hands it is because I WANTED TO BE YOU.

I rub my red-rimmed eyes, pluck at my grey and haggard cheeks to bring blood to them. I am fainting.

"Oh, I say, look to him," calls out my King crisply, and rises to his feet. His brow darkens with irritation, and he purses his lips.

"Put him on his feet. We must have an end to this whole blab of our dear Dean."

Two of Queen Henrietta's sweet-smelling minions rush forward to enfold me in their arms and coax me from my swoon.

"There was nothing more free, more voluntary, more spontaneous than the death of Christ. 'Tis true, he died voluntarily, *libere egit*, but when we consider the contract that had passed between his Father and him, there was an *oportuit*, a kind of necessity upon him . . . "

Charles is staring at me with an expression of owlish bewilderment.

This is my last sermon. Farewell my King.

Historical Note

Historical Note

Campion's Ghost is a work of fiction based upon a diversity of factual sources and my own speculation about the nature of John Donne from his poems and his prose writings. The character of Underhill is wholly a novelist's creation: an "other self", a projection or personification of what I believe Donne felt to be missing in himself. In many ways Underhill conforms with one of the prototype heroes of the age, the Catholic martyr of this golden age of Catholic martyrs. I cannot claim, as does R.H. Benson for his more straightforward and much more documentary account of the pursuit and martyrdom of Catholics during the Babington Plot (*Come Rack! Come Rope!*) that "very nearly the whole . . . is sober historical fact"; but I must express gratitude to him and his book, on which I have drawn, as well as to other sources in common with his including Bede Camm's *Forgotten Shrines*, John Gerard's *The Autobiography of an Elizabethan* (in my case translated by Philip Caraman) and a score or more historical works or biographies covering the period. The standard Donne biography, by R.C. Bald, is excellent, although my own interpretation of his character differs largely from Bald's; while notable critical works on Donne which I have also consulted are John Carey's *John Donne: Life, Mind and Art* and *John Donne* by George Parfitt. I have quoted from the Nonesuch Press edition of *John Donne*, edited by John Hayward. The best short biography of Edmund Campion is by Evelyn Waugh; but there are a host of others which I have consulted. I should also mention J.J. Scarisbrick's *Henry VIII*; Lacey Baldwin Smith's *Treason in Tudor England*; *Ben Jonson: A Life* by David Riggs; and *Tudor London Visited* by Norman Lloyd Williams. Roland Connelly's *No Greater Love*, and works by Keith Thomas, R. Houlbrooke and Lawrence Stone should also join a list of important background reading.

Perhaps I also ought to say that it has become increasingly clear to me that John Donne's life covers the beginning of the disastrous suppression of the Catholic spirit in English literature. Graham Greene, one of the few English writers since the seventeenth century to grapple with the themes of sin and redemption (at the heart of nearly every one of his novels is a persecuted saint or sinner) has summed up the effects of this suppression which may be worth quoting in the context of *Campion's Ghost*:

> To the religious sixteenth-century mind there was no such thing as a commonplace young man or an unimportant sin; the creative writers of that time drew characters with a clarity we have never regained . . . Rob human beings of their heavenly and their infernal importance, and you rob your characters of their individuality.
> (Graham Greene, *Collected Essays*)

> If Shakespeare had sat where Bacon had sat and given the orders for the torture, one wonders whether into the great plays which present on the inner side, however much on the outer Lear may rave or Antony lust, so smooth and ambiguous a surface, there would have crept a more profound doubt than Hamlet's, a sense of a love deeper than Romeo's.
> (Introduction to John Gerard's *Autobiography*)

More recently other writers such as Ted Hughes and Peter Ackroyd have in different ways echoed Greene's observation. Hughes, for instance, has written, "The poetic imagination is determined finally by the state of negotiation . . . between man and his idea of the creator."

That Shakespeare was the highest point is of course undisputed, but that he can be seen as the beginning of the end is also suggested by Anthony Burgess in his story "A Meeting in Valladolid", in which a Spanish character tells Shakespeare that his work compares unfavourably with Cervantes' *Don Quixote*:

> I have seen your plays. I have read his book. You will forgive me if I say that I know where the superiority lies. You lack his wholeness. He has seen more of life. He has the power to render both the flesh and the spirit at one and the same time.

John Donne certainly turned against his earlier "sins" and repudiated some of the former self he expressed in words: no gentleman at the time published in his lifetime anything that might declare private life and feeling. He could be insincere and misleading: for example in a letter he once claimed to be "no great voyager in other men's works; no swallower nor devourer of volumes nor pursuant of authors"; yet after his death his first biographer Isaak Walton found "the

Historical Note

resultance of 1400 Authors, most of them abridged and analysed with his own hand".

Donne also displayed an unpleasant side in his anti-Catholic writing: as Thomas Fitzherbert, his contemporary, complained:

> He sheweth such a venomous malignity towards Catholics, that it may serve for a symptom to discover another more malignant, and dangerous disease bred in his heart, from whence he hath belched out so many Lucianical, impious, blasphemous and atheistical jests against God's saints and servants.

Anyone who wishes to confirm this should read *Pseudo-Martyr* and *Ignatius his Conclave*.

That Donne became Egerton's Secretary is fact; that he was at Court and involved with the Queen is fictional but not impossible. Men in Elizabeth's England felt a strong erotic as well as matrimonial stimulus in having a virgin on the throne even well into her old age. As late as January 1597 Simon Forman recorded a dream in his diary that he was with the Queen:

> ... she a little elderly woman in a coarse white petticoat all unready. She and I walked up and down through lanes and closes, talking and reasoning. At last we came over a great close where there were many people, and there were two men at hard words. One of them was a weaver, a tall man with a reddish beard [supposed to be Lord Essex] distract of his wits. She talked to him and he spoke very merrily unto her and at last did take her and kiss her. So I did take her by the arm and did pull her away ... I led her by the arm still, and then we went through a dirty lane — she had a long white smock very clean and fair and it trailed in the dirt and her coat behind. I took her coat and did carry it a good way, and then it hung too low before. I told her she should do me a favour to let me wait on her, and she said I should. Then said I "I meant wait *upon* you and not under you, that I might make this belly a little bigger to carry up this smock and coat out of the dirt ..." When we were alone, out of sight, me thought she would have kissed me.

A month after this suggestion, Forman dreamt once again of the Queen, this time coming to him all in black and wearing a French hood – which signified the deep-rooted English fear of a French marriage.

In our own day, once again, not only is England's national and spiritual identity at the crossroads, but there are grave doubts raised about the present Royal Family's ecclesiastical status, especially in relation to some of its members' behaviour and their attitude to divorce. The historical roots of both these profound problems lie deep in the conflicts I describe.

One late discovery I have made is that the Elizabethans did have in their houses a primitive, static form of television. They called it a dummy board. Painted life-size in the likeness of a favourite servant, or even perhaps of a dead relative, such boards alleviated loneliness, while sometimes members of the household would even set places for them at table.

Finally, I can only add that every novelist is himself a maker of myth, as Carl Jung explains in his Prologue to *Memories, Dreams, Reflections*: "I can only make direct statements, only 'tell stories'; whether or not the stories are 'true' is not the problem. The only question is whether what I tell is *my* fable, *my* truth."

The perfect epitaph Donne wrote in the most famous of his *Devotions* may perhaps serve for Donne himself:

> All mankind is of one author, and is one volume; when one man dies, one chapter is not torn out of the book, but so translated into a better language; and every chapter must be so translated; God employs several translators; some pieces are translated by age, some by sickness, some by war, some by justice; but God's hand is in every translation; and his hand shall bind up all our scattered leaves again, for that library where every book shall lie open one to another.